# Extreme American Makeover

# Extreme American Makeover

FIRST DAUGHTER Book 1

Mitali Perkins

HARPER

First published in India in 2010 by Harper
An imprint of HarperCollins *Publishers*

Building 10, Tower A, 4th Floor, DLF Cyber City, Phase II,
Gurugram Haryana – 122002, India
www.harpercollins.co.in
2 4 6 8 10 9 7 5 3

Reprinted by arrangement with Dutton Children's Books, a division of Penguin Young Readers Group, a member of Penguin Group (USA) Inc.



ISBN: 978-81-7223-965-7

This is a work of fiction. Names, characters, places and incidents are either the product of the author's imagination or are used fictitiously, and any resemblance to actual persons, living or dead, business establishments, events or locales is entirely coincidental.



Typeset in 11/15 Ehrhardt MT Std
InoSoft Systems

Printed and bound at
MicroPrints India, New Delhi

*for Timothy*

# One

Eight buff, gorgeous guys from six different countries hoisted Sameera Righton onto their shoulders and paraded her along the river in front of the cheering crowd, chanting 'SPARROW! SPARROW!' Then they tossed her into the water and jubilantly hurled themselves in after her, cavorting to the music of the jazz band.

As her multicultural entourage of hunks splashed around her, Sameera wished someone could press a celestial pause button so she could savour the moment. She was celebrating much more than a first-place finish in a race. For months, she'd been griping long-distance to her cousin-slash-best friend Miranda about staying in Europe to finish out her sophomore year. With Dad's presidential campaign gathering steam in the States, her parents had become jet-setting celebrities travelling back and forth between the continents, and *she'd* been stuck in Brussels trying to grasp the mystery of isosceles triangles.

But now she was done. Done with school, done with the newspaper, done with packing and organizing. And last but not least, she'd coxed her team to this big end-of-the-season win. She was ready to join the campaign.

Her request for a heavenly pause button was denied. The band stopped playing; the crowd began to disperse. A dozen or so girls, ranging from willow thin to voluptuous, beckoned to their soaked boyfriends. The guys obeyed, of course, but not one of them climbed out before throwing his arms around Sameera, holding her close, and kissing her goodbye.

'I'll come up to visit you en La Casa Blanca next summer,' Adorable Antonio, the son of a Mexican banker, promised extravagantly. His girlfriend was the tall, toned Eritrean stunner tapping one stiletto on the shore, and making Sameera feel like an Oompa Loompa.

'Get one of those fancy guest rooms ready for me, too,' said Delectable David, the only other American on the team. 'I hear they have an amazing movie theatre inside the place.'

'Dad could lose, you know,' Sameera reminded her teammates, looking around at their affectionate faces.

After the California primary, which was only a few days away and predicted to be a slam dunk for Dad, he'd have enough votes to win the Republican nomination. Then, in the November nationwide election, if he beat the Democratic candidate, James Righton would become the next president of the United States of America.

'No chance of him losing,' said Jacques, their coach, sighing. 'Looks like he's going all the way to the top, great for him, lousy for us. Where are we going to find a cox as good as you, Sparrow?'

'I wasn't good when you recruited me,' Sameera told him, remembering the day in the fall of her freshman year when he'd asked her to join the team. 'You just picked me because I was the smallest kid in sight. I had no idea what I was getting myself into.'

It had taken only one practice for Sameera to realize that she couldn't sit like a lump and expect her backward-facing team to get to the finish line safely. She started using the inflections of her voice and encouragement to get them to go where she wanted. She practised steering and shifting her weight, mastered a cox box, and made charts about the strengths and weaknesses of each of her teammates. And she learned how to issue commands from her gut, not her throat, which made all the difference.

'Hey, coach,' Antonio said. 'How'd you know a little bird like Sparrow could shout *con mucha fuerza?*'

Sameera made a face at the 'little bird' comment, and Jacques ruffled her hair affectionately. 'I could tell she had a bossy streak a mile wide. Stay in touch, sweetheart. I'm off to say goodbye to your mother.' He tucked in his shirt and surreptitiously sniffed an armpit as he headed for the parking lot, where Sameera's mom was leaning against the long, black U.S. ambassador's car.

'You haven't blogged in days, Sparrow,' complained Amazing Ahmed, the muscular, soft-spoken son of the Pakistani ambassador to NATO. 'I've been checking in regularly and there's nothing since your last post.'

'I know. I've been so busy. But I promised to keep you guys up to speed, didn't I?'

Magnificent Matteo was the last to leave. 'We will be cheering for you,' he whispered, kissing her on the lips right in front of his *'novia'* who was also a Spaniard.

Sameera tried to keep her heart rate normal; a quick lip-on-lip kiss between friends was nothing in Europe. And she certainly wasn't in love with Matteo. But did all of her teammates have to be so... beautiful? And couldn't their girlfriends at least *pretend* to be threatened by their boyfriends' obvious affection for the team coxswain?

She watched them saunter off into the sunset pair by pair, almost expecting credits to roll across the orange sky like they did in one of Miranda's favourite chick flicks. Sameera preferred classic black-and-white romances like *Roman Holiday* and *Casablanca* or romping old-style musicals like *My Fair Lady*. She and Miranda were both avid fans of makeover shows, getting teary-eyed together as they watched home, heart, or hair redos on the tube. Trivial pursuits compared to parents out saving the world, maybe, but the girls loved them.

The scene involving Sameera's mother and Jacques looked like it belonged either in a chick flick or a makeover show, with Jacques bending low to kiss Mom's manicured, red-tipped hand. Sameera still wasn't used to the glam 'after' version of her normally makeup-free, hairy-underarmed, out-of-shape, jeans-clad, tennis-shoe-wearing, human-rights-activist mother. But Dad's campaign staff had gathered an expensive team of three last-name-free Hollywood experts to take Mom in hand at the start of the campaign season last year. Thanks to 'Camera-Ready Constance' (hair and makeup), 'Vanessa: Stylist for the Stars' (fashion), and 'Manuel: He Moves You' (a personal trainer licenced to pummel famous middle-aged bodies into shape), Elizabeth Campbell Righton had achieved a look that could easily be labelled 'twenty-first-century first lady.' She was tall, blonde, thin, and elegant in tailored suits, lip liner, and French perfume, and guys of all ages worried about their body odour in her presence.

Sameera yanked off her T-shirt to squeeze the water out of it—an out-of-character move that she usually reserved for the privacy of the girls' locker room. She never felt comfortable racing in a sports bra, like some of the other coxswains. Sadly, nobody paid any attention to her brazen act. *Hello? A girl just peeled off a wet T-shirt.* But this was Europe, where a shirtless woman in June was as common as a pair of golden arches in an American minimall. Besides, a petite, flat-chested girl shaped like a twelve-year-old boy didn't show up on 'sexy' radar anywhere on the planet. *They probably think my sports bra's an extra-small undershirt.*

But all that was about to change. As soon as Sameera arrived in L.A., Vanessa and Constance were going to descend on her (Manuel: He Moves You focused on bodies over thirty). The breaking news item on her myplace.com site this week:

> The moment we've all been waiting for is upon us. I'm going to bring my friends (that's you!) along for the amazing, never-been-reported-on-before journey of a President's Daughter in the Making. Your good old blogger buddy is about to morph from drab to glam, from drudge to diva, from unknown spectator to talked-about celeb. Stay tuned for the inside scoop.

She always ended her blog posts with the same tagline:

> Comments? Remember: keep them short, clean, and to the point. Peace be with you. Sparrow.

# Two

Sameera folded her first-class seat from a bed into a chair again and peered down at the flat plains of Kansas. They were almost there. Get some sleep, Dad had advised. You're going to have to hit the ground running. He was right. The next few days promised to be a tornado of activity. But after the California primary, she'd be heading off to spend the summer in Maryfield, Ohio. She'd have time to relax on the farm and take stock of her first plunge into fame before rejoining her parents just before the Republican National Convention in the fall.

Mom was hunched over her laptop, working on a report about internally displaced people. These people were attacked by their own country's army and couldn't flee across the border. Hiding in jungles, mountains, or caves in their own countries, they weren't technically refugees, so they didn't get much international aid money. Mom's hope was that this report would convince international foundations and charities to reserve some of their dollars for IDPs.

Sameera groped under the seat for her own laptop, safely ensconced in the waterproof, airtight case her parents had given her for her sixteenth birthday. Dad claimed that if either she or Mom were caught stark naked in a fire, they'd both grab their laptops and run for the hills. He was probably right. These days, Sameera mostly used her computer to blog and to track her father's campaign.

Her myplace.com site and blog could be accessed only by a list of twenty-nine 'buddies', which included Miranda, her crew guys, the newspaper staff in Brussels, a few keeper friends from schools she'd attended in Cairo, Moscow, and London, and Mrs Graves, the ancient but techno-savvy Maryfield librarian, who'd begged to be added last summer and was the only person over twenty on the list.

Sameera reread her most recent post:

> My Top Four Campaign Goals (Not Listed in Order of Importance): (1) Get the Makeover—check out the 'after' version and let me know what you think; (2) Explore America—I might be there to stay this time; (3) Give YOU the Skinny on Life As a Celeb; and (4) Help Dad Win. Comments? Remember: keep them short, clean, and to the point. Peace be with you. Sparrow.

She certainly wasn't anywhere close to being a celebrity yet. So far, the press had summed up her existence as a brief postscript to her parents' list of accomplishments: 'Righton, previously a popular three-term congressman and currently serving as Ambassador to the North American Treaty Organization, has been married for thirteen years to Elizabeth Campbell, a human-rights activist who consults for organizations like Amnesty International, Bread for the World, and the United Nations. The couple has one adopted daughter.' Sameera had no idea why reporters wanted to announce immediately that she and her parents weren't genetically connected. In the international trade and aid circles where the Rightons travelled, lots of kids were adopted, and it wasn't a big deal.

She opened the mailbox she had created in her email account for Tara Colby, a staffer whom she'd privately nicknamed the 'Bench', short for 'The Bossy Wench'. Tara was in charge of spinning James Righton's personal life for the media; she'd been the one who'd hired Constance, Manuel, and Vanessa to morph Mom's image from middle-aged hippie to Middle-America hip. The Bench had started sending memos a few weeks ago, and Sameera reread a few of the crisp, terse commando-style emails that had come barreling across the Atlantic. *Wow. The woman would probably make a great coxswain.*

The most recent memo listed some questions that Tara thought reporters might ask Sameera along with ready-made answers. *I'd better look at them again,* Sameera thought. *Not that she came up with anything I haven't thought of myself.*

> ***Q. Why did you wait so long to join your father's campaign?***
>
> *A. I had a TON (emphasize) of responsibilities to finish, like coxing and writing for the paper.*

That Tara-generated answer was half true. The other half was Sameera's parents wanting her to have as 'ordinary a life for as long as possible.' *Some ordinary life,* Sameera thought. Three years in an orphanage in Pakistan. Being adopted by parents whose job descriptions included simple tasks like putting an end to global warming and eradicating poverty. Moving every three years to a new diplomatic post. The closest she ever came to feeling ordinary was during the summers she spent on the farm in Maryfield.

> ***Q.*** ***How do you feel about your father's strong stand against terrorism? (Or any other political question)***
>
> *A. Dad's going to be the best president America's ever had. Mom and I know him better than anybody. He's loyal, and smart to the core.*

That was true, too, even though she'd never say anything that clichéd. Dad's campaign team was spinning his image into something called 'crunchy conservatism,' hoping that he could be pro-environment, pro-peace-and-justice, pro-free-enterprise, *and* pro-family-values at the same time. This was convincing his supporters, but his opponents were skeptical. It helped that he'd served three terms as a congressman *and* fifteen years in the foreign service, so he knew how to make things happen inside the country and around the globe. Last year, for example, he'd brokered a groundbreaking anti-terrorist treaty between fifty-three nations that had made headlines everywhere. He was perfect for the job, in Sameera's opinion, and that's what she planned to tell the reporters.

> ***Q.*** ***Do you know anything about your birth parents in Pakistan? Do you hope to find them?***
>
> *A. No, I don't. Maybe someday.*

Sameera rolled her eyes. She'd been answering unwanted inquiries about her adoption from strangers for years—she certainly didn't need the Bench to get her ready for those. A couple of years ago, just before they'd moved to Brussels, she'd wrestled heavily with the fact that she wasn't the biological child of her parents. Curiosity about her birth family still came in cycles, but the bottom line was she was grateful to them for giving her life, and to Mom and Dad for raising her.

> ***Q. What's it like to have such high-powered parents?***
> *A. I'm proud of them. They're proud of me, too.*

Okay. She could say that now. But that didn't mean a younger version of herself hadn't struggled with guilt over their differences. It was easier for Sameera to pick a savoury new recipe for the chef to try out, plan new borders for the gardens, and redecorate and create a cozy retreat for her stressed-out parents than to save people hiding in the jungle. In Brussels, she'd come to accept that both skill sets were important and had commandeered the job of managing the Residence from Mom, with Mrs Mathews's expert help, of course.

'Earth to Mom. Earth to Mom. We're almost there.'

Mom sighed, powered down her laptop, stretched out her legs, and rotated her ankles. She was five foot ten in bare feet; Dad was six three; Sameera was barely five foot one. 'I'll have to pull some all-nighters to finish this freakin' report.'

'Careful, Mom. You know what Gran says about trash talking. You slipped up twice in New Hampshire and the reporters were all over it.' In spite of the makeover, the campaign staff was still worried about feisty, passionate Elizabeth Campbell.

'That was early in the campaign,' Mom said, sighing. 'I've gotten better, haven't I? Besides, all I said was 'crap'. I can't bring myself to say any *really* juicy words, thanks to your grandmother.' Mom's voice changed as she mimicked her own mother's advice: 'Swearwords are used by unimaginative people too lazy to convey feelings with more creative language.'

'Gran's got a point.'

'She usually does, but four-letter words are so handy. What am I going to do, Sparrow? The current first lady's so d—*darn* perfect. It's a good thing your father's campaign team's such a well-oiled machine. I just follow their directions like some kind of... mindless wimp.'

'You're doing great, Mom. Dad's won most of the primaries so far, and you've been right there by his side.'

*Looking like a forty-seven-year-old fembot,* Sameera thought. She didn't say it; Mom hated the fuss and expense of her makeover and submitted to it only because Tara Colby insisted. Style was one of the few things Mom didn't have an opinion about; Sameera figured she sat thinking deeply about IDPs while the last-name-free people ran around rearranging her clothes, hair, and makeup.

Just yesterday, a Brussels-based stylist had sprayed and polished Mom up (with strict on-the-phone instructions from Constance) so that her hair and nails could survive the long journey. And Vanessa had emailed detailed instructions to her about what to wear for the journey. Sameera, on the other hand, had been left to her own devices, which were about as glam-challenged as her mother's. She'd asked Tara via email if they could start The Makeover in Brussels, but the Bench had nixed that idea. 'Those European places can't pull off the all-American look we need,' she'd written. 'My people want a clean palette. Anyway, I doubt many reporters will be waiting for you at LAX. I'll whisk you away as soon as you land.'

Sameera hoped Tara was right. She didn't really want to make her American debut on the 'don't' page of some fashion magazine. After a long-distance consult with her cousin (who as an infant had probably snagged the most stylish blankie in the hospital for herself), Sameera had settled on a pair of jeans, a blue button-up blouse, and ankle-high black leather boots. At the last minute, with a shadow of foreboding over what Miranda might say, she'd put on the poncho that Mrs Mathews had knitted as a goodbye present. It had proved to be comfortable on the chilly flight, and she was still wearing it now.

'Flight attendants, prepare for landing,' the pilot announced.

Sameera loosened her hair and brushed it out so that she could rebraid it neatly before they landed.

'Your hair's gotten so long, darling,' Mom said, fingering one long, fine black strand with her red-tipped fingers. 'Don't let Constance cut too much off.'

'Are you kidding? I'm going to sit back and let the amazing Vanessa and Constance go wild. I'm so tired of feeling invisible and SO ready for this to start, Mom.'

For months now, she'd been watching reruns of *The West Wing* and *Commander in Chief,* renting every flick featuring a president's daughter she could get her hands on, and fast-forwarding and rewinding through movies like *All the President's Men, Dave, Head of State,* and *The American President.* She'd been browsing celebrity websites to glean insights on how to manage the paparazzi (never be rude, set boundaries, always smile and wave). And with her myplace.com buddies travelling along to keep her steady, she couldn't wait to be a part of the sure-to-be-crazy ride of a presidential campaign.

# Three

A dazzle of flashbulbs blinded Sameera as she and Mom emerged from the customs and baggage claim area of the international terminal. *Here we go! But it looks like the Bench was wrong; tons of reporters, cameras galore, and I'm still the* before *version.*

Mom was peering into the crowd like a miserable deer confronting a traffic jam of headlights. 'Where's Tara?' she muttered.

'No idea,' Sameera answered.

A voice rang out from the crowd: 'Who's been taking care of your daughter while you've been campaigning this year, Mrs Righton?'

'She's done a pretty good job taking care of herself,' Mom answered, still scanning the crowd for any sign of a staffer coming to greet them.

'But she looks so young, Mrs Righton,' another voice said.

Sameera felt the same rush of adrenaline that came before the sound of her voice made eight oars start slicing through the water. 'I'm sixteen,' she called out. 'In Brazil, sixteen-year-olds get to vote.'

'Your father's running for president in America, my dear.'

People laughed nervously.

Sameera couldn't tell which reporter had made that tongue-in-cheek comment, but she didn't let it faze her. 'And he's going to win in America, too,' she said.

More laughter.

Reporters cruised along with Sameera on every side. 'Miss Righton, why did you wait so long to join your father's campaign?'

'I had a lot of responsibilities to finish up, like coxing and writing for the paper.' Smile. Wave. *Hey, this isn't bad. I'll wow them with my conversational skills and they'll overlook my lack of style.*

'This is your first time in Los Angeles, right? Why haven't you visited your father's hometown before?'

The Bench hadn't prepared Sameera for this one, and she hadn't anticipated it herself. 'Er... we've been too busy,' she managed.

That was probably true enough. But the other reason was that her high-powered father was as much of an orphan now as she had been before her adoption. Sameera's grandparents had died when their only child was serving his third term in Congress. Almost immediately after that, he'd sold his parents' house and joined the foreign service. Sameera was almost as curious about the Rightons as she was about her birth family—and that curiosity, too, ebbed and flowed with the years, but was always there.

'Stay close, Sparrow,' Mom threw over her shoulder, striding down the corridor so fast that the reporters had to jog to keep up. Doggedly, Sameera pushed the luggage cart along as fast as she could. *How do celebrities smile so constantly?* she found herself wondering. Her face muscles felt like they did when the hygienist cleaned her teeth.

Microphones angled toward her, reminding Sameera eerily of the blackened hot dogs on sticks at Maryfield's annual Fourth of July picnic. 'Miss Righton, you've just finished the tenth grade, right? Are you going to enroll in a public school this fall? Are you going to cox here in the States?'

Too many questions were coming from every side to process and answer coherently. Sameera settled for nodding and shrugging and keeping that wide dentist's-office smile in place as she steered the baggage cart through a maze of reporters, photographers, and gawking travellers. *Where is a Bossy Wench when you need her, anyway? Slow down, Mom!*

Mom finally stopped near the airport exit and flipped open her phone with an impatient gesture. Cameras clicked and flashed, capturing every gesture and expression. Sameera powered up her own phone, shielding the small screen from curious eyes trying to see over her shoulder. Miranda had told her to check in upon arrival, so thumbs flying, Sameera speed-dialed the familiar number and started text-messaging.

S: WHASSUP?

Miranda's message came right back; she'd probably been staring at her screen, waiting for Sameera's message to appear.

M: R U OK?

S: PAPPAZ! B4 MAKEOVER!

'Whom are you text-messaging, Miss Righton? Where are you staying in L.A.? Do you have a boyfriend? What are your first impressions of California?'

M: KEEP EYZ WIDE.

S: ?

M: 2 B HOT IN FOTOS.

'Sparrow!' Mom hissed. 'She's here.'

A thirty-something brunette wearing a tailored pinstriped suit, a crisp white blouse, and funky tortoiseshell sunglasses was pushing through the crowd. *Finally,* Sameera thought. She slid the phone back into her pocket, trying to hold her eyes wide while still smiling as broadly as she could. *My head feels like a jack-o'-lantern.*

'I'm Tara Colby,' the woman announced, extending a hand to Sameera and taking her sunglasses off, her eyes raking over the jeans, boots, braid—and the rainbow-coloured poncho Mrs Mathews had made, which Sameera had forgotten to remove.

Like the best of ventriloquists, the Bench managed to whisper without moving her lips: 'Take that thing off. It's seventy degrees outside.' Then, nonchalantly, she tapped her front tooth with one manicured fingertip, and followed the gesture with more ventriloquism: 'Food in your teeth. Get rid of it.'

Sameera whipped out her phone again and gazed at her reflection in the small black screen. *Oh no!* This whole time, while she'd been grinning like a pumpkin, a tiny chunk of airplane peanut had been wedged between her two front teeth. She flicked the peanut away immediately. It was harder, though, to remove a piece of clothing in front of so many watchful eyes, so she kept the poncho on.

'It was chilly at home... we left before dawn—' she said, holding on to the poncho like a baby clutching a comfort blanket.

'Does Brussels feel like home to you, Miss Righton?' a voice called out immediately.

'Yes, but—' Sameera started, but stopped when she felt a hand on her shoulder.

'Home is where the heart is,' Tara said loudly. 'Which means this young lady's heart is with her father. He's been counting the minutes till the two of them get here, of course.'

The Bench's polished smile didn't affect the upper half of her face, but at least now all eyes were fixed on her. Sameera seized the opportunity to slip out of the poncho and tuck it into her carry-on.

'She's just glad to be back on American soil,' Tara was saying. 'And I'm sure both of the Righton women can't wait to be reunited with the man in their life. Isn't that right, Elizabeth? Sammy?'

'Of course,' Mom answered, blinking as several more meteor-bright flashes exploded in their faces.

*Sammy? Who's Sammy?* Sameera thought as Tara pulled out two more pairs of tortoiseshell sunglasses and handed one to Sameera and one to Mom.

The pack of reporters followed them into the afternoon sunshine where palm trees lined the busy, wide avenue. 'The hotel's not far from the airport,' Tara said, leading them to a long white limo waiting at the curb. 'We're staying on the beach.'

A driver leaped out, loaded their suitcases into the trunk, and opened the door. *The getaway car,* Sameera thought, feeling more like a celebrity than ever, thanks to the dark glasses, stately palm trees, and a crowd of strangers wondering which famous person was being hounded.

She was only a few steps from the limo when someone blocked her way. 'Are you an American citizen, young lady?'

a gruff voice barked. Sameera looked up at the grizzled man looming over her and got a whiff of the pizza he must have eaten for lunch. He shoved a microphone into her face.

'Don't answer him,' Tara called sharply from inside the limo.

*Don't worry, I won't,* Sameera thought, trying to get around the foul-smelling man, who seemed about three times her size. *If I open my mouth, I'll hurl on him.*

'I asked: ARE YOU A CITIZEN OF THE UNITED STATES?' Mr Halitosis sounded like he was speaking to somebody with a hearing problem. The other reporters had kept a respectful distance, and most of their questions had been friendly. This pit bull made them seem like poodles.

Sameera faced him, holding her breath so she didn't have to smell the pepperoni marinating in his digestive juices. She didn't want to make a fuss in front of so many interested eyes, but as Mom always said, bullies needed to be confronted. 'I—' she started.

Suddenly Mom leaped out of the limo and pushed her way in between them. 'Let *me* take care of this, Sparrow,' she said.

'Did you get your citizenship recently? Do you speak English fluently?' the man persisted, still trying to angle his mike around Mom's substantial presence.

'THAT is none of YOUR freaking business,' Mom snarled, swinging his mike away with her open palm.

Eager photographers and cameramen leaped forward to capture the moment. Tara jumped out of the limo and somehow managed to pull Sameera and Mom inside. The Bench slammed the door shut, and they screeched away from the curb.

# Four

'That fool writes for one of those reactionary rags that aren't fit to be in print,' Tara said, breaking the silence. 'That's why I told you not to answer him.'

'Are you okay, Sparrow? That *Neanderthal!* How dare he—'

'I could have handled him, Mom,' Sameera interrupted, frowning. She'd been about to deliver a few well-chosen words in just the right crisp tone of voice before Mom had pounced into the scene. *And* I *wouldn't have lost it in front of all those cameras,* she thought.

Mom took a deep breath and cleared her throat. 'I'm sorry, Sparrow. I don't know what came over me. I felt like—like a lion watching her cub get attacked, and I couldn't help my-self.'

*'I'm* sorry I wasn't waiting when you came out of security,' Tara said. 'I had an intern call to get the flight info, and *he* told me your plane was *delayed.* What a disaster! As if we didn't have a tight enough schedule over the next couple of days.'

She emphasized a few words with such venom that Sameera felt a twinge of pity for the unknown intern. *Passing the buck. Nice,* she thought. Her first impression of Tara Colby certainly didn't measure up to Mom's rave reviews about 'superb organizational skills' and 'state-of-the-art campaign savvy'.

Of course, Mom wasn't a detail-oriented person; passionate, yes, practical, no.

But now Mom herself didn't seem at all pleased with Tara. 'How are we going to keep my daughter from being harassed like that again?' she demanded, her inner maternal feline obviously still growling.

'I'm *okay,* Mom,' Sameera said again, fighting another wave of irritation. *You're the one having a meltdown.* Her parents had been quick to realize that the petite Pakistani they'd adopted was tougher than she looked and could handle most things that came her way. Why, then, was Mom acting so hyper-parental now?

'This won't happen again, I promise, Liz,' Tara said. 'And even if it does, I'm going to equip Sammy to respond to it.' Sameera opened the fridge in the limo and pulled out an iced cappuccino. *I'm already equipped, thank you very much. And stop with the 'Sammy' already.*

'I've been pretty hands-off so far, Tara, but I refuse to let my daughter be harmed by this campaign in any way,' Mom said, still sounding all riled up.

'Calm down, Mom.' *I'm not one of those IDPs or child laborers you have to fight for.* 'Here—have something to drink.' She handed Mom the icy bottle and grabbed another one for herself. 'Want something?' she asked Tara.

Tara smiled, and this time the faint lines around her eyes deepened into grooves, making her face seem older but friendlier. 'No thanks. Liz, listen, I don't want either you or James to worry about what's going to happen to your daughter during this campaign. I was a politician's daughter myself, remember?'

'I remember,' Mom said, sighing. 'But James is used to campaigning, like you. I'm not.'

'Speaking of which, where *is* Dad?' Sameera asked, taking a big swig of coffee.

'He's had meetings all day, but he'll be in your suite by the time we get to the hotel. Only two more events before the primary—tonight's party and a Faculty Club event tomorrow. Which reminds me—you only have a couple of hours to rest before you need to start getting ready.'

*A couple of hours?!? Could a girl go from blah to beautiful in a couple of hours?* 'Are Constance and Vanessa meeting us at the hotel?' Sameera asked.

Tara didn't meet her eyes. 'Er… no. With your mom away, they took some time off to work with another client. He's an actor with a new movie coming out; the premiere's tonight, and then they'll be available to us again. I've got them booked from then on as long-term consultants until November.'

'You'll be fine, darling,' Mom told Sameera. 'Tonight's party is strictly fund-raising, right? That means no press passes.'

'Right,' Tara said. 'Did you pack anything dressy, Sammy? I can come up and help you get ready if you want me to.'

Sameera sighed. 'As long as there aren't any reporters there, I'll be okay. Thanks for the offer, though.'

She'd packed two party outfits, just in case something like this happened. The first was a three-piece salwar kameez that Mom had bought for her in India, which included a green calf-length flowing tunic worn with matching loose-fitting pants and scarf. The second was a simple chocolate-coloured dress that Sameera had bought for herself at a mall in Toledo the summer before. Miranda had tried to talk her out of buying the dress because the fabric matched her skin almost exactly. 'You look invisible, Sparrow,' she'd moaned, holding up a blue dress with a plunging neckline instead.

'I'd get that one if I could borrow your shape, Ran,' Sameera had answered. It was humiliating to be so underdeveloped, especially when her teammates had such curvy girlfriends. Ahmed's squeeze-bottle-shaped companion was rumoured to be a 36D on top, with a teeny tiny waist that was smaller than Sameera's.

'… Marina del Rey,' Tara was saying, gesturing out the window.

Sameera peered through the tinted glass; dozens of tan, toned people were walking dogs and taking the Southern California sunshine for granted. Sailboats swayed and danced on the sparkling blue water as though they, too, were looking forward to a relaxing weekend.

Mom was rifling through the fridge. 'Hungry, Sparrow? They've stocked this thing with all kinds of goodies.'

Tara's laugh sounded like a chandelier in the breeze. '"Sparrow"! What a sweet name. Don't you think "Sammy" suits her better? It sounds a bit more… American, don't you think?'

Mom was ominously quiet. Sameera suddenly felt like she was coxing a boat with two rowers pulling in opposite directions. *Get it together, girls*! she should yell. But she didn't; she was curious to see how this middle-aged conflict played itself out.

She opened her cell phone stealthily. I AM SAMMY, she informed her cousin via thumb.

M: WHA? WHERE R U NOW?

S: LIMO W/ MOM & BENCH.

'You don't mean you want me and James to start calling our daughter "Sammy", do you?' Mom was asking. Sameera noticed that she didn't use any salty adjectives or adverbs. That was a bad sign. It meant the steam was still building inside.

M: U C MOVIE N LIMO? *I Am Sam*, starring Sean Penn and Dakota Fanning, was one of Miranda's top tearjerker picks on a Friday night.

S: NO. BENCH RENAMES ME.

M: WOW.

'Yes, that's exactly what I'm suggesting,' Tara was saying brightly.

M: NAME U LIKE?

Sameera didn't hesitate. She'd been planning a name change for the campaign, but her choice involved going back to the three syllables on her birth certificate.

S: SAMEERA.

M: WHA? BUT I CALL U SPARROW!

S: OK 4 U. NOT 4 PLANET.

She was starting to feel like she'd outgrown the nickname that her friends and family had used since she was three. 'Sparrow' seemed to underline that physically she was as easy to overlook as the gazillion commonplace birds that shared the name. Besides, it didn't really fit; she hadn't chirped into the cox box as she led her team to yet another win. She hadn't twittered when she'd written articles for the paper, or posted entries on her blog. She was hoping to ease her circle of twenty-nine away from 'Sparrow' and into 'Sameera'—everyone except Miranda, of course. She couldn't see anyone in her family switching from the name they'd grown so used to through the years—that would be an impossible feat.

Mom didn't need to be sitting in a boat to raise her voice; the back of a fancy limo, apparently, was just as good. 'I am forty-seven years of age. I do not need ANYBODY to tell me what to call my daughter.' *Yep,* Sameera thought. *Mom was right—she's definitely more feisty than the current first lady.*

M: WHA UP NOW?

S: CATFIGHT!

That glassy laugh came again. 'We'll have to work on keeping that passion in check, Liz, won't we? Especially if you want to help James win this election. I'm sure the team's going to have a lot of damage control after that airport incident.'

Defeated by this below-the-belt blow, Mom slumped against the leather seat, sighing. 'I know. I'm sorry. But when it comes to my daughter—'

'I know how much you adore your daughter, Liz. Listen, call her "Sparrow" in private if you want, but she's going to have to be "Sammy" in public.'

M: PR GURUS KNO BEST. GO W/ SAMMY.

S: NO WAY. L8R.

M: OK. LUV U.

Sameera was sure her cousin was off on this one. 'Sameera' sounded much more mature than either 'Sparrow' or 'Sammy', and it added an urban, international edge that felt *right.* And besides, even celebrities surely didn't let other people *rename* them without permission. Or did they? Well, too bad. She certainly wasn't about to morph into a 'Sammy' just because the Bench was a power player.

She snapped her phone shut and leaned forward to make her announcement. 'I'd like to be called "Sameera" publicly. That is, during the campaign. "Sparrow" is fine for my family—I know it might be hard for you guys to make the switch, since you've been calling me that for so many years.'

'But, Sparrow—' Mom said, looking surprised.

'Why don't we talk about this later?' Tara interrupted smoothly. 'We're almost to the hotel, and we're all a bit stressed out from the fiasco at the airport. I'm sure we'll be on the same page once we've had some time to recover.'

*The same page?* Sameera thought. *I'm not even sure we're in the same book.*

# Five

The limo turned a corner, and Sameera glimpsed the Pacific Ocean curving into the bay and what looked like an extremely cool amusement park. 'That's the Santa Monica Pier and Boardwalk,' Tara informed her. 'Your parents had a photo shoot there earlier this week.'

They pulled up in front of a hotel that backed up onto the beach.

'After you, Sammy,' Tara said as the driver opened the door.

'You first, Sparrow,' Mom added grimly, not giving an inch.

Sameera led the way past two burly, tattooed doormen guarding the entrance to the hotel. Probably thanks to them, no reporters waited in the airy, tiled lobby, where French doors led out to the bright sand and the blue waves. *I caught the show about California minimalist on the Home and Garden Channel, but this is ridiculous,* Sameera thought, looking around for any signs of furniture. Three older, tight-faced women wearing white cotton pajamas were sitting cross-legged on the floor, eyes closed as they faced the ocean.

'Wait till you see your suite,' Tara said, commandeering an elevator. 'Not a bit of colour anywhere. Or comfort, sadly. But this is *the* place to stay in L.A., and they gave our campaign team a huge discount. You're sure to spot someone famous doing yoga in the lobby or sipping a health shake at the bar.'

'We're only here three more nights, right?' Mom asked.

'Right. Then we head back to D.C. for the summer.'

'You mean you guys head to D.C.,' Sameera corrected. '*I'm* flying to Toledo.'

'Yes. Well, we need to discuss your summer plans, Sammy, but perhaps we should save that conversation for later, too.'

Mom and Sameera exchanged glances as they followed Tara down the hall. A couple of months on the farm in Maryfield had always been a non-negotiable in Sameera's calendar. Besides, this summer, with Gran still recovering, an extra pair of hands was really needed there.

The top floor of the hotel only had one door along the entire passageway. Gilt lowercase letters were etched into the natural wood: *presidential suite.*

'Aptly named, don't you think?' Tara said, handing Mom the room keycard.

Before Mom could get to the door, it flew open, and there was Dad, arms wide and face full of delight at the sight of them. He seemed a bit grayer at the temples, and there were a few new lines at the corners of his eyes, but he was the same old Dad. Unchanging. Solid as a rock. Sameera threw herself into his arms; she hadn't seen him in two long months.

'Sparrow!' He dropped a kiss on her head, like he always did, hugging her tightly and keeping his eyes closed for a long moment, as though he'd recovered a lost treasure.

'James.'

Dad's eyes flew open and zoomed in on something above and beyond Sameera. Of course. The love of his life was standing in the hallway, and she'd uttered his name.

'Liz.'

Sameera barely managed to get out of the way before they collided. This was the longest her parents had ever been apart in their married lives—almost three weeks. Their squeeze was so tight she couldn't see where Mom left off and Dad began.

Sameera put down her laptop case and carry-on and glanced around the suite. There wasn't a fleck of dust or dirt anywhere. A slim, grey screen covering an entire wall was the only non-cream, non-glass item in sight. She couldn't help mentally replacing the sleek cream-coloured modern couch, two stiff-looking chairs, and hard ottoman with a squashy, chintz-covered sofa and leather recliners. After all her travelling and settling into different diplomatic residences, she'd developed the ability to make even the most sterile place feel like home. This room, however, felt beyond help.

'I think they want to be alone,' a voice murmured behind her.

It was Tara, and she was right. Sameera's parents' reunion had progressed from a close embrace into a long, juicy kiss.

*You've got an audience, people,* Sameera thought. *Get a room.*

Oh, yeah. They had one.

She could see the master bedroom from where she was standing; the French doors leading into it were thrown open, the lights inside dimmed, and imitation flames flickered in a faux fireplace. Another closed door off the living room probably led into a private bedroom for Sameera, and she fought off a wave of exhaustion as she pictured sinking into a comfy bed. If this hotel *had* beds; she didn't think she'd get much sleep on a yoga mat.

'I'd like to show you something, Sammy,' Tara whispered. 'Want to come down to campaign headquarters for a while?'

Sameera didn't look closely at her parents' intertwined bodies as she eased around them, and they didn't seem to notice that she was leaving. *A forty-seven-year-old woman and a fifty-three-year-old man shouldn't make out like teenagers,* she thought. *Someone might have a heart attack.*

Tara didn't say anything as they rode the elevator, and Sameera was glad for the chance to gather her wits as she watched the floor numbers light up one by one. When they got off at the fifth floor, she heard ringing phones, loud voices, and televisions blaring down the hall, but she stopped and faced Tara before they walked any farther.

'We need to settle the question about my name, Tara. Mom will go with my decision; we can leave her out of it. I'd also like to have the conversation about summer right now, because I've already booked my ticket to Toledo. I leave the day after the primary.'

Tara shrugged. 'Okay. Let's face facts—you're not quite the all-American type, are you? And a name like "Sameera" just underlines that.'

'I've lived overseas a lot, but this doesn't feel like a foreign country to me, if that's what you're worried about.'

'I'm not worried about how America feels to you. You've got to realize that *you're* going to seem foreign to America.'

Sameera tried to keep from rolling her eyes, but she couldn't help it. 'This isn't the last century, you know,' she said. 'People don't think like that anymore.' *Lady, you need to get out more.*

'Values in America don't change as fast as they do in Europe,' Tara answered, shaking her head. 'You're going to look like an outsider to some Americans—not to everybody, of course, but there are still some people like that out there. And they vote.'

'So we're supposed to cater to a few narrow-minded people?' Sameera asked. 'That seems like we're giving them a ton of power.'

'Not at all. What *I* want to do is help you—the real you—survive what could become an ugly campaign. A more… American image can act as a shield to keep the real Sameera safe and sound. I'll show you what I mean once we get inside.'

*I might as well see what she has to say.* 'Fine. But what about the summer?'

'After your dad clinches the Republican nomination the day after tomorrow, the race is going to heat up. Senator Banforth, the front-runner on the Democratic side, has a son campaigning heavily for her—Banforth Junior's a law student, handsome *and* articulate. And Governor Tom Dorton, the other strong Democratic candidate, has a lovely wife—who leads Bible studies, by the way—and three adorable children, all under the age of seven. The paparazzi *love* to photograph a political father bouncing a toddler on his knee.'

'That's nice, but Dad's certainly not going to bounce me on his knee.'

'Your role as your father's only daughter, my dear, is going to be crucial all the way through the summer and into the fall.

If you head off to Maryfield for the summer, people are going to wonder why you're being "sent away". Your father's opponents could have a field day with a move like that.'

'No way,' Sameera said. 'I'm going to Maryfield. My grandparents are expecting me. I'm not going to let them down.'

Tara sighed heavily. 'Well, let's forget about the summer for now. You might change your mind down the road. Come inside and I'll introduce you to "Sammy", okay?'

Following Tara into the temporary headquarters of Campaign Central, Sameera wrinkled her nose against cigarette smoke, the smell of sweat and stale coffee, and the unmistakable odour of Chinese take-out containers. Five enormous screens that were tuned in to different channels splashed colour across the walls. A dozen people watched intently and scribbled notes; some of them were groaning audibly.

Sameera glanced at the televisions to see what was evoking so much agony and then did a double take. On every screen, a tall, blonde woman dominated the scene; a short, thin, dark-skinned girl was trotting along behind her, half hidden by the luggage cart she was pushing. *Oh, my,* she thought. *I look like a before version of Michael Jackson. Minus the 'fro. Either that, or... Mom's baggage cart attendant.*

The cameras followed the two figures through the airport. You couldn't get a good look at the girl because she was either blocked by bodies that were much bigger than hers or huddled over her cell phone. But American viewers certainly got a close-up of the woman's furious expression as she slapped away a burly man's mike. In fact, that angry gesture was being repeated again and again, on channel after channel. From most angles, you could clearly see Mom's lips forming the word 'freaking'.

'Oh, no!' Sameera gasped. 'They're making it seem like Mom attacked that awful guy. I wish she had let me handle him.'

'Don't worry,' Tara said. 'I'm sure the team's already got a response strategy hammered out.'

The tension in the room over the on-screen Sameera and Mom was so thick that nobody seemed to care much about Sameera's live appearance. Following Tara into the adjoining room, Sameera overheard one-ended snippets of phone conversations. Some of them were definitely damage-control related: 'Mrs Righton was defending her daughter, just like any American mother would.' 'Yes, he did block her way into the limo.' Others were more general: 'Mr Righton was absolutely thrilled when we told him about your generosity.' 'Yes, the Rightons plan to be there. Of course they're bringing their daughter to the Governor's Ball. They don't like to go anywhere without her.' The woman who said this looked up and smiled distractedly at Sameera.

The third room, which was just as smoky as the other two, was obviously Cyber Central, with at least ten people surfing the Web on laptops. *Ah, the fun room,* Sameera thought, feeling much more at home.

A dapper man in a perfectly tailored suit was reading something over the shoulders of three staffers clustered at the same laptop. Catching sight of Sameera and Tara, he stubbed his cigarette into one of the many overflowing ashtrays and strode over to greet them.

'I'm so sorry about this afternoon. I'm Jerry Cameron, Sammy.'

*My! New names certainly spread fast,* Sameera thought, shaking the campaign manager's outstretched hand. 'It's okay,' she said. 'It was no big deal.'

'*Why* wasn't I given up-to-the-minute info about the Rightons' flight, Jerry?' Tara demanded. 'All the press seemed to know their arrival time. I can't do my job when nobody else does theirs.'

'I know, I know,' Cameron said, sighing. 'I've already fired that intern.'

A desperate voice called out from the television room and he dashed out, followed by most of the staffers who'd been sitting in front of their computers. In thirty seconds flat, the room was practically deserted; Sameera was reminded of firefighters racing off to battle an inferno.

# *Six*

Only one person stayed with Tara and Sameera. He was a plump, thirty-something man wearing thick-lensed glasses, black jeans, and a Hawaiian print shirt. He was fingering his goatee as he approached them, and Sameera wondered if he was trying to distract their attention from his baldness.

'This… this is Marcus Wilder, Sammy,' Tara said almost breathlessly, as though she were introducing a rock star. 'Marcus is one of the top marketing-to-teens communication experts in the business. He's simply… amazing.'

Sameera looked at her suspiciously. Why did this sophisticated, confident woman suddenly sound like a groupie in a mosh pit?

'What do you think of my work?' the man asked, his voice high-pitched and intense. The emphasis he put on 'my work' made whatever he was talking about sound like a masterpiece he'd spent a lifetime creating.

'What work?' Sameera asked.

'I haven't shown her the site yet,' Tara said. 'Bring it up, Marcus, will you please?'

Wilder flipped open a laptop with a flourish. 'Welcome to SammySez.com,' he said, sounding as dramatic as an announcer at the Academy Awards.

A cartoon that looked like an anime girl was forming on the screen, accompanied by background music. The red-lipped, big-eyed manga creature was wearing a Vote for Righton button on her shirt. A bubble of words appeared, and Sameera read them under her breath: 'Welcome to SammySez.com, the online journal written by the gurl who knows our next president better than anybody on the planet. I'm Sammy, and this is my virtual crib. Click on the Vote for Righton button, come on in, and hang a while.'

Sameera stared at the manga art, her mind frozen for a moment in cyberspace. 'Wait a minute,' she said finally. 'That's supposed to be ME!'

'You got it, babe,' Wilder crowed. 'She got it, Tara. You were right.'

'Of course she did, Marcus. It is your work, after all.'

*What is this, some kind of mutual admiration society for workaholics?* 'Is this site live?' Sameera demanded.

'Of course not,' Tara said. 'We're waiting for your approval, of course. This is the demo "persona" I was trying to tell you about, Sammy.'

'My job is to package you as an asset in your father's battle against the Democrats,' Marcus added, giving his goatee one more caress.

*I already* am *an asset, you morons. With me around, Dad gets to show off how compassionate and caring he is—how many rich, white golden boys adopt babies from Pakistan? Don't you* get *it?* 'What's that song playing in the background?' she asked out loud.

'Oh, I picked that tune out myself. Just click the reload button. Or should I say, "Play it again, Sammy"?' Wilder chortled at his own stupid pun.

Tara giggled like an eight-year-old at a slumber party. 'Marcus, you are *so* funny.'

*You're no Bogart, dude,* Sameera thought. *Casablanca* was number two on the list of her favourite movies, with Humphrey Bogart at number seven on her top-ten-sexiest-movie-stars list. When *he* said 'Play it, Sam,' Sameera always got the chills.

She clicked the button that made the page load again. Wilder turned up the volume, and Sameera listened carefully. The tune sounded familiar. She hummed along under her breath until she got it. It was a hip-hop-ized version of a patriotic country song—one that Miranda had sung in the shower at the top of her lungs a couple of summers ago: 'I was born, I was raised, in the U.S. of A…'

He's using as many tricks as he can to create a… a red, white, and blue virtual version of me. Subliminal. Clever. But not true. The truth is that 'Sammy' was born in an unknown village somewhere in Pakistan.

She clicked on the Vote for Righton button, and the manga girl disappeared. The cursor turned into a glitter pen that could be moved across what looked like a crisp white scrapbook page edged with one blue stripe and cut-out red stars. More manga art served as links to pages called 'da blog,' 'vote for Dad,' 'hot guyz,' 'gurl style,' 'hip toonz,' 'fun-n-gamz'.

Tara was studying the expression on Sameera's face. 'Marcus knows pop culture inside and out; if anyone can morph you into an all-American girl, he can. You *do* want to help your father win this election, don't you?'

'Of course I want to help Dad win,' Sameera said, sitting back in her chair. 'But this won't work.'

'Why not?'

'First of all, letting somebody else write stuff that's supposed to be mine? That's just not right.'

'It's wonderful to be so ethical, my dear,' Wilder said condescendingly, as if she were a precocious child. 'But this kind of thing is done all the time. It's called "custom blogging".

'Celebrities hire experts to create content on their websites, and so do politicians,' Tara added. 'Heavens, I wouldn't have suggested it if it wasn't legit, right, Marcus? Your father's got a custom blog, too. Want to see it?'

She directed the browser to display the campaign's official site, and there was Dad's home page, featuring a photo of him saluting the American flag. 'Read Righton's Weekly Blog on the Top Issues of Our Day' announced a banner across the bottom of the page. Sameera clicked on the banner and a long, five-paragraph essay about welfare reform opened up. She skimmed it, frowning. There was nothing personal about this writing; her Dad's writing style, at least in the emails he sent when he was on the road, was funny and lighthearted. This post, or essay, or whatever it was, sounded downright stodgy.

'Let's get back to SammySez.com, shall we?' Wilder interrupted. 'Any other objections?'

'It seems much more "tween" than "teen". I'm not twelve, you know. I'm sixteen.'

Wilder gave a dry laugh that sounded more like a cough. 'Based on the nice cheques they send me, ZTV and Podtunes seem to think I know the difference between "teen" and "tween".'

Sameera stood up. 'None of it sounds anything like *me.* I think Americans can handle a more truthful version of me.'

He hesitated, and Sameera could tell he was fighting to keep his eyeballs from rolling in their sockets. 'Which part *especially* doesn't sound like you?' he asked.

'The whole thing, really. I have a blog already, you know. On my site at myplace.com. I never use emoticons and—'

'But emoticons make Sammy seem so hip,' Wilder interrupted, completely ignoring the information about her own website. 'Teens *love* emoticons.'

*You were my age a quarter of a century ago.* 'I guess I'm not hip, then,' she said, shrugging. Why'd she bring up her blog, anyway? She'd have to list him as one of her 'friends' on her myplace.com site for him to see her writing, and she had no intention of doing that.

'Anyway, now that I've gotten to know you better,' Marcus said, 'my mind's overflowing with ideas to make the site more authentic. So, are we good to go, then?'

*Yeah, we know each other so well now,* Sameera thought sarcastically. 'Tell you what—I'll take a closer look at the whole site later and let you know my decision.'

'Take a couple of days,' Tara said, as though she were offering Sameera a three-week luxury cruise.

Wilder obviously wanted his stamp of approval right now. 'But—'

'It's okay, Marcus,' Tara said. 'You and I can talk about this tonight. Right now Sammy's got to run upstairs and get ready. Do you have any communication hints that might help her at tonight's event?'

He held up one hand, palm outward, bent his knuckles, opened them again, and repeated the gesture a couple of times. 'This is how American girls wave. *Don't* do that British-I'm-Royalty-Wrist-Twist thing you did at the airport.'

'What about conversation skills?' Tara asked.

'You need to use "uh-huh" a lot more,' Wilder said immediately. 'And when you *want* to answer no, say "I'll have to talk that one over with my father" instead. Also, use a phrase like "this rocks" or "totally". And giggle as much as you can.'

Sameera was appalled. 'Are you SERIOUS?' she blurted out.

'Extremely serious. Practise the wave and a decent-sounding girly laugh a *ton* of times,' Wilder said.

'Thanks, Marcus,' Tara said. 'I'll be right back.'

She walked Sameera to the elevator. 'Keep your hair loose tonight,' she commanded, appraising Sameera from head to toe, as though she were an outdated product on the verge of being junked. 'And cake on some bright, light undercover if you have it. Your skin colour's beautiful, don't get me wrong, but it's going to make you disappear in front of the cameras.

'I usually don't wear much makeup,' Sameera said. 'Just a touch of lipstick.'

'*That's* going to change,' Tara said grimly. 'You've got to accept *some* things without debate. When you get in front of cameras, you wear makeup. What have you got to wear for tonight?'

'Er—let's see. I packed a salwar kameez and a dress.'

'Whatever that first thing is, bag it,' Tara said immediately. 'Wear the dress. We start your makeover first thing in the morning. Don't forget to practise everything Marcus told you to do tonight.'

Sameera fought the urge to salute and click her heels as the elevator doors closed in Tara's face.

# Seven

Thankfully, there was furniture in her bedroom. Sameera gazed longingly at the queen-size bed, but the day wasn't over yet. After she showered and got dressed, she checked the living room for any sign of Mom and Dad; the room was empty and the door to their bedroom still closed.

*That's some reunion they're having,* Sameera thought, going out to the balcony that overlooked the beach. A breeze was spinning lightly across the bay, and it sifted through her unbraided hair like a caress. It felt strange to wear her hair loose; it was long but so fine that it felt thin and lank hanging down her back. The graceful curves of the coastline and mountains reminded her of the French Riviera, where she and her parents had vacationed the year before. Couples strolled along the beach, savouring the sunset. Sameera sighed. Was she always doomed to watch guys disappearing into the horizon with other girls?

Heading back to her room, she stretched out on the bed and dialed her cousin's cell.

'Sparrow! Are you okay?'

'Oh, I'm fine. Ran, do you think I'm… normal?'

'What? Of course you are. You're wonderful.'

'Remember Drew Barrymore in *Never Been Kissed?* I feel her pain, Ran.'

'So what? I've never had a boyfriend either. And I'm almost seventeen.'

Sameera's once-scrawny cousin had matured into a tall, curvy blonde with a farm-fresh wholesome sweetness. She worried about Miranda, whose goal in life was to leave the dairy farm forever and make it big in Hollywood. Ran was actually quite a decent actress, starring in Maryfield's local theatre productions and moving everybody to tears or laughter with her performances. Now that there was a chance her cousin might be discovered by the camera hounds, Sameera had started keeping a mental list of other once-sweet blonde starlets from small towns who'd gotten trashed by fame. Everybody in Maryfield knew that Miranda Campbell was smart, gorgeous, and talented, but... she hadn't been out and about in the real world the way Sameera had.

'Yeah, but that's because you're waiting for Mr Perfect,' Sameera said. 'You've had guys drooling at your feet since you were twelve.'

Miranda sighed. 'It's not easy being a guy magnet. I know I could always find someone to kiss if that's all I wanted.'

*Not every girl gets to know that, Ran,* Sameera thought, but she didn't say it aloud. 'Okay, so you're like a rich person who's fasting for religious reasons. I, on the other hand, am a starving beggar.'

'You are not. You've just got outrageously high standards.'

'Yeah, well, it runs in the family. How's Gran doing?'

Their grandmother was under strict orders to slow down after a heart attack had landed her in a Toledo hospital last fall. 'She seems better to me, but Poppa won't let her do any milking. And I'm so sick of cows I might butcher them all in a frenzy. Only three more days till you get here. We're counting the hours; Mom has your room ready with fresh linens on the bed.'

'I can't wait either. But get this—the Bench actually suggested that I hang out in D.C. all summer where I don't know a soul. How's that for nuts? She's also created a whole new *PAR-SO-NAH* for me.'

She wasn't sure why she'd switched to a Pakistani accent to lilt her voice up and down but she'd wielded it perfectly as usual. She'd always been good at making the retroflex *t* and the *dh* sound when she pronounced the few Urdu words she knew—sounds that her parents had a terrible time with no matter how hard they tried. *I heard it in the womb, after all, and for three years after that. I probably spoke my first words in it.*

'What in the world is a "persona"?' Miranda asked.

'Remember how the Bench wanted to change my name? Well, she's hired some marketing dude who wants to launch a virtual online image for " Sammy".'

'Wow! That's great.'

'WHAT? It's terrible.'

'You're giving us the inside scoop on the celeb life, aren't you? They always get funky new names and hire PR people to spin their images.'

'Yes, but what they've done for "Sammy" is so... horrible.'

'So what? You're supposed to be *delegating*, remember? Having fun? "Sammy" actually sounds like someone who's into fun. It's definitely a more kissable name than "Sparrow".'

'I thought you were into kissing abstinence.'

'I am. But *being* smoochable and smooching are two different things.'

'Whatever. For someone who doesn't want to be kissed till you're at the altar, you've sure thought about it a lot. Speaking of fun, though—Hey! Didja catch my campaign debut at the airport? Now THAT was fun! Wahoo!'

Her cousin's tragic Shakespearean groan travelled from Ohio to California without losing any intensity. 'Oh, Sparrow, Sparrow. *Why* did you put on that *poncho?* Or should I say that *sack?* It looked like you had *absolutely no shape at all* until you took that thing off.'

'And then I had a shape? Yeah, right. Mrs Mathews knitted it for me; I had to wear it. The Bench ordered me to dump it as soon as she set eyes on it.'

'See—the woman has sense. Even though I can't believe she wants you to skip your visit here.'

'Yeah, she's not half as savvy as Mom described; she hasn't been able to schedule The Makeover until tomorrow, and I've got to show up at some fancy fund-raiser tonight.'

Miranda was quiet for a few seconds. 'Please, *please* tell me you're not going to wear that Harry Potter invisibility cloak you bought last summer.'

Sameera looked down at herself. She was already wearing the dress, along with black hose and black pumps.

Her silence was a dead giveaway. 'I *told* you to buy the blue one. *And* one of those miracle bras. But no! You wouldn't listen. Oh. My. Gosh.'

'Nothing I can do about it now. Did you see Mom take on that reporter at the airport?'

Another groan. 'They keep playing it over and over again. Gran's getting all worked up about it.'

'Send her to the sunroom,' Sameera ordered, sitting up. 'Tell her to meditate. And turn *off* the television.'

'She won't let us. She flinches every time your mother throws that punch.'

'It wasn't a punch,' Sparrow said. 'She just sort of slapped his mike away.'

'Sparrow!' Dad was calling her from the main room of the suite. 'Come out here and talk to me.'

'I have to go, Ran,' Sameera said.

'Wait—Gran's here. She wants to talk to Aunt Liz.'

'She does? Oh, no.'

'Hello? Liz? This is your MOTHER. I can't BELIEVE—'

'It's me, Gran.'

The voice changed completely. 'Oh hello, sweetheart. Are you all right? I can't believe you had to face that terrible crowd at the airport.'

'Don't worry, Gran, I'm fine.'

'We can't wait till you come home, Sparrow. Your room's ready and waiting. Let me talk to your mother, darling.'

Sameera took the phone into her parents' bathroom, holding it up as she passed her waiting father. 'It's Gran.'

The room was so steamy she could barely see Mom's shower-capped head peering around the curtain. 'It is? Do I have to talk to her?'

Sameera nodded. 'Might as well get it over with,' she whispered, handing her mother the phone.

Dad was pacing in the living room, looking stunning in his

tuxedo. 'It's so good to see you, darling,' he said, coming to meet her with both hands outstretched. 'I've missed you so much.'

She put her hands in his. 'Me, too. I can't believe I'm finally in California. Whadja think of our arrival?'

'I try not to watch the coverage of the campaign unless the staffers ask me to,' he said. 'But your mom told me what happened. I'm so sorry that you had that kind of entry shock, Sparrow. That's one of the reasons we wanted you to stay in Brussels for as long as you could.'

'What? And miss out on all the action? *I* was fine at the airport. *Mom* was the one who lost it.'

'I know. But if I'd been there, I might have punched the dude myself.'

As they sat down in the uncomfortable chairs to wait for Mom, Dad glanced at his watch. 'Where *is* your mother? She used to get ready in five minutes flat before they turned her into Mrs America.'

'Still showering. Don't you like what they've done with her?

'Want the truth? I fell in love with her natural, sweet look, and I sort of miss it. Don't tell her that, though.'

'Do you have to give a speech tonight?'

He sighed. 'Yes, and I'm not sure if I completely agree with what they want me to say. I've been out of politics for so long I don't know if I can toe the party line anymore, Sparrow. I was a black-and-white kind of thinker when I served in Congress, but after living overseas for fifteen years—and being married to your mother for thirteen—I can at least *see* more grey now. And not just in my own hair.'

'But that's good, isn't it?'

'The problem is that there are so many issues I need to be on top of that I'm rubber-stamping anything Cameron's people write... something I vowed never to do.'

'Like welfare reform, right?' She couldn't help saying it.

'Right. How'd you know that?'

'I skimmed your blog post.'

Dad groaned. 'I don't even have time to read my own blog. Can you believe it, Sparrow? Even the jokes I'm going to make tonight aren't mine. I used to come up with my own bad jokes, at least.'

'That's hard, Dad,' Sameera said. 'I know how you feel; they've come up with a "custom blog" for me that's awful.'

'Well, if you don't like it, tell them. They won't go live with it unless you agree. You don't have to sell your soul just because I am, Sparrow.'

'You haven't sold your soul, Dad. You *have* to delegate stuff to people you trust or you won't survive.'

'You're right. And I do trust Cameron. He'd take a bullet for me if he had to.'

She didn't want to think about bullets coming his way; when she and Dad watched reruns of *24* together, she always fast-forwarded through the assassination attempts. 'What's your speech about tonight?' she asked.

'My so-called stand on bioethics; I'm not allowed to mention anything controversial like cloning.'

Sameera grinned. 'Mom and Gran got into a huge fight about cloning last summer. Mom thinks it's a good way to end famine. Gran thinks human cloning's against the will of God. I'm not sure what to think myself.'

'Me, either. Most of these issues don't have easy answers. I'm a diplomat and an ex-congressman, Sparrow, not a life sciences ethicist.'

Sameera was wishing desperately that she could help, but she wasn't sure how. 'You can't expect to know the answers to everything, Dad.'

'You're right. But the American people seem to want an omniscient president—that's the problem. And I'm far from divine.'

Sameera didn't answer. It was strange how she and her father could talk freely about everything except religion. Mom, on the other hand, prayed and read her Bible almost every morning, and loved to talk about faith. She and Sameera had attended international church services wherever they'd lived but Dad only joined them every now and then. Sameera herself wasn't sure *what* she believed, but she'd stayed up many a night with Mom, asking questions and debating theological issues into the wee hours of the morning. 'If God loves us, why is there so much suffering in the world?' could keep them going for weeks.

Mom didn't claim to have all the answers, but at least she liked to talk with Sameera about the questions. Not Dad. There was a boundary around Dad when it came to religion, and Sameera wasn't sure why.

# Eight

Mom came out and handed Sameera her phone. 'I am now officially deaf in one ear,' she said, but she sounded chastened. 'Your grandmother knows how to heave on the guilt, that's for sure. She's still *furious* about the airport incident, even after I explained what happened.'

'Don't worry about it, honey,' Dad said. 'We're late. Are you ready?'

'I think so. How do I look?'

Sameera fought a pang of jealousy at her mother's post-makeover sophistication. Mom's hair was twisted into a bun and a pair of enormous, sparkling diamonds dangled from her ears; she was definitely an 'after' version.

'You both look lovely,' Dad said, throwing a vague, distracted look at Mom's peach-coloured wool suit and Sameera's chocolate dress. 'Now let's go.'

Once they were in the limo, Mom brought up the airport arrival fiasco. 'I was surviving this campaign just fine until I brought you along, Sparrow,' she said. 'Watching your daughter get harassed by a bully would send most women over the edge.'

'Mom, you know me better than that. I can handle it.'

Judging by her frown, her mother wasn't convinced. 'You

don't know how rough it can get during a presidential campaign, Sparrow.'

'There's little or no privacy,' Dad added.

Mom: 'People want a piece of you for the wrong reasons.'

Dad: 'And you get constant criticism and praise, none of it deserved.'

What was this about? They hadn't used back-and-forth scare tactics like this since the Mom/Dad co-lecture on peer pressure and drug abuse that she'd yawned through when she was ten. 'I'm not backing out now; I just got here. And besides, what if you win? I'm sure the fishbowl gets even more intense then. This could be good training for life in the White House.'

Dad shook his head. 'The president gets a press secretary to manage the media, a staff of at least a hundred people to take care of his family, and Secret Service agents to protect them 24/7. There's a much wider buffer between his family and all the negativity.'

'It's not long until the election,' Sameera said. 'I can make it if you guys can.'

'Well, at least you'll get a break when you head to the farm,' Mom said. 'I'm pretty sure reporters won't follow you to *Maryfield,* of all places. You can't even find the town on a map.'

'Mom! Don't talk about Maryfield like that.'

The Rightons had never owned their own house; they'd moved from one government-owned diplomatic property to another. Maybe that's why her grandparents' dairy farm was the gold standard that Sameera set for herself when she tried to make a place feel like home.

The limo drove up a twisting road, and the city below them glittered like a Lite Brite board. The driver stopped outside the Hollywood Hills Country Club, and the three Rightons climbed out. Tara had actually been right this time; there were no journalists here.

'Stay close to your mother and me, Sparrow,' Dad muttered as they walked toward the entrance.

*Hello? I've been attending diplomatic events for a dozen years. Not to mention planning the bashes that we hosted at the Residence.* But she didn't say it out loud; Dad was already stressed out enough about his speech. She'd have to complain later about the epidemic of overprotection that had infected her parents.

Inside the reception area of the swanky club, hordes of old, well-dressed people were waiting to greet them. To make things more interesting for her blogging circle of twenty-nine, Sameera decided to try everything Wilder had suggested. She answered dozens of inane questions with 'uh-huh' and 'this is amazing' until the phrases started to sound strange in her ears. She opened and closed her fingers in the California-friendly wave that Wilder had shown her. She even tried a giggle once, managing to produce only a manic chuckle that made the woman she was talking with take an inadvertent step backward.

Tara came over to guide them into the next room. 'You're doing fine, Sammy,' she whispered before fading into the background again.

The Rightons made their way slowly into the dining room, working the crowd as they headed toward the podium and the table of honour. Waiters and waitresses were weaving through the crowd, carrying platters of hors d'oeuvres and refilling drinks. Dad stopped to chat with a group of prosperous-looking older men, and Mom smiled and shook hands with their dowager wives. Sameera stood behind them, trying to chew and swallow a rubbery calamari that a waiter thrust into her hand.

A portly, cigar-smoking man turned to her. 'Bring another platter of that shrimp by here, will you?' he asked.

'Uh-huh,' she answered through the calamari, still on autopilot with her prepared phrases. But why did this man want her to bring him food? Surely a server would pass by again soon.

Then the truth dawned. This man thought she *was* one of the waitresses. Her dress did resemble the simple dark uniforms worn by the staff—the only other non-white people in the room.

'I'm sorry,' Sameera said. 'But I'm not a waitress.'

The previously chatty circle had grown quiet. Mom looked shaken, and Dad was scowling. 'This is our daughter, Grady,' he said, his voice frosty.

The man choked, spluttered, and coughed, and the cigar shot out of his mouth. Dad ground it into the carpet with his heel.

'I'm sorry, Righton,' the man managed to say. 'I had no idea—I'm sorry.' He turned to Sameera, his face as red as the dipping sauce for the shrimp. 'How can I make it up to you, my dear?'

'It was a mistake,' Sameera said. 'Don't worry about it.'

Then she caught sight of her mother. Elizabeth Campbell Righton's face had taken on her familiar 'I'm-on-a-crusade-to-combat-evil' expression; her lips were about to form a host of four-letter words that she'd probably regret forever.

*She's gonna blow!* Sameera thought. *I've got to get her out of here!*

'Excuse us, will you?' She grabbed Mom's arm and pulled her out of the ballroom, hardly noticing that Tara was hot on their heels.

Mom sputtered and protested but somehow Sameera managed to get her into the ladies' room. Tara made herself useful by confronting the startled attendant: 'Twenty bucks if you get out, guard the door, and keep everyone else out for fifteen minutes.' The woman nodded, terrified, and scuttled outside.

Mom let loose once they were alone: 'THAT RACIST JERK!'

'Take a breath, Liz,' Tara said. 'Mr Grady's one of James's biggest supporters.'

'I don't care. He's a BIGOT, and he needs to be called on it!' Mom was pacing the carpeted floor, clenching a fist and punching it in the air like Russell Crowe in *Cinderella Man.*

Sameera rolled her eyes heavenward. Why did her mother have to make everything so... *big?* After all, it *could* have simply been an honest mistake. 'Maybe he's not a racist, Mom,' she said. 'Every other guest in there besides me is white. And my dress does look like the outfits that the servers are wearing.'

Tara threw her a surprised look. 'You're... not offended?' she asked.

'I've dealt with stuff like this before. In Maryfield, I'm usually the only dark-skinned person for miles around, and a couple of strangers who don't know me have sometimes acted... odd. Gran always told me to ignore it; that it was their problem, not mine.'

Mom groaned as she kept walking and knocking out imaginary enemies. 'Oh, so you're supposed to just TAKE treatment like that, like in the pre-civil-rights days? That's just great coming from my mother, who never had a relationship with a non-white person until you came along.'

'Mom! I set Mr Grady straight. I didn't "just take it".'

'We need to prevent this kind of thing from happening, especially as the campaign gets more heated,' Tara interposed quickly. 'What we need to do is get Sammy out there ASAP so your daughter can be known and loved. Can't *you* convince her to let us go live with the website, Liz?'

'What website?' Mom asked, stopping in her tracks.

'We hired a marketing expert to create an online blog and site for Sammy so that we can be proactive with her image. If we create a public persona for her, we might be able to retain some privacy for her. And keep her safe.'

Sameera was shaking her head, but Mom was nodding slowly. 'You might be right, Tara,' she said. 'America's so… odd and divided when it comes to race. James and I certainly don't want Sparrow to pay the price.'

'Why is it up to everybody else to decide what price I'm willing to pay?' Sameera asked. 'Why don't I get to choose how I want to do this?'

That was when she noticed the tears in Mom's eyes. It was typical for Elizabeth Campbell to get fired up about something, but she rarely cried.

The door swung open. 'I *paid* that woman to—' Tara started.

It was Dad. 'I had to give that attendant twenty-five bucks to let me in. Are you okay, Sparrow?'

'I'm fine. But aren't you supposed to be giving your speech?'

'I wanted to talk to you first. Tara, do you think you could—'

'Of course, James.'

After Tara left, Dad put his hands on Sameera's shoulders and looked intently into her eyes. 'That was rough, what happened out there. Especially right after you had to face that jerk at the airport. Listen to me, Sparrow: if my running for president's going to hurt you or your mother in any way, I won't go through with it. It's not worth it.'

There was so much love in his eyes that Sameera had to look away. She hadn't flinched when that reporter had breathed pepperoni fire over her. She hadn't gotten ruffled when she'd been mistaken for the hired help, or when Mom had been so irate over how she'd been treated. So why was the intensity of her father's concern making her throat feel tight?

Mom had ducked into a stall to grab some toilet paper, but now she came storming out again, blowing her nose. 'We've had two race-related incidents in our first six hours here as a family, James. I'm not going to survive many more of these, even if Sparrow thinks she can. Tara thinks it's going to get even more intense as we head toward the election.' She turned to Sameera, and her voice shifted from hard-nosed boardroom to nursery croon. 'For my sake, sweetheart, *please* give Tara carte blanche. Just for a while.'

Sameera turned to her father. 'What do *you* think, Dad?'

He hesitated. 'It's up to you, Sparrow. But Tara's gone through it herself, you know. She was smeared during her father's re-election run, and she vowed to do whatever it takes to keep other political kids safe. That's the main reason we hired her.'

Sameera hadn't known that, and it did make a difference. Besides, if rubber-stamping the creation of 'Sammy' meant that her parents could be a little less stressed-out… and as Miranda had pointed out, celebs *did* hire publicists and marketing gurus to create spin. It might be kind of interesting to find out what happened once you gave the image makers free rein. 'Okay,' she said, sighing. 'I'll sell my soul.'

Dad groaned. 'Did you have to put it that way?'

'Thank you, darling,' Mom said, wrapping her arms around Sameera and holding her tight.

'Come on, you two,' Dad said. 'I have to give a speech that I didn't write and tell some stupid jokes I didn't come up with. I need all the moral support I can get.'

# Nine

The day was finally over. It felt like weeks since Sameera had kissed Mrs Mathews goodbye at the Residence. But now it was the middle of the day again in Brussels and she was too keyed up to sleep. She got in her jammies, flipped her laptop open, and immediately felt the tension subside. Something about sitting in front of her screen, connecting to the Internet, and placing her fingers on the keyboard always made her relax.

The first thing she did was check for comments from her myplace.com buddies, and found several nice cliches of praise about her widely publicized flop of an airport appearance. *Liars, the bunch of them,* she thought, but she let herself bask in their affectionate (but undeserved) admiration. Not all of her buddies knew one another when she'd started blogging, but as they responded to one another through comments made on her site, they became cyberlinked into what she liked to call her 'strange little intergalactic circle'. When marvellous Matteo's beloved, ancient *abuelita* had died a few weeks ago, for example, two dozen succulent homemade chocolate chip cookies had winged their way to Brussels from Maryfield (baked by Mrs Graves; packaged by Miranda).

For some reason (inspiration, maybe?), she skimmed through the archives of her blog before posting a new entry. Lists always elicited comments from her buddies, and she had posted plenty of those.

*Five Keys to Good Coxing:* steer a straight course; keep your cox box in repair; invest in great sunglasses that block the sun and glare from the water; record your calls and listen to yourself; and figure out ASAP how to take a turn at high speed. Her guys had debated and re-prioritized this list for days.

*Five Cafe Must-Haves:* lyric-free music; private booths; cushioned benches; free muffin and croissant samples; and servers who leave you alone. Her newspaper buddies, many of whom frequented cafes, had strong opinions on this list.

*Five Traits of Head-Turning Guys:* kindness to babies, dogs, and old people; great conversation skills; strong, clean hands; longish, curly hair; and a mother tongue other than English, thereby creating a sexy foreign accent when English is actually spoken. Girls and guys had argued ferociously over this one, but Sameera's teammates had generally approved, as they all had at least three of these traits.

*Three Must-Dos for High-Powered Parents:* coordinate calendars so you don't travel at the same time; give offspring unlimited cell phone privileges; set aside two weeks of vacation together every year no matter what. Sameera's parents had been good about all three of those items for years. When Dad headed to D.C. or to London, Mom had made sure not to plan any meetings after three o'clock. And when Mom travelled to Dhaka or Dar es Salaam on a crusading trip, Dad had telecommuted from his home office during the afternoons. Even now, they checked in with each other and with Sameera via phone and email when they were away, and they always set apart a couple of weeks every summer to visit the farm. Sameera had always liked their hands-off-we-trust-and-love-you parenting approach and the freedom she got to enjoy as a result. *Let's hope they get over this strange fussy stage soon,* she thought.

Three of her lists were direct responses to her mother's work. In *Three Tips to Survive the Womb As a Girl,* Sparrow had fumed about how girl foetuses were aborted more often than male foetuses in many parts of the world. In *Four Truths About Kids and War,* she'd written about the plight of child soldiers. And last but not least, she'd come up with *Three Reasons Human Beings Buy and Sell Each Other,* which talked about the horrible practice of slave trafficking. She read the piece over; she was especially proud of it because of what it had led to.

> Dubai airport. I'm twelve, flying back to the States with a bored-looking flight attendant assigned to escort me. In the boarding area next to mine, where a plane is about to leave for Oman, I see four terrified girls, all younger than me, sitting with a man. I can tell right away he isn't their father. None of the girls look alike; none of them look like him; and he looks. . . downright mean. Their plane is boarding. Mr Evil steps aside for a minute, and I ask the oldest girl: 'Are you okay?' She begins to cry, quietly though, tears streaking down her cheeks. The man returns, glares at me, barks something at the girl, and they scurry after him to board the plane.

> The older girl throws a desperate look over her shoulder and catches my eye before disappearing. And I? I do… nothing. It's time for me to board my plane to Cairo, and my own escort is hurrying me along.
>
> When I tell Mom about it, she says that they were probably being sold as housemaids or something even worse. Why? I ask. How can that still be happening? She gives me three reasons:
>
> 1. Their parents are so poor they have to sell one child to keep the others alive.
> 2. Professional kidnapping groups grab them out of their villages and make sure their families can't trace them.
> 3. Nobody knows how widespread the practice is; nobody cares enough to try and stop it.
>
> I'll never forget that oldest girl's eyes. I see them sometimes in my dreams. But always, again, again and again, I do… nothing. When I wake up, I'm crying.

Comments on this post had revealed a growing desire in her circle to *do* something tangible about trafficking. Thanks to their encouragement, Sameera submitted the post as an op-ed article in the school paper. The piece had inspired the school's social action committee to adopt the issue as their annual charity project during the holidays. They'd organized a banquet/ auction, raised a huge sum of money, and made a big year-end donation to an anti-trafficking organization. That donation had been a big item on Sameera's 'I-need-to-stay-in-Brussels-until-these-things-are-done' list.

She opened a fresh blog box and titled her post 'Three Essential Non-verbals for Teen Icon Wannabes.'

> (1) GRIN. Do this constantly. Until your cheeks hurt. Don't stop. But check teeth for snoogies first. (2) WAVE. Not like the queen of England. Don't turn your hand so that your own palm faces your face. This might be taken as an obscene gesture in some countries with a name ending in 'stan.' (3) GIGGLE. Whenever. About whatever. Don't make it sound like you're taking strong doses of medication.
>
> Okay, intergalactics, despite your sweet words, I'm not quite there yet, but tomorrow, after The Makeover, I get a second chance to burst onto the scene as a star. We face the press at some event on campus at UCLA, Dad's alma mater, where I'll be looking (hopefully) less like Michael Jackson/a baggage handler and more like the glam princess I promised you I'd be.
>
> Also, check out SammySez.com in a couple of days if you want to meet the 'persona' they've invented for me. Can't wait to hear what you think about Sammy Righton, all-American girl. Remember: keep your comments short, clean, and to the point. Peace be with you. Sparrow.

After she published the post, she went back to Wilder's site and clicked on 'da blog'. Another crisp white page opened, surrounded by that familiar red, white, and blue border. A glitter pen graphic began writing across the screen, just a bit faster than Sameera could read. The cursive was rounded, the i's dotted with doughnuts like her cousin Miranda's i's. In fact, the computerized penmanship eerily resembled Miranda's handwriting.

Words were curling out across the white background:

> I'm finally on the campaign trail with my dad and we're staying at the **Santa Monica Seaside Hotel**. I'll be heading to **Petite Pizzazz**, which is this hot boutique for small-scale chicks like me, so check out my outfits over the next few days. L.A. is full of **hot guyz**, and I love So Cal! Go **Dodgers**! Go **Lakers**! Sammy.

One by one, she clicked on the phrases in the post that were links. Not surprisingly, the name of the hotel opened the hotel's website, 'Petite Pizzazz' led to some store's website, 'Dodgers' took her to the Dodger Stadium website, and 'Lakers' took her to the 'Official Site of the Los Angeles Lakers'. 'Hot guyz' led to another page on the SammySez website that was splashed with photos of current screen and music hotties (none of whom Sameera thought deserved the label) and a shot of the Harvard crew team (who were hunks, she had to admit, but not as hot as her own guys).

She browsed quickly through the other pages on the site.

'Vote for Dad' was set up as a FAQ page, with manga 'Sammy' answering the questions:

> ***Q: What's a party? Are you throwing one? Can I come?***
>
> *A: Sammy: If it were that kind of party, you can be sure I'd invite ya, but it's not. We have two big parties in America, or groups of voters who tend to think the same way on most of the issues—the Republican and the Democratic parties.*
>
> ***Q: Are you going to be at the Republican Convention in September?***
>
> *A: Definitely. Every state sends a group of delegates to the Republican Party's National Convention. So during a primary, registered Republican voters in that state decide which candidate their delegates should pick at the convention. The person who gets the most votes from the convention delegates runs against the Democrats in the November presidential elections. I've already got a hot outfit picked out for the convention, so check it out.*

These 'I'm-teaching-but-trying-to-pretend-I'm-not' answers were nothing like her own writing; they sounded so condescending that Sameera fought the urge to gag.

She clicked on 'hot outfit' and was taken to a page called 'Gurl Style', which was nothing more than beauty tips and product endorsements, along with a buxom but headless mannequin wearing a red leather dress labelled 'My Un-Conventional outfit.' 'Fun 'n' Gamz' provided links to free gaming sites galore; 'Hip Toonz' had a list of songs that were titled 'Sammy's Top-ten Playlist'. Sameera didn't recognize any of the pop songs on the list; thanks to her crew team, she knew a lot of hip-hop and reggae music, but she also knew a ton of country songs, thanks to Miranda.

Groaning, Sameera powered down her laptop. It was going to be humbling to let this... falsetto version of herself go live in the public eye. But apart from the twenty-nine people on her buddies' list and the folks back in Maryfield, she didn't really care *what* the American public thought about her. What counted was helping Dad achieve his dream—and finding interesting stuff to write about on her real bios.

# Ten

The next morning, once Mom and Dad headed off for a personal training session with Manuel in the hotel fitness centre, Sameera posted again:

> Four Insights into Life As a Celebrity: (1) When facing the media, your tongue may get heavy and thick and make you feel like you're having an allergic reaction. And your armpits will get itchy and sweat. A lot. (2) Limo fridges are stocked with excellent goodies. (3) Sunglasses make you feel braver. (4) Image makers, PR people, and marketing experts think they're a lot cooler than (a) you, (b) everybody else on the planet, and (c) their actual over-the-hill selves. Comments? Keep them short, clean, and to the point. Peace be with you. Sparrow.

She raced downstairs to meet Tara in the lobby of the hotel. The older woman was carrying a briefcase and wearing a pantsuit and heels that looked stylish but comfortable; Sameera was in her jeans again, but this time she was wearing a University of Ohio fleece that her grandfather had given her. The coastal breeze was chilly, and her teammates always teased her about not having any extra insulation on her body.

'Our time is short, Sammy,' Tara said briskly, stepping over several white-clad bodies concentrating on prone, silent yoga moves. 'We have a busy day ahead. First, we meet Vanessa at a boutique on Rodeo Drive. She's got some outfits waiting for you. Next, we head down the street to a salon where Constance has arranged for hair, makeup, and nails. In the afternoon, you'll have a brief session with Marcus. He's going to give you some tips on how to handle the press tonight.'

'Wait. I have something to tell you first, Tara.'

The two of them settled into the now-familiar leather seats. 'Rodeo Drive,' Tara commanded the driver. 'Make it fast. And *don't* get us stuck on the freeway.' She turned to Sameera. 'Well? I'm all ears.'

'I'm giving you and Wilder my okay on the website,' Sameera said.

Tara's eyebrows lifted. 'Really? I know your mom wanted you to go for it, but… how do *you* feel about it?'

Sameera was surprised by Tara's question; she'd figured her feelings weren't important to this PR queen. 'I think you guys are selling the American people short,' she said slowly. 'But it's going to be interesting to see if you're right and I'm wrong, or vice versa.'

Tara reached into her briefcase and pulled out a book. 'I brought something to show you,' she said. 'Take a look at this.'

*Political Progeny* was a pictorial history of kids with parents who were governors, senators, or presidents. Turning the pages, Sameera recognized Jenna and Barbara Bush, Chelsea Clinton, Amy Carter, Susan Ford, and the Kennedy kids, as well as several others.

'Jackie Kennedy protected her kids' privacy fiercely,' Tara said. 'That's why they survived emotionally—even though poor John Jr died so young. I had a crush on him for years. I even danced with him once at some event, but he always preferred the tall, thin, model types. Besides, he was a Democrat, and my dad was a Republican.'

She flipped to a page somewhere near the middle of the book and pointed to a photo of a plump girl at a picnic who was obviously relishing her ice-cream cone. The girl was perched on an overturned barrel, and the newspaper caption read: 'Ten-Year-Old Tara Colby Enjoys Porky-Barrel Benefits.'

'Oh, no!' Sameera said, with a rush of sympathy. 'Poor you!'

'It took years of therapy to get over the times the press poked fun at my body.'

'But you're not fat now,' Sameera said. 'You *are* one of those "tall, thin, model types".'

'Nah. I'm still "Porky Colby" inside, trying to prove that I'm more than just a senator's daughter. But enough about me. I just wanted to show you that I know how rough it can get for a kid during a political campaign. I'm so glad you're willing to accept our help.'

The palm trees along Rodeo Drive stood at attention as the limo stopped in front of Petite Pizzazz. Impossibly leggy mannequins in the display windows flaunted jeans, leather jackets, flared, pleated skirts, and blazers. *They don't look very petite,* Sameera thought, frowning up at the one in the middle, who looked at least six foot three.

Vanessa was a superbly maintained older woman who looked great from a distance. When you came closer, however, you saw that her skin had been stretched and lifted so often that it was physically impossible for her to smile. She didn't (or couldn't?) say much but escorted Sameera immediately into a dressing room. Tara followed them inside, leaving the door open so that salesclerks could come and go with different outfits.

Sameera took stock of the situation. She was sixteen years old, her 'bra' was a tube vest, and her underwear was so small she ordered six-packs online from the girls' department. She felt shy changing in front of her cousin, and even in front of her own mother. Now she was supposed to undress in front of Tara, Vanessa, and the clerks, one of whom was a guy? No way.

'I'd like privacy, please,' she said firmly. 'I'll come out once I have an outfit on, and take the next one in with me. Could one of you pick something out so we can get started?'

Vanessa shrugged, but she backed out of the dressing room as a clerk handed Sameera a blue wool dress, black boots, and a red, white, and blue scarf.

'You might need help tying that scarf,' Tara called through the closed door. 'Should I send someone in?'

'I can do it,' Sameera called back.

She squeezed in and out of a myriad of outfits, emerging from the dressing room only to have Vanessa shake her head and frown. Other clerks brought over shoes with heels so high Sameera felt like she was standing en pointe, like a ballerina.

After a whispered one-word suggestion from Vanessa, the clerks also began handing in shaped undergarments. Most of these had so much padding that Sameera felt like she was putting an extra body on top of her own.

After two long, arduous hours, she came out wearing an outfit that finally made Vanessa clap her hands (smilelessly, wordlessly).

'That's it!' Tara said. 'It's perfect; demure and sweet with a hint of sexy. Consider tonight's event your real debut, my dear, because tomorrow the press is going to be raving about the new you. Take a look.'

The salesclerk unbuttoned a couple of the buttons on the jacket Sameera was wearing and moved out of the way. Sameera took stock of herself in the three-way mirror, and her lower jaw dropped. She was wearing a beige leather miniskirt and matching jacket. Black high-heeled boots made her legs look shapely and… long. Actually long. The jacket was opened just enough to reveal a black, scoop-necked clingy shirt underneath it. And there was even a glimpse of hidden curves at the top of the shirt.

*Where did THOSE come from?*

But Sameera knew the answer to her own question. The undergarment was lifting, squeezing, and pushing together the little she had on top, and the cups were chock-full of synthetic stuff that 'felt natural when you're hugged', as one clerk discreetly put it. 'It does look good, but isn't it a bit… low-cut?' Sameera asked.

Vanessa rolled her eyes heavenward and gave her head a small shake.

Tara translated. 'A hint of cleavage is perfectly modest for a teen girl, especially by L.A. standards. Wear it to the salon, and keep the boots on, too. You've got to learn to walk naturally before tonight.'

Tara was right; Sameera needed practice. She could hardly make it over to the cash register without toppling over—how was she supposed to wear these boots through the entire event scheduled for that night? And no matter how demure Tara thought she looked, Sameera had never emerged into the public eye with even a 'hint' of cleavage. Even Miranda, for all of her desire to be stylish, rarely got away with wearing low-cut shirts. Gran and Aunt Bev both thought they made a girl look 'starved for attention'.

'While you're in the salon with Constance, Vanessa will pick out some casual clothes, bags, and shoes,' Tara said. 'Now that she's seen what works on you, she doesn't even need you to be there.'

*She should just take the undergarment along,* Sameera thought. *It could probably sashay around by itself.*

Just before they left the store, Tara stuffed Sameera's discarded jeans, T-shirt, and fleece into a bag and handed them to one of the clerks. 'Could you get rid of these, please?'

Sameera almost fell over to grab the bag before it was whisked away. 'I'll hold on to this,' she said. Poppa had bought his granddaughters the matching fleeces when he and Gran had attended their college reunion, and Sameera knew he liked to see the girls wearing them.

'Suit yourself,' Tara said. 'But I don't recommend you wear those clothes again. Take a look at these photos.'

She pulled out a copy of *Los Angeles Currents* from her designer handbag. The front page of the 'Life' section featured a big photo of James Righton's daughter grinning into the camera with a chunk of airplane peanut caught in her teeth. The Mathews-made poncho, which did hang around Sameera like a sack, made her body underneath seem even more tiny. 'Righton's Adopted Daughter Joins Father on Campaign Trail' the headline read.

'That stupid peanut,' Sameera said, sighing.

'It wasn't the peanut who wore that poncho,' Tara said, taking back the paper.

They walked down Rodeo Drive to the salon, where Camera-Ready Constance scanned Sameera's face and hair with the intensity of a master artist appraising an empty canvas. In response to her commands, a triad of stylists clustered around Sameera. Tara called back a final reminder as she headed out the door: 'A trendy but feminine appearance, please. Nothing too edgy.'

'We absolutely *can't* let you look in the mirror till we're done,' Constance told Sameera. 'Makeovers are more *dramatic* that way.'

*Don't worry, sweetheart,* Sameera thought. *I've seen the shows.* She could hardly wait to describe this experience to her intergalactic circle. The only problem was that she was starving. She hadn't eaten anything for breakfast. Did celebrities *ever* eat? Did Tara Colby ever eat?

The Makeover began with the application of a facial mask that smelled hauntingly like Gran's homemade pesto. Sameera continued to battle hunger pangs as they cut, styled, and blow-dried her hair, doing her best to focus on what they were doing. She took mental notes on technique, texture, and colour while they manicured her hands and applied makeup to her face, trying not to think of oatmeal scotchies or a Sunday feast of roast chicken, fresh-baked crusty rolls, green salad, and rosemary potatoes.

But when the stylists spun her around to face the mirror, any temptations to fantasize about food vanished. She couldn't believe what she saw. *Wow! This girl is... stunning.* And she was. A short, layered haircut framed her face and showed off her slim neck. Foundation and blush emphasized the high cheekbones and brought out her big, almond-shaped eyes. The lipstick made her lips look red, rich, full... downright *smoochable.* Even her skin looked more alive, glowing, fresh.

'Stand up *immediately,* Sammy darling,' Constance commanded.

Slowly, Sameera obeyed, appraising her reflection in the full-length mirror. The hair, the makeup, the leather outfit, the boots, the tantalizing glimpse of cleavage... WHO WAS THIS HOT GIRL IN THE MIRROR?

Tara came back, clutching two extra-tall cups of coffee. 'I picked up some lunch for... SAMMY!' For once, the cynical facade lost its grip on Tara's face and her mouth fell open. 'Oh my! You look... AMAZING!'

Constance blew on her own freshly touched-up white-tipped French manicure. 'I'm sure you'll have my website link up and running as soon as the photos of *this* version of Sammy hit the press.'

Sameera caught the slightly flustered look on Tara's face. 'We're always looking for ways to save your dad money,' Tara said, giving that tinkly laugh that Sameera was starting to recognize… and dislike intensely.

'And what if I hadn't agreed to letting SammySez.com go live?' Sameera asked.

'Oh, we'd have put the link somewhere else—on your father's website.'

*Yeah, right.* They exited the store and Sameera glimpsed the limo parked at the corner. The driver was nowhere in sight; he must be somewhere eating lunch, like most normal human beings. As she and Tara walked down the street, Sameera realized she was drawing attention from a lot of people. Especially a couple of young construction workers, who were checking out the 'after' version… and obviously liking it. *Look out, world, Sameera Righton is definitely on the radar. I AM FINALLY VISIBLE!*

One of the construction guys put a hand over his heart as she walked by. 'Whassup, baby?'

*He's talking to me. Okay, girlfriend, if you want to know what it's like to be a celeb, you've got to act like one.* She tried smiling and gave her head a little shake so that her hair moved around her face, like shampoo models did in commercials.

'Looking good, girl.' The second guy pursed his lips as he checked Sameera out from head to toe.

She tried adding an extra swing to her hips but almost fell over on her high heels.

'Sweet boots.' It was the first guy again.

*Is this all it takes to get some male attention? It's like putting a slab of steak in front of hungry dogs.* Sameera fought an impulse to snap her fingers in front of his face as his glazed eyes focused on her push-up bra. *He did say 'boots', didn't he?*

Hurrying to keep up with Tara, she gave up the attempt to swing her hair and hips around and focused instead on keeping her balance.

# Eleven

The limo was locked, so they had to wait on the sidewalk. Sameera tried to stay in her aloof-but-gorgeous celebrity mode as the construction workers still pledged undying love—or lust—from a distance.

'Your parents called from Orange County,' Tara said, handing over the iced cappuccino she'd bought for Sameera's 'lunch'. 'They're meeting us in the hotel at six, and we'll head to UCLA in a caravan. Where *is* that driver?'

'The students are gone for the summer, right? So who's going to be there?'

'A few students might be there, but you're right—most of them aren't on campus right now. About two hundred alumni and faculty have been invited to the banquet. You'll want to come across as smart, stylish, and absolutely loyal to your father. Marcus can prep you for that. *Where is that driver?*'

'Here I am. Sorry, Ms Colby.' Sheepishly, the driver opened the door for them, and Sameera tried not to lunge for the doggy bag of leftover Mexican food he was carrying.

As they walked into the frenzied din that was Campaign Central, Sameera downed the last of her coffee in big gulps. Thankfully, someone on the staff had ordered a pizza and there was one wedge left. As she chewed and swallowed, she was careful not to spill on her new outfit, but Tara kept reaching over to brush imaginary crumbs off her skirt.

'She looks perfect,' Wilder said to Tara, as though Sameera wasn't there.

'She needs to. The primary's tomorrow, and the press is going to be there tonight in full force.'

'Don't let her sit while the two of them are standing, or vice versa. Always put her right between the two of them during any photo ops. And, please, don't let her ever be seen carrying *anything* for them, for heaven's sake.'

Sameera knew Wilder was referring to what had happened the day before at the reception. *How had he found out about that?* 'Don't worry,' she said wryly. 'I don't think anybody's going to mistake me for the Righton family servant two nights in a row.

'Especially now that you look so look fabulous. Right after we're done, I'm going to blog about your makeover for your first live post; I'm so glad you agreed to go for it. Now, let's practise some Q and A to get ready for tonight, shall we?'

'I think I can handle it.' *How many times did she need to say it before they believed her?* 'I've been a diplomat's daughter for thirteen years, you know.'

The Sammy-makers exchanged looks. 'You probably could swing it without help,' Tara said. 'But this is standard protocol for candidates and their families. Even your parents are prepped thoroughly for each appearance; it helps a public figure stay in charge of the event.'

'And that's what you are now, Sammy,' Marcus added. 'A public figure.'

*Let the games begin,* Sameera thought as Marcus and Tara began throwing out odd questions that might come from left field and coming up with 'suggested' answers. She repeated their answers, trying not to roll her eyes, and amused herself by coming up with the truth in her head.

Q: 'Do you go to church?' A: Oh, yes. Every Sunday. (True Answer: Yes, but I'm still confused about religion.) Q: 'Do you agree with your dad on most of the issues?' A: Of course. He's the smartest guy I know. (True Answer: No, but we love a good debate, and we can both admit when we're wrong. That's why Dad's going to make a great president.) Q: 'Do you have a boyfriend?' A: Not yet. My parents want me to focus on my studies, and I'm too busy with all my activities. (True Answer: Know anyone who's smart, funny, eligible, *and* attracted to the Oompa Loompa type?)

And there was more. Much more. By the end of it, Sameera was so tired and jet-lagged that her second evening on the campaign trail felt unreal. Bits and pieces played afterward in her memory like a montage in a movie trailer: Dad's and Mom's open-mouthed response to her new 'look', the admiring stares of the few college guys sitting at the lone students' table in the back of the room, the wine that was poured into her goblet despite Mom's frown. Sameera didn't touch it, of course, but still... to be thought grown-up enough to be served Chardonnay... that had certainly never happened before.

The reporters were there, dressed in tuxedoes themselves, and Sameera delivered her pre-rehearsed phrases perfectly. Q: 'Are you glad to be here?' A: 'Yes, it's *great* to be part of Dad's campaign. I'm lovin' it!' (True Answer: It's quite interesting from a journalistic point of view, but my tootsies are already starting to ache in these boots.) Q: 'How'd you spend the day today, Sammy? A: 'Shopping on Rodeo Drive. L.A. is awesome!' (True Answer: Purchasing the most intensely padded undergarments in the universe.) As her 'true answers' got more and more zany, she was grateful for the dry-run rehearsal she'd had with Marcus and Tara. Repeating memorized lines was a lot easier than thinking up decent answers, especially when mikes were shoved into your face and cameras started dancing at the sight of you.

'Blow the reporters a kiss,' Wilder had told her. 'Pout your lips like this, and then let them go with a soft puff of air. They'll love it, trust me.'

Sameera hadn't been able to bring herself to practise this particular manoeuvre in front of him. 'I've *never* blown a kiss at anyone in my life,' she'd told Wilder.

Now, in her I-wannabe-a-starlet mode, she decided to risk it and find out if he was right. Amazingly, the kiss seemed to come naturally, as though her lips were designed to blow them at strangers. But, of course, she wasn't herself—she was 'Sammy', the celebrity whose sole purpose in life was to wow her fans and convince them to vote for her dad.

She had to admit that, in this case, Wilder was right. Most of the reporters and photographers grinned affectionately at the gesture and a few even blew kisses back. Sameera glimpsed the pleased expression onTara's face. Yes, the Bench was there as usual, hovering in the background with a few staffers in case the Rightons needed damage control. *Don't these people have lives?* Sameera wondered. They'd travelled constantly with Dad throughout the campaign and would do so until November. What about their families? Who was watering their plants, collecting their mail, feeding their pets?

During dessert, while Dad gave a carefully rehearsed speech about his commitment to public-private partnerships in revitalizing America's cities, the Righton women smiled and gazed at him, just as they'd been coached. Sameera managed to stay steady on her boots but kept fighting the urge to tug the neckline higher or button up her leather jacket. *Stop being so shy,* she commanded herself. If you took stock of the room, cleavage was definitely in style; alumni and faculty members alike were showing off even the most ancient of curves.

When it was finally time to leave, a young woman pushed her way over to Sameera through the reporters. Sameera had noticed her when she'd first walked into the room partly because the stranger was a large, striking girl, but mostly because she and her mother were either Indian or Pakistani.

'I'm Sangita Singh,' the girl said in a low voice, slipping a small business card into Sameera's hand. 'My mom's on the faculty here, but I'm a student at George Washington University. Everyone there calls me Sangi. Come join us for coffee in the fall when you're back in D.C., if you can get away from *them.*' She tipped her head in the direction of the reporters, and a dimple deepened in her round cheek.

A refrain formed itself in Sameera's tired mind: *Sangi Singh, Singi Song, Songi Sing.* As she grinned back at the girl, a vague part of her brain registered that this was her first genuine smile of the entire evening.

'Keep walking, Sammy, keep walking,' Tara's voice said behind her. She managed to edge Sameera away from the

South Asian girl just before a photographer snapped another picture.

Sameera kept a tight grip on Sangi's card as she and her parents made their way to the limo. She forced herself to stay in character and blew one more of Wilder's kisses at the cameras before climbing in, and Dad rolled down the window so that they could all wave as they drove away.

# Twelve

In the limo's dim light, Sameera held up the card. SARSA@GW, she read. Fridays from 3-5 p.m. Revolutionary Cafe. Foggy Bottom Station. She tucked the card inside the small glittery clasp bag that was part of her outfit, wondering what SARSA@GW stood for.

Dad leaned back and loosened his tie. 'It's going to take me a while to get used to this new version of you, Sparrow. You gave your old man a heart attack when you walked in the hotel room.'

'Me, too, Sparrow. You look about… twenty-three,' Mom added. 'Do you *like* what they've done to you?'

*What? YOU get to look glam and I don't?* 'It's awesome,' she insisted, even though her feet were screaming in agony. 'I actually felt like a celebrity tonight.'

'There's a downside to fame, you know,' Mom said.

'I KNOW, Mom. I'm not stupid.' *Don't you get it? I'm a journalist TRACKING the life of a celebrity*. But how could her parents get it? They weren't members of the elite twenty-nine; she'd wanted to keep her myplace site parent-free. She didn't write anything that she'd be embarrassed for them to read, but… well, Mom would probably be a bit too enthusiastic and offer 'suggestions' for things Sameera could write about. And

Dad? Well, she wasn't sure what *he'd* think about some of her crew teammates' off-colour comments. He was so… well-bred and polite. No, Mrs Graves was the only exception to her twenty-or-under age limit.

Mom looked surprised and a little sad. 'Okay, Sparrow. I… just don't want to see you getting—'

Sameera relented, sighing. 'Hurt. I know, Mom.'

'Just wait till you're a parent,' Mom said. 'You'll tell me, "*Now* I get how you were feeling during the campaign".'

Dad looked from his wife to his daughter, who were both concentrating on taking the instruments of torture off their tired feet. 'How about we head out early tomorrow, just the three of us, and I give you a tour of my old stomping grounds?' he asked.

'But James, tomorrow's the primary.'

'I know. But I want to show off my surfing skills for the ladies in my life.'

'Are you sure you still have 'em, Dad?'

'You bet. A surfer never forgets how to catch a wave, dude,' Dad answered, making the hang-ten sign with his hand. For a second, Sparrow glimpsed the blond, teenaged California boy he used to be all those years ago.

'That sounds great, Dad, but don't we have to visit polling stations? And there's another party tomorrow night, right?'

'Leave that to me. We will have to kiss some babies once the polls open, and take some photos, but I'll figure something out. What do you think, Liz?'

'I'd like that, James,' Mom said. 'But tonight I'm going to have to stay up late to work on that freakin' report.' It was getting to the point where Sameera couldn't hear the word 'report' uttered by anybody without mentally adding 'freakin'' in front of it.

When she finally got back to her room, she realized that someone had been hard at work. New tubes and pencils of makeup, vials of perfume, and glittering jewellery were arranged neatly in a case. When she opened it, drawers rose and slid forward and out, so that everything could be accessed while travelling. More new clothes were layered in the dresser and hanging in the closet. Sameera glimpsed angora sweaters, flirty skirts, blazers, and scarves, along with countless pairs of shoes and even more undergarments that felt like armour when you put them on.

'WHO'S BEEN IN MY ROOM?' Sameera growled, feeling like the three bears after Goldilocks barged into their lives. She was glad that her laptop was password protected; there and the changing room were the two places where her privacy was a non-negotiable.

She picked up the hotel phone and dialled Campaign Central. 'I'm looking for Tara Colby,' she said, figuring that the entire team was gathered in front of the televisions and computers, analysing the coverage.

'This is Sameera,' she said when Tara's voice came on the phone. 'Who was in my room?'

'I gave housekeeping some extra money to put away the stuff Vanessa and Constance sent over for you. What do you think of it?'

*Oh. The hotel cleaner came in every day anyway; I can't really get ticked about that.* 'I haven't looked through the clothes. But I'm sure they'll be fine.'

'The white dress is for tomorrow night's celebration,' Tara told her. 'Vanessa thinks you need something a bit more elegant for that event; it's a father-daughter dance—the perfect place to announce that he's secured the party's nomination. You did great tonight, by the way. The coverage is superb and more than makes up for yesterday's disaster.'

'Am I meeting Vanessa and Constance tomorrow before the event? Sounds like we're on a tight schedule.' *I hope we can squeeze in that early morning tour,* she thought.

'I've got it all taken care of. Don't forget to read your blog; you don't want to say something that seems out of character.' For a moment, Sameera thought Tara was talking about her real blog, but then she remembered that SammySez.com had gone live, maybe even as they were talking.

Dad's voice came on the line. 'Oh, sorry, Sparrow.'

'It's okay, Dad. I was just talking to Tara.'

'Good. I'll need to speak to her about tomorrow's schedule. Tell me when you're off the phone.'

'I'm done, Dad.'

'I'm here, James,' said Tara. 'What about tomorrow?'

Since nobody had told her to get off the line, Sameera listened as Dad explained his idea of heading out at dawn to take his daughter and wife on a brief, personal tour. 'I know the schedule's tight, but Sparrow's leaving for Ohio the day after tomorrow, so we—'

'I've been meaning to talk to you about that, James. Your daughter simply cannot spend the entire summer in Ohio apart from you and Liz. Not now; not when we're about to take on the Democrats full force. The race may get ugly, and she needs to stay by your side.'

'No.' Dad's voice was firm. 'Sparrow spends the summer in Maryfield. If she decides to end her visit early and join us in D.C. before the convention, that's up to her. Otherwise, Liz and I want this to be as normal a summer for her as possible.'

Tara sighed. 'Okay. But I'll be waiting for a call from Ohio, Sammy. I'll come and pick you up myself and bring you back to D.C.'

*How'd she know I was still on the line?* 'Fine. See you tomorrow.'

She replaced the land-phone receiver in the cradle with a hard click so that they both knew she'd exited the conversation. Then she flipped open her laptop to visit SammySez.com. Wilder's (live!) Sammy post of the day was in line with the rest of his creative offerings:

> what do you guyz think of my new look? I've always wanted to be a hottie; what gurl doesn't? so we did a little nip and tuck, and the results were sort of amazing... **petite pizzazz** is an awesome boutique, and the **rodeo drive salon** rocks... the boots were my favourite part... it was so great to be at UCLA tonight... my dad went there you know and graduated head of his class... he's a genius... in a couple of years I might get in, too... college apps and sats are such a drag but everyone's gotta do it...

Sameera stopped reading. If *she* rolled her eyes constantly while reading Sammy's posts, what would other visitors think? *They're loving it if they're insomniacs,* she thought, yawning widely. *Works like a charm.*

But before she went to sleep, she had to find out what her cousin thought of The Makeover. 'It's me,' she said when Miranda answered the phone. 'Or at least I think it's me.'

'Sparrow, turn on the television *right now.*' It was Miranda. 'You're on every channel, practically. We can't *believe* it's you… I mean… *how* did you…'

Sameera headed into the living room with her cousin still sputtering in her ear. 'Hush up, Ran,' she said. 'Let me check it out for myself. I'll call back in a minute.'

She put the phone on the coffee table, but Mom didn't look up from her laptop. 'Miranda said we're all over the news. Can we watch?'

Dad wearily reached for the remote. 'Tara told me the coverage was positive,' he said, nipping through channels to find the news.

He found a local station first: 'James Righton, the front-runner Republican candidate who has practically locked in his party's nomination, was joined by his charming wife and daughter at UCLA's Faculty Club tonight.'

The camera zoomed in on Sparrow's face as she blew a kiss to America. 'She's a beautiful girl, isn't she?' the newscaster in the studio said. 'And such a joyful spirit, too!'

The Celebs! channel was featuring side-by-side before-and-after shots of Sparrow, just as Tara had predicted. 'Cinderella in Hollywood? In twenty-four magical hours, Sammy Righton's style changed from schoolgirl to posh princess. Angeleno sophistication oozed from this young lady as she stood by her father's side tonight at the UCLA Faculty Club. Righton is expected to sweep the California primary tomorrow and clinch the Republican nomination.'

Sameera dialed her cousin again. 'I look so different. I hardly recognize myself.'

*'What happened to your body?'* Miranda demanded.

'These people are miracle workers, Ran. Look at what they did to Mom.'

'But… but *you* grew new parts. You didn't let them… add anything surgically, did you?'

Sameera glanced over at her father, who was frowning at the television. 'No way,' she said in a low voice. 'It's just the magic of underwear. Hey, I'll call you tomorrow.'

She sat next to Dad on the stiff, uncomfortable couch. He was tuning in to coverage of the Democratic primary, which was a much closer race than the Republican one. Sameera noticed that Senator Banforth came across as earthy and natural, making people laugh with her well-timed, witty, incisive comments. The other Democratic front-runner, Tom Dorton, was always swinging one of those adorable kids of his around, tossing a baseball with another one, or riding the third one on his shoulders. He looked young and energetic and vibrant. Sameera couldn't help feeling that Dad came across a bit staid and stuffy in contrast to these contenders, despite his charm and polish. He did better with people when he was actually with them, chatting in off-the-cuff conversations that showed off what a good listener he was.

*Tara said the Republican race would be easy compared to what's ahead. Things are going to heat up.* A part of her did want to stick around as the campaigning got more interesting over the summer, but she couldn't let the Maryfield folks down. Everybody was doing their own chores *and* taking over a big chunk of Gran's work so she could recuperate. This was one summer when they actually needed her help.

'I'm heading to bed,' Dad said, switching off the television. 'We're going to meet Vanessa and Constance before sunrise.'

'Why so early?' Sameera asked.

'Tara's asking them to come in two hours ahead of schedule. That way, we start the day camera-ready and can hit the polling places right after our tour. And guess what? Because they're predicting a low voter turnout, they'd already planned a midday photo shoot on the beach to generate some interest. And when I suggested surfing, Tara leaped at the idea. You and your mother are going to get to see me hang-ten!' His grin made him look like a kid without a care in the world. *If only the voters could see him now,* Sameera thought.

'Sounds great, Dad,' Sameera said. 'I'm so glad we can do the tour. Get some sleep, Mom. G'night.'

Mom hadn't tuned in to the television and now she didn't answer either member of her family. She was crouched over her laptop in a writing frenzy and didn't seem to notice that Sameera and Dad were leaving the room.

*Have a freakin' good time, Mom,* Sameera thought, sending some mental goodwill in her mother's direction.

# Thirteen

Looking as immaculate and wide awake as ever, Tara Colby met them in the salon, accompanied by Vanessa and Constance. It was a bonding experience to be made over together, Sameera realized, as she and her parents modelled different outfits, laughing and teasing each other. When Dad came out in one of Mom's skirts and a floppy hat, he looked so ridiculous that even stretch-faced Vanessa's tight lips moved in the memory of a smile.

Sameera loved the combination that they settled on for her—tight jeans and a beaded pink T-shirt, sunglasses, a floppy straw hat banded with pink ribbon, and strappy, high-heeled faux-jewel-encrusted sandals. If only she didn't have to don the uncomfortable body-shaper underneath the ensemble, but she didn't complain when she checked herself out in the mirror. California words like 'hot' and 'babe' came to mind.

With Mom and Dad attired in equally appropriate West Coast chic, a sleepy-looking Constance quickly touched up their hair and makeup (she slathered bronzing lotion with a 'natural glow' over Sameera's parents to fake a tan).

'White dress. White sandals,' Vanessa grunted at Sameera, just before the Rightons left. Sameera nodded. 'Got it.'

'I'll see you in your hotel room at around five o'clock, Sammy,' Constance said. 'We'll doll you up nicely for tonight.'

'Meet me at Zuma Beach at noon,' Tara added as the Rightons ducked into the limo. 'The press will be waiting for you at each voting station; we sent them a timed list of your appearances, so don't be late.'

Dad gave the driver directions to the house where he'd grown up. It was a big home on a bluff overlooking the ocean, gated now with an alarm system, but Dad said that the intense security was new. 'We were a neighborhood then,' he said. 'Kids playing on the street, riding bikes, playing Red Rover on summer nights…' His voice trailed off.

Sameera felt a pang that she'd never met the people who'd built the house and lived there for years—James Righton Sr and Mary Righton, his wife of forty-three years. Would they have liked her? Would she have felt as close to them as she did to Gran and Poppa?

'I can imagine you riding your bike down to the beach, Dad,' she told him as they cruised around the quiet, tree-lined streets. Her father had worked summers as a beachboy, setting up umbrellas and beach chairs, and as a lifeguard, racing into the waves to rescue people caught in riptides or in over their heads. *He's still into saving people,* she thought.

The limo took a detour, and Dad leaped out to buy a bouquet of stargazer lilies ('my mother's favourites from a twenty-four-hour grocery store,' he muttered) before heading to the nearby cemetery. Sameera's grandparents' graves were simple, flat, side-by-side stones marked with crosses. Sameera and Mom helped Dad strew the lilies over them as the morning sun climbed higher in the sky.

'Can we pray before we go, James?' Mom asked, reaching for his hand.

'You go ahead, Liz,' he said, gazing into the distance at the blue line of the Pacific Ocean.

As Mom recited the Lord's Prayer in a low voice, Sameera reached for her father's other hand. If only she could help him when it came to religion! But she had no easy answers herself to share.

The three of them walked back in silence to the waiting limo; it was time to re-enter the campaign fray. They stopped at several polling places throughout Los Angeles and even drove into Ventura County, all three of them shaking hands, making small talk, waving and smiling at the cameras, and kissing a few babies.

At noon, the limo drove them to Zuma Beach, where Dad changed out of California casual into a wet suit. Sameera and Mom squinted into the sun, watching him catch waves on a borrowed surfboard while the cameras filmed nonstop. Dad was right; he hadn't forgotten how to surf, even though he didn't bend and swerve quite as smoothly as the twenty-somethings the campaign team had recruited to join him for the photo op.

Sameera could have sworn that Mom was drooling as Dad showed off in his skintight Lycra. *I hope the cameras aren't zooming in on the lust in her eyes,* she thought, anticipating correctly that her parents would disappear for an 'afternoon nap' when they got back to the hotel.

She herself seized the one quiet hour in this fast-paced day to check in to her myplace.com site. Comments were pouring in about her transformation the day before. First, she savoured the comic book-style responses from her teammates: WOW! ZOWEE! GADZOOKS! KAPOW! Most of them thought she looked tremendous, although Amazing Ahmed claimed to worry that he might not feel comfortable teasing her like 'a sister' anymore. Miranda's wordless comment was a photo of herself with her hands on either side of her head, eyes wide and startled-looking, mouth forming a huge O. A couple of Sameera's more radical newspaper buddies in Brussels asked her to alleviate concerns that she was selling out to The Man. Mrs Graves tuned in with a typically strong opinion, arguing that she much preferred the simple 'before' look to the 'Barbie Doll version of our sweet Sparrow', as she put it.

Sameera described The Makeover briefly before weighing in with the truth about how it made her feel:

> For once in my life, I'm VISIBLE. Those of you who are naturally eye-catching don't know what it's like to walk into a room and feel like nobody notices you. There's a downside to visibility, of course: I didn't like the leers from middle-aged men, my made-up skin feels like it's painted on with plastic (a good laugh might mess up my look, so I stay serious all the time), the do is so hair-sprayed that a head-butt from me could take someone out, and the pointy shoes torture my toes until they confess all my sins.
>
> But on the whole, it's fun to turn heads for a change. When you're power-dressed on the outside, the eerie part is that you feel more powerful on the inside. I don't get that. I'm not sure I like that. Okay,

yesterday was mostly fogies and geezers (with the exception of one interesting girl I met), and today all the voters were over twenty-one, but tonight's my first real event with people my age. We're going to celebrate Dad's winning the primary at a father-daughter dance. (Mothers are invited to watch and socialize, so Mom's coming, too.) The problem is that I'm so zonked that I might make a total fool of myself. Comments? Keep them short, clean, and to the point. Peace be with you. Sparrow.

She was powering down and fighting an immense wave of sleepiness when Tara came up to the room. 'We clinched the primary, but nobody's surprised. Get dressed and I'll send Constance in, Sammy; she'll do your mom first.'

A shower helped a bit, and Sameera managed to slip into her dress, but she kept her eyes closed for a few blissful minutes while Constance made her up and fixed her hair.

'You're *snoring,* Sammy,' Constance told her.

'Time to go!' called Dad from the living room, and Sameera staggered out on another newly acquired pair of four-inchers.

# Fourteen

'I don't like it,' Dad growled when he saw his daughter in the white dress.

'But it's sexy *and* sweet, James,' Tara said. 'That's the look we need for tonight. All the other daughters are going to be dressed in much more revealing outfits.'

'She's only sixteen, Tara. I don't think sexy is an appropriate way for her to dress.'

Sameera yawned and plopped down on the couch. She felt about as sexy as a turtle.

'Californians want their sixteen-year-olds to be a little on the glamorous side, James,' Tara said, giving one of those brittle laughs that made Sameera's eardrums feel like they'd been scraped.

'When it comes to my daughter, it doesn't matter what anybody wants,' Dad said, lacing his normally courteous voice with the steely undercurrent that took down opponents in any debate. 'I expect her to dress her age. And she's wearing entirely too much lipstick.'

'I agree,' said Mom, coming in and leaping into the discussion. 'Can we take it down a notch? Last night she was offered *wine* to drink. And I saw men twice her age practically undressing her with their eyes. It was disgusting.'

Sparrow didn't have the energy to say anything. Did her mother have to be so... *crass?* Besides, those weirdo-perverted types hadn't really been ogling her body; they'd been checking out a body-shaper with underwire and padding, even if they didn't know it.

'Didn't you see the coverage after her debut last night, James?' Tara asked, standing with her feet apart, arms folded across her chest. 'They loved Sammy. They loved how she looked and how she sounded. They loved how the three of you looked together. And besides, you won today—this is a celebration.'

Dad sighed, giving up as he glanced at his watch. That was another thing about him; he didn't die on every hill. 'You just look so... different. I guess every father struggles when his daughter starts growing up.'

*STARTS growing up? I'm SIXTEEN, people!*

'I won't be coming with you tonight,' Tara told them. 'Just remember Wilder's instructions, Sammy, and we should have a repeat of last night's success.'

They got stuck in traffic on the way to the dance. Battling to keep her eyes open as the limo crawled along, Sameera held together the slit in her dress so that Dad couldn't see how much thigh it revealed. Not that he'd notice; he was ensconced in paperwork, and Mom was still working feverishly on her report.

'I'm sad you're leaving tomorrow, Sparrow,' Mom said, looking up from her laptop and rubbing her eyes wearily. 'We'll try to get to Maryfield for a couple of days in August. In the meantime, it's good to know that you'll get a nice long break.'

'I *am* tired, Mom. How about you?'

'Shattered. When I'm done with this report, I'm going to crash in our D.C. apartment with a good novel while your poor old dad plans the next phase of his campaign.'

Dad peered at them over his reading glasses. 'Tara warned me that anti-Republican reporters could turn up at this event tonight. Get ready for some unfriendly fire.'

Vanessa had chosen strappy white sandals to match the dress, with heels so long and thin they looked like lethal weapons. As it turned out, Sameera was tempted to use them to defend herself more than once. Tara was right; reporters were swarming outside the entrance to the hotel, and they descended the minute the Rightons arrived. Not all of them were friendly, either.

*You're a cute, doting, excited president's daughter wannabe,* Sameera's tired brain told her when she discovered photographers and reporters inside the hotel, too. But it took a huge effort to stay in character.

Trapped by half-a-dozen interrogators at the entrance to the ballroom, Sameera looked around desperately for help. Where was her mother? She glimpsed a crowd of women on a balcony smiling as they overlooked the dance floor, trying to catch sight of their daughters and husbands. Mom must be somewhere up there. And Dad was in a faraway corner of the huge room, facing a battalion of microphones of his own. Because she was so exhausted, new questions were throwing her off balance, so she stuck to one-word answers and relied on the non-verbals that Marcus had suggested.

'Where were you born, Miss Righton?'

'Pakistan.' Smile. Wave. Giggle-slash-manic-chuckle.

'Has it been easy being raised by white parents? Do you wish they looked more like you?'

'Uh-huh. I mean, no.' Giggle again.

'Do you feel uncomfortable being the only minority in the room, Miss Righton?'

Another reporter guffawed. 'How about in the entire Republican Party?' he added.

'Er…I'll have to talk that over with my father.' Oh no! She'd completely stopped making sense. They were looking at her like she was nuts.

Dad came over and took her hand. 'Dance with me, darling?' he asked. 'They're playing our song.'

The reporters parted like the Red Sea, and Dad led her out to the dance floor, where other, less famous fathers were whirling their daughters around to the orchestra's music.

'What was happening back there?' Dad asked. 'You looked besieged.'

'I'm so tired that I think I'm babbling.'

He sighed. 'If they don't like me, Sparrow, they'll take anything you say and use it for their purposes. That's the name of the game, especially from here on out.'

'We haven't danced in a while, Dad,' Sameera said, recognizing the three-quarter-time beat as a waltz. When she was seven years old, she and Dad had taken dancing lessons at the American Club in Cairo, along with a lot of other diplomats and their daughters. They'd always danced well together, and she loved it when they did.

She closed her eyes as Dad spun her effortlessly around the room. Leaning her head against the front of his tuxedo, she let herself savour the feeling of floating safely in his arms, the way she always did when they danced. Dancing made her feel *connected* to him, without words, and she was so glad they were getting the chance to do it before they'd have to part ways again for the summer.

But when the song ended, and *they* descended again, Dad had to shift his attention back to answering their questions. The mothers cloistered in the balcony upstairs were sipping cocktails and chatting; Sameera hoped Mom was holding up better than she was. She managed to ease out of the circle and head to the ladies' room for the third time that night. There was a chaise longue in the entry, and she plunked herself down on it. She waited out ten more minutes, imagining a front-page shot of herself coming out of a door marked 'ladies': 'Righton's Daughter Battles the Runs at Father-Daughter Dance.'

A couple of girls about her age came in, giggling and whispering in unmistakable camaraderie. They fell silent when they caught sight of Sameera slumped on the chaise.

'Hi,' she said, suddenly missing Miranda with a pang. Why did they have to live so far apart? *I'll see her soon,* she comforted herself. *I'll be safe on the farm this time tomorrow.*

'Hey.'

'Hi.'

More silence.

'Congratulations,' one of them said. 'Your dad's clinched the nomination, I guess.'

'Thanks.'

'Aren't you… excited?'

She couldn't muster up the energy to be bubbly… or fake. 'Right now I'm so tired I can't see straight. And a few of those reporters got in my face. It's been a tough night.'

The girls exchanged glances. 'Stick with us,' one of them said. 'We know how it is; my dad's the CEO of his company. And hers is a senator.'

'Yeah, we'll protect you.'

They put Sameera between them, and arm in arm the three of them re-entered the ballroom just as Dad and Mom were heading up front for their first appearance as the Republican presidential candidate and family. Sameera's female escorts accompanied her all the way to the foot of the stage, where she climbed the stairs to join her parents.

'Hang in there, sweetheart,' Dad muttered to Sameera just before turning to grin and lift both hands high, bringing a roar of applause from the crowd.

'Thank you, California!' he said.

Sameera managed to make herself smile Sammy's smile one more time, focusing on the two girls' faces in the front row. If only she were in Maryfield, dancing wordlessly to blaring music in Miranda's room or lolling on the family room couches watching a flick. Or even back in the hotel room, blogging about surviving this night. Anywhere safe. Anywhere private.

Thankfully, Dad kept his speech short. As the crowd cheered and stomped their approval, a DJ appeared out of nowhere and put on a hip-hop record, cranking up the bass. Someone switched off the chandeliers and turned on some strobe lights. Everyone over twenty-five got the message and raced for the exits.

As reporters surrounded her parents and hustled them out of the loud, now dimly lit ballroom, Sameera's self-appointed teen girl guards flanked her again. Before she knew what was happening, she was at the centre of a singing, pulsating solidarity of dancing daughters. For the first time that night, she felt protected from curious eyes and cameras, and she let her body relax into the joyous beat of the music.

# Fifteen

Tara strode into the presidential suite on Sunday morning, pulled a folder full of newspaper and magazine clippings out of her briefcase, and spread them across the table in the living room. 'I hear you zonked last night and didn't tune in to the news,' she told Sameera. 'Here's what you missed.'

Sameera had slept most of the morning, then packed and dressed for the flight; her parents had been out and about, so they were still getting ready in their room. She took a deep breath before looking at the clippings; she *had* purposely avoided the news to give herself a break. The first thing that struck her was how dark she looked in the photos. She'd loved the feel of the pristine white silk dress Vanessa had chosen, but in the newspapers and magazines, the colour made Sameera look like a black-and-white graphic imported into a full-colour spread.

'I would have brought these up yesterday, but your parents thought you needed a rest,' Tara said. 'I thought it was important for you to see this before you left.'

> Sammy Righton, who arrived in the United States only a few days ago, seemed overwhelmed by the fact that she was the only minority at a father-daughter dance

> in Orange County last night. 'I'll have to talk that over with my father,' she answered, when asked how she felt about standing out in the crowd. Perhaps the Rightons have been hiding the truth from their daughter, just as they'd previously been trying to hide Sammy herself from the public eye: 'You're Pakistani, Sammy,' they need to inform their daughter. 'And we're not.'
>
> 'THAT'S A PERSONAL QUESTION!' Elizabeth Campbell Righton said, refusing to answer questions about how the Rightons ended up adopting a baby from Pakistan. 'Why not an American baby?' our reporter asked. 'No comment,' said Campbell Righton, who seemed overwhelmed and exhausted by her husband's overextended campaign schedule.

*Poor Mom!* Sparrow thought. *She'd stayed up till 3 a.m. the night before, working on the freakin' report.*

The worst was a photo of Dad smiling down into Sparrow's freakin' face as they waltzed on the dance floor. 'Righton: Soft on Muslims?' read the caption.

> As he clutched his Pakistani daughter in his arms, observers wondered if James Righton's foreigner-friendly approach during these frightening times might not be tough enough to fight the war on terror. We interviewed...

Sameera stopped reading. This was lousy journalism, and they were trying to tarnish the beautiful dance she'd shared with Dad. Well, she wouldn't let them. She was going to treasure that memory until they were able to be together again. 'I'm sure there was a lot of positive coverage, too,' she said. 'Why didn't you bring any of that up to show me?'

Confirming her suspicions, Tara didn't meet her eye. 'I wanted you to understand how rough it might get in the weeks ahead. And why it's so important for the three of you to stick together. There's still time to change your flight if you decide to come with us to D.C.'

'No thanks,' Sameera said, forcing herself to sound polite. 'I promised my cousin I was going to help out on the farm this summer. You take care of Mom and Dad; I'll be fine.'

Tara shrugged. 'Okay. The good news is that SammySez.com has already gotten a decent number of hits, and Marcus did some damage control on the site. Check out his post when you get a chance. Now, where are your parents?'

Sameera gathered the clippings together and shoved them back into the folder. 'Don't show them these just yet, Tara. Especially not Mom. It's going to be much harder than usual for them to say goodbye; let's not make it worse.'

Tara shrugged and tucked the folder back into her briefcase just as Mom came out. 'The reporters are going to head straight for Maryfield as soon as they find out you're there. You're the human-interest angle. Reporting on you brings in the younger viewers. They're not going to let you escape.'

'You don't know my family,' Mom said. 'My father won't let the media get anywhere near Sparrow. I'll be so relieved once she gets there.'

'*You* don't know the press,' Tara said. 'James's enemies are looking for an 'issue' to focus on, and Sammy's the perfect target.'

'I really *hate* it when you call her that,' Mom snarled. 'Can't that Marcus fellow come up with something better?'

'What could be better than "Sammy" ?' Tara asked. 'Besides, it creates a shield for your daughter. You gave us carte blanche to keep her safe, remember?'

'I don't mind it anymore, Mom,' Sameera added quickly—and truthfully, she realized. *I've never liked Sparrow much either, but who cares? It doesn't really matter what other people call you.*

'What I'm worried about is what the American people are going to think if you send your daughter away,' Tara said, aiming this last verbal punch at Mom with just the right amount of doubt in her voice.

Mom's face fell. Sameera frowned at Tara; obviously the woman hadn't gotten her point about not making this parting hard. 'Get Wilder to spin something about me getting in touch with my mother's country roots or something,' she said. 'You're probably paying that guy a bundle; let him do his job.'

'That's an idea, Sammy,' Tara said slowly. 'A good idea, actually. I'll tell him. But remember—call me if you change your mind. I'll fly to Toledo and bring you back myself.'

Mom was still looking troubled. 'A decent mother would go with her daughter to Maryfield, wouldn't she, Sparrow?'

'I'll be fine, Mom,' Sameera said. 'I've flown alone dozens of times, and when I get there, Gran will take good care of me.'

It was the wrong thing to say. 'How could I forget?' Mom asked, looking even more despondent. 'You'll be with the Ultimate Good Mother. Why can't every woman run a farm, a church, and an entire town, still manage to cook everything from scratch, knit, and garden?'

'Gran's stopped doing most of that stuff now, Mom.'

Mom sighed. 'I know. A decent daughter would visit her recuperating mother, wouldn't she? After she had the heart attack, did I take the time to visit her? No.'

'You had to campaign with Dad, Mom, and you used every spare minute to come back to Brussels and see me. Gran understands. Besides, you're going there in August.'

'She *might* go there in August,' Tara said. 'Otherwise, you can definitely visit at Thanksgiving, Liz, *after* the election.'

The limo transported the unusually silent family to the airport and took Sameera to her airline first. After saying goodbye to her parents, who held her much closer and tighter and longer than normal, Sameera made her way through security. She was wearing her old jeans and her sweatshirt again, and no makeup; she wanted to feel like herself as she travelled to the farm. It was a relief not to draw attention as she walked through the busy airport to her gate; the past few days had been an intense dive into the deep end of celebrity life. She was ready for a break before wading back in again.

The plane wasn't boarding yet, so she logged onto the Internet to check out Wilder's 'damage control' post. Now that Tara had shown her some of the coverage, she wanted to check things out for herself.

> i went to the **rodeo drive salon** again for my hair and nails... they do a fantastic job... last night's party was a total blast, but i was so tired i couldn't think straight... i thought how lucky i am to be growing up in America instead of someplace where kids can't dance or laugh or sing... we're so free here,

> it's awesome... speaking of freedom, i'm thinking of getting another piercing somewhere on my body, probably ears again... my parents are really cool, but they might not let me get SOME parts pierced... vote in this survey for YOUR favourite body part to pierce.

Sameera clicked on the survey to discover that people were able to vote on six choices: lip, belly, chin, elbow, throat, or nose. Well, *she* certainly wasn't about to put holes in any part of her body, no matter how the readers of SammySez.com voted. The virtual manga girl would have to do it on her behalf.

She checked in to her real site, where her buddies had poured out words of support, praise, and encouragement, along with their congratulations to Dad for securing the Republican nomination. 'Sparrow, you looked exhausted in the news coverage,' Mrs Graves wrote. 'Make sure you take care of yourself and rest when you get to the farm.'

Sameera closed her eyes for a minute, and a picture of the farm shimmered in her mind. The rolling hills and pastureland. The familiar paths and trees and people who loved her. No strangers anywhere in sight. She wrote back in a comment:

> I'm bound to get some rest in Maryfield. But I might not be able to blog as much. Poppa cut off Internet access on the farm as part of the huge family effort to de-stress Gran. So talk amongst yourselves, and I'll tune in when I can.

# *Sixteen*

Sameera was looking forward to visiting the small brick Presbyterian church in Maryfield; the service was predictable and down-to-earth, and people didn't give you dirty looks if you sang off-key, didn't know the liturgy by heart, or worst of all, weren't even sure *what* you believed. Nobody in the Campbell family settled for just warming a pew, even though a break had been enforced on Gran. Miranda taught the third-grade Sunday school class, Aunt Bev played the piano, Poppa was an elder, and Uncle Jake sang baritone in the choir.

As soon as Sameera got off the plane, she dialed her cousin to see which Campbell was going to skip out on churchly duties to make the three-hour drive to the airport.

'I'm here already,' Miranda said, sounding extremely proud of herself. 'I'm sitting in the *driver's* seat of *my* Jeep at the curb. Didja get that, Sparrow? *My* Jeep.'

After passing her driving test two months ago, Miranda spent all her savings to buy a second-hand fire-red Jeep that Sameera hadn't seen yet.

'Isn't this your first time driving to Toledo?' Sparrow asked doubtfully, keeping an eye out for her suitcase.

'It is! And I only got one ticket!' Miranda said. 'Now get

out here and hug me right now. I'm tired of watching you on a screen; I need to see your sweet cheeks with my own eyes.'

Ever since they'd met thirteen years ago, the cousins' friendship had stayed strong, and they were always inseparable during the summers. An outsider might think that it would be easy for Sameera to envy her tall, lovely cousin, but she'd never struggled with jealousy when it came to Miranda. What she did battle was a bit of the overprotection she'd glimpsed recently in her own parents. Miranda was so… unsullied. She was popular and beloved in Maryfield, but that was a safe place where everybody had known one another from the cradle.

After their usual rapturous reunion, Sameera gushed sufficiently over the Jeep, and they headed home.

'Why don't you get your licence this summer?' Miranda asked her. 'I'll let you drive this baby any time you want.'

'I'd love to,' Sameera said. 'Do you think Poppa has time to teach me?'

'He's already talking about it. Sorry, Sparrow, I can't drive and talk at the same time,' Miranda told her as they pulled out of the airport exit. All the way to Maryfield, she concentrated fiercely, clenching her jaw and furrowing her brow as she steered the Jeep around the curves.

Sameera didn't mind the silence. She gazed out the window, feasting her eyes on the familiar scenery. They reached the first stoplight in town, just before the big brick courthouse building and statue of the town's founder, and drove past a train station, bar, the combo grocery-hardware-variety store, diner, library, and beauty shop before turning left at the high school. If they'd kept going, Sameera knew exactly what they'd find before reaching the hayfields that stretched away on the other side of town—two churches, two restaurants, a few offices, the school building that housed grades K-8, and one more stoplight.

With a sigh of relief, Miranda turned off the paved road at the entrance to the farm, and Sameera jumped out to open and close the gate. 'Are Poppa and Gran still debating what to name the farm?' she asked her cousin, climbing back in.

'Yeah. We're stuck with "The Campbell Farm" because either one or both of them nixes every suggestion. Maybe you can come up with something, Sparrow.'

The narrow, plowed lane curved for five miles into 'The Campbell Farm', cutting through the thousand acres of fenced-in, rolling pastureland. It was a small farm, with only two hundred Holsteins, and Poppa liked to let the stock graze freely during the spring, summer, and fall instead of keeping them inside year-round and buying feed. Every Campbell could tell which cow was which by the pattern of their spots; Sameera relied on the numbered tags in the cows' ears. After they crossed a wooden bridge, the road took one last turn, and Sameera caught sight of the familiar three-storey yellow clapboard house set behind a wide expanse of summer-green lawn.

She jumped out before Miranda had a chance to turn off the engine, and the first Campbell to race up to her was Jingle, the family's grizzled-but-still-yellow Labrador retriever. During Sameera's first summer on the farm, the puppy version of Jingle had started dogging the three-year-old version of herself, and every summer since then he had claimed her as his own. It always took her a few weeks to get over missing him when she left. Now he lavished her with wet kisses and a wildly wagging tail and she kissed him right back on the nose, a joyous refrain singing through her heart: *Safe, safe, I'm finally safe. Home, home, I'm finally home.*

Then Poppa was there, hugging her, and Gran, pushing Poppa aside to hold Sameera tightly. Everybody had already changed out of their fancy church clothes. Sameera scrutinized her grandmother's face; she *did* look more tired and pale than she had last summer. Uncle Jake and Aunt Bev kissed Sameera and unloaded her suitcase and laptop case from the truck, and Miranda escorted her arm in arm into the house that had been built by their great-grandfather over a hundred years ago.

The atmosphere on the farm always felt different on Sundays, beginning with mandatory church attendance and followed by afternoon coffee, a rest, and a lavish supper. After that, the family played board games by the fire—thanks to Poppa's 'no-screens-on-the-Sabbath' rule, a practice that Sameera secretly liked. Now it was coffee time, so they gathered in the big kitchen, which had been designed as a place where a large family could cook, eat, and commune.

Aunt Bev poured cups of coffee and passed around the plate of still-warm oatmeal scotchies. *Dad's campaign team might he positioning him as a 'crunchy conservative',* Sameera thought, restraining herself to three cookies, *but Aunt Bev's the real thing.* Her stocky, curly-haired aunt was a passionate advocate of smaller government bureaucracies and greater individual and community responsibility. Clothed in flannel shirts tucked into high-waisted jeans that she'd probably bought at a yard sale in the 1980s, she grew most of the produce for the family in her organic garden, composted fervently, and wrote articles about the waste and excesses of consumer culture.

'How's your mother doing with the campaigning, Sparrow?' she asked now. Aunt Bev was a huge fan of her sister-in-law and a champion of all of Elizabeth Campbell's causes. But her own daughter's life goal to become a pop culture icon was driving her nuts.

'I don't know,' Sameera answered truthfully. 'Mom didn't meet her deadline on the—the report she was working on, which always stresses her out. Plus she's worried about Dad.'

Gran sighed. 'I know. I get nervous every time they mention your father in the news. My heart starts racing.'

'That's why you've got to turn off the television,' Miranda said. 'You're addicted to the coverage. I'm sure Poppa's going to get rid of our satellite dish next. I'll be the only girl in America who has to check her email at the town library *and* miss my favourite shows.'

That pushed Aunt Bev's buttons. 'Miranda Campbell! There are plenty of girls your age on this planet who don't have any computers or televisions—'

'I know, I know, Mom,' Miranda interrupted. 'My point was that Gran needs to stop tuning in to the news every day for hours on end. It's making her crazy.'

'Are you starting to... feel like yourself again, Gran?' Sameera asked hesitantly.

Until last fall, Sarah Campbell had been an elder and a member of the Ladies' Aid at church, a well-known leader and advocate in Ohio's community of small dairy graziers, and a founding member of Celebrate Country, a movement that aimed to 'eliminate stereotypes about country living and promote awareness of the rich intellectual and cultural traditions of the

Heartland'. After her hospital stay, she'd agreed to resign from her umpteen committees at church and in town. But that wasn't as hard as giving up the care and feeding of her family and her home, which is what she was being asked to do this summer.

'I'm fine,' she said now. 'Bored out of my mind, though. Everyone's treating me like I'm made of porcelain, and that doctor told me to take a break from coffee and drink green tea. Can you believe it?' She grimaced at the pale, grassy-smelling liquid in her cup.

Poppa and Uncle Jake came in. 'Well, Sparrow, when can we go pick up your permit?' Poppa asked. 'I'd like to start logging in some of those hours you'll need to get your licence.'

'ASAP, Poppa,' said Sameera, who'd been longing to get behind a wheel ever since her birthday. She'd taken a driver's ed courses in Brussels and passed with flying colours—but that hadn't been the real thing.

Her grandfather looked pleased. 'We'll pick up a permit for you in the next couple of days, Sparrow.'

'I think *my* daughter needs a few more lessons, Dad,' Uncle Jake said, frowning at the ticket Miranda had received on the way to the airport. 'I still feel like fasting and praying every time she's on the road.'

Miranda threatened to smack him with a rubber spatula, and the family talked and laughed together until the coffee was gone. Glancing at her watch, Gran sent Miranda off to practise piano and Sameera to shower and unpack.

Sameera climbed the stairs to the third floor with Jingle at her heels. Their great-grandfather had purposely built this house to hold an extended family. Gran and Poppa had a bedroom on the first floor; Uncle Jake, their oldest son, lived with Aunt Bev and Miranda in a spacious, newly renovated second-floor apartment; the guest quarters were up on the third floor, where two bedrooms and a bathroom were always reserved for Sameera and her parents during their visits.

She always stayed in the smaller room, which had once belonged to her mother. It was an alcove that overlooked the maple grove and was furnished simply with a rag rug and white cottage furniture. Uncle Jake had put her suitcases, makeup case, and laptop bag in one corner. Tara had packed an extra suitcase for her Vanessa outfits, and Sameera left that unopened, along with the makeup case that Constance had stocked for her. She might need to access them down the road, but for now, she was going back to the comfy 'before' version, so she only unpacked the stuff she'd brought with her from Brussels.

After unpacking and taking a shower, Sameera stretched out with a sigh on the four-poster bed. Since the farm wasn't connected to the Internet, she'd have to blog or surf the Web at the library. She didn't mind; it was going to be good to take a break for a while. *Gran's not the only one who needs a bit of de-stressing,* she thought. Jingle jumped up on the bed, too, and Sameera rested her head against his stomach. *Perfect. Fur therapy.*

Sameera's cell phone rang 'Yankee Doodle', which was the ring tone she had assigned to her father. 'Hi, Dad,' she said into the phone, running her fingers through Jingle's coat.

'Hi, sweetheart. You made it.' She could hear sirens and horns blaring in the background as he talked.

'Yeah. Miranda picked me up at the airport and we drove straight here. No reporters anywhere in sight.'

'That's great. Lots of them on our end; we're just leaving the airport now after facing them.'

'Guess what, Dad? Poppa's going to teach me to drive. I might be able to get my licence this summer!'

Silence.

'Dad? What's wrong?'

'My father taught me to drive,' Dad said. 'I should be doing it, not your grandfather.'

'Poppa taught Miranda, too. Uncle Jake said it's too stressful to teach your own kid.'

'Oh. Well, that's okay then. It did get a bit hairy, with my dad gripping the dashboard and praying out loud. I'll talk to you soon, darling. Here's your mom.'

'How's your grandmother?' Mom asked right away.

'She seems... okay,' Sparrow said. 'Still trying to be in charge around here, that's for sure.'

'I've been thinking, Sparrow,' Mom said. 'Maybe we could invite your cousin to join you when you come back in the fall. She'd be great company; the two of you always have such a good time together.'

Sameera was surprised by her reaction, which was a strong reluctance even to consider her mother's idea. 'What about school?' she asked. 'Miranda can't miss school.'

'Oh, there are ways around that. She wouldn't have to stay for long. Let's see how it goes.'

After they hung up, Sameera stretched out again without bothering Jingle, who was fast asleep. Miranda had a knack for making everything more fun. Why *wouldn't* she want her cousin to join her on the campaign trail? It wasn't jealousy;

she'd always loved her cousin's visits overseas despite the fact that Miranda attracted so much attention. And she'd never begrudged her cousin her natural gifts of grace and beauty—or even her genetic connection to the family she loved so much. No, what worried Sameera was what might happen to Miranda if she were yanked into the public eye.

'Sparrow! Come help set the table!'

Sameera and Jingle raced down the familiar stairs side by side. By the smells wafting out of the kitchen, she hoped that supper would be roast chicken, rosemary potatoes, and warm, flaky biscuits straight out of the oven—her favourite.

Gran was overseeing the supper preparation, even though Aunt Bev and Miranda were doing the actual cooking. 'YESSSS!' Sameera said when she saw what was cooking. Some dreams did come true.

# Seventeen

The entire family participated in the early morning feeding and milking, which was the same every morning, even on Sundays. Poppa and Uncle Jake were at work by three o'clock, rain or shine, day in and day out, 365 days a year, and Miranda and Aunt Bev by five o'clock. Gran, too, when she used to milk.

During previous summers, Sameera had always made it a point to get up and join them, even though she hadn't actually been much help. She'd been too small to attach the milking machines to the cows when they were up on their elevated platforms, she didn't know how to drive a tractor or work the motorized manure scraper, and she'd always kept her distance from the bull. This summer, though, she'd promised herself to learn all that stuff and more, mostly to (1) give her cousin the chance to escape the milking routine (which Miranda hated) and take over the household work so that (2) Gran could have a break from constantly cooking, cleaning, and doing the laundry.

Sameera got up when her alarm buzzed, pulled on overalls and boots, and stumbled through the still-dark morning with Aunt Bev and Jingle. After Poppa and Uncle Jake prodded eight cows into place with the crowd gate, she and her aunt cleaned the udders and dipped them into anti-bacterial solution. After a couple of weeks, Sameera got used to the smell and sounds and feel of the udders as she washed them, and she even forced herself to squeeze each teat, just like Aunt Bev did, to make sure the milk ran clear. Then they attached the milking machines to the teats. The automatic milkers sensed when the udders were empty, detached themselves, and swung back into place. Aunt Bev and Sameera cleaned off the teats again, led the cows out, and waited while the next eight milkers were prodded into the parlour.

Meanwhile, Miranda was trying to get all the indoor work done so they could have some free time. Sameera's cousin was the hub of the Maryfield teen social scene, and the phone was always ringing with bored people asking what they were doing. Sameera slipped easily into the relaxed climate in Maryfield—a couple of Miranda's best friends had even made it into the intergalactic myspace.com circle. In summers gone by, they swam at the high school pool in the afternoons, basking in the sun, or Sameera helped her cousin memorize lines for whatever 'Shakespeare in Maryfield' play she was about to star in every August. Later in the day, they'd help Aunt Bev in the garden, or swing luxuriously in hammocks in the shade of the weeping willows, flipping through magazines, talking, listening to music. And after the afternoon chores were done, they might head over with a bunch of people to the arcade, ice-cream parlour, and bowling alley twenty minutes away in Canobie. They'd usually end the day by catching a sitcom or a reality show, tuning in to their favourite makeover channels, or making popcorn and watching a chick flick.

But this summer was different from the start.

First, Miranda was discovering that working inside the house was just as hard, if not harder, than doing the milking twice a day. She was so overwhelmed with chores that Sameera and Aunt Bev found themselves chipping in to help. It was even more stressful with Gran calling out instructions, comments, and suggestions from her forced place of 'rest' on a rocking chair in the sunroom.

Second, Sameera's main priority was squeezing in a morning driving lesson from Poppa; she was learning fast and loving it. Miranda was letting her practise on the Jeep.

And third, *everybody* in Maryfield was into her father's campaign. In Brussels, or even during her brief stint on the campaign trail, Sameera had been too distracted and busy to get nervous for her father, but here on the quiet farm, the intensity of the race was nerve-wracking. Different family members gathered in front of the television at any hour of the day or night, watching Sameera's parents in action or getting updates on the campaign. The family even tuned in on Sunday evenings instead of playing board games or reading aloud. Poppa, who always looked guilty and flustered when someone mentioned the word Sabbath, was a regular in one of the recliners, with a remote clutched in his hand. But by far the most frequent visitors to the Shrine of the Big Screen were Gran and Sameera, who ran into each other in the family room every hour or so. They both spoke to Mom and Dad regularly on the phone, of course, but there was a constant need to track the campaign coverage on national news. Dad was now neck and neck with Senator Banforth, with Dorton falling behind them in the polls.

One sunny morning, when Sameera came down after her shower, Aunt Bev was slicing a loaf of zucchini bread. 'I'll pour you some coffee to go,' she told Sameera. 'And here's something to eat with it. Miranda's in the Jeep; she said you wanted to get online at the library?'

'I do. I want to find out how Dad's doing on the web—and if anybody online has discovered I'm MIA yet. Because they certainly haven't mentioned my absence on the tube. Thank goodness.'

They both jumped at the sound of the horn. Miranda was leaning on it, hard, probably to show off the extent of its blast. She was going to scare the cows if she didn't let up, and Poppa and Uncle Jake would be furious.

Jingle raced around the kitchen, barking loudly, and Gran's head popped in from the adjoining sunroom. 'That Jeep's gone to Miranda's brain,' she said. 'She needs to calm down. And somebody keep that dog from barking!'

Sameera and Aunt Bev exchanged looks. 'Take a deep breath, Mom,' Aunt Bev said. 'We'll do some yoga together this afternoon.'

'I hate yoga,' Gran growled.

*Beep! Beep!*

Sameera raced out to the Jeep, clutching her coffee and her zucchini bread. 'Ran, stop! Gran's getting all red in the face.'

'Okay, okay. Want to come to Save Mart with me? The library doesn't open till eleven.'

'No thanks. I'll wait at the diner until Mrs Graves shows up.'

Sameera drank three more cups of bitter brew across the street from the library, watching through the big plate-glass window as people opened their shops and exchanged greetings. Most of them waved and grinned, and people coming in for breakfast kept stopping by her table to give her a hug or offer words of support for her father.

This was another aspect of life in Maryfield that Sameera loved—everybody knew her story; they'd known her since she was little. Nobody asked intrusive questions about her past, or her adoption, or her life as a diplomat's daughter moving from one international capital city to the next. Maryfield folks kept up during the year via Gran's prayer requests and caught up with Liz Campbell during her summer visits; they felt like Sparrow Righton was one of their own, too.

'It's good to see you here again, Sparrow,' said Mayor Thompson, who was also the owner of the hardware store. 'We weren't sure you'd make it back this summer what with all the hubbub.'

'We're glad you came, darling,' said his wife, leaning down to kiss Sameera's cheek. 'How's your mother doing? And your grandmother? I haven't seen Sarah much lately; we've been missing her in our board meetings.'

'Mom's fine. And Gran's going to be okay, too. *You* know how tough they both are.'

Mrs Thompson laughed; she'd taught Sunday school for years and claimed that each grey hair on her head had sprouted in response to a challenging theological question from Liz Campbell. And she'd had plenty of tussles with Gran on the Elder Board before Gran had resigned.

Sameera spotted the librarian unlocking the front door across the street. She tried to open her bag to pay for her coffee, but Mayor Thompson called out, 'Put Sparrow's breakfast on my bill, Stan.'

# Eighteen

Maryfield folks loved their library; farmers stopped by to vie for the computers after their morning work, book clubs met to discuss the hottest bestsellers, and students from the high school gathered to do homework. The main draw was Mrs Graves, the tiny, bubbly librarian who was one of three unofficial co-leaders of the community, along with Mrs Thompson and Sameera's grandmother. Mayor Thompson was sort of a figurehead sent to represent Maryfield at county gatherings and such; the trio of older women made the real decisions.

Mrs Graves enfolded Sameera in a big hug. 'I've *loved* reading and commenting on your blog, sweetheart,' she said. 'And getting to know your friends. I'm so glad Matteo liked the cookies.'

'He loved them. And everybody enjoys *your* comments, Mrs Graves. They're so… spicy.' She'd worried that when the librarian joined her circle she might have to censor herself on certain topics, but Mrs Graves was actually more open to new ideas than some of Sameera's peers.

'How's your grandmother?' the librarian asked. 'Your poppa's gone overboard with all the restrictions he's put on her life.'

'Well, he wants her to live for a long time. And so do we.'

'Women my age don't want to slow down, Sparrow. We need satisfying work, and to keep learning, or we get all crotchety. I've been updating all our terminals with the latest technology—it's been a delight to get up to speed.'

Mrs Graves hurried off to greet another patron, and Sameera sat in front of one of the library's two fast, sleek, state-of-the-art computers. She checked and de-spammed her email first. There wasn't much of value because most of her friends used her myplace.com site to connect. The inbox did contain a note from her English teacher, one from Mrs Mathews, and one from her crew teammates with an attachment that had been too large to post on her myplace.com site.

Saving the best for last, she started with her teacher's note.

> I'm thinking of you through this difficult, amazing journey, Sameera. I encourage you to start writing in the journal I gave you. You're like me; your true self is best expressed through the written word instead of the spoken word. Journalling will help you to process your thoughts and feelings, as well as serving as a record of a once-in-a-lifetime experience. Affectionately, Ms Banning.

Sameera sighed. How could she explain that she couldn't 'express her true self' using a pen to write words that only she would read? She needed a keyboard, screen, and buddies who commented frequently and passionately on her true self's expressions. The journal was still packed in a corner of her suitcase, blank and untouched.

Mrs Mathews's note was full of juicy tidbits about life in the diplomatic enclave, the most shocking being the Canadian ambassador's gardener running off with the Brazilian ambassador's nanny. She wrote in closing:

> I miss you so much, Sparrow. You looked so beautiful in that poncho, sweetheart. I hope you're having a nice rest in Maryfield; it's good that you're getting a break from being famous. I grew up in a small town, too, remember, and I'm starting to miss it lately. I'm still not used to the continental lifestyle, even after all these years. I don't know what I'll do if your dad wins in November. I'm not sure if I could work with a new family. What if I don't get along as well with them? Well, as your mother reminds me, I should probably stop worrying and start trusting. Much love, Doris Mathews.

Sameera's crew teammates had attached a video clip of themselves dashing to the shore, flinging themselves into the boat, and beginning to sob, weep, and wail as they noticed the empty place where the coxswain usually sat. The whole scene had been filmed in slow motion, and Nat King Cole's voice crooned 'Unforgettable, that's what you are. Unforgettable, though near or far…' in the background. Sameera played it three times, noticing Matteo's calf muscles rippling as he ran and how absolutely gorgeous all eight of them were. *I had every girl's dream assignment,* she thought.

She grinned as she read their written message; the email server obviously didn't have an obscenity filter.

> Sparrow. Come back. We need you. We saw you get harassed on TV. Don't let them do that to you. Here's what you say the next time someone like that comes after you:

A list of choice phrases and insults in a host of different languages followed. She'd never minded that they all swore constantly, but she didn't do it herself. How could she? She was Sarah Campbell's granddaughter. Even Mom, still trapped in some extended teenage rebellion against her mother, couldn't bring herself to say anything really off-colour.

After thanking her teammates and responding to her teacher and Mrs Mathews, Sameera took a deep breath and opened a browser window to check the online coverage on Dad—and herself. She skimmed through different news sources, radical, liberal, conservative, middle-of-the-road, non-partisan. Some critics were worried about his lack of experience with national issues like unemployment and the economy. Supporters were touting Dad's international experience, but critics complained that he was more of a 'world citizen' than an American. 'So what?' Sameera muttered. 'What's good for the planet is good for America. We share the same space, people.'

Along the same lines, an editorial in the *New York Times* wondered if a diplomat could lead the nation in tax reform and health care, or handle an aging population. *He served in Congress for three terms,* Sameera thought furiously. *Get a clue.*

*He must have learned something then.* A few popular conservative blowers wondered about Righton's faith. He'd never made a strong statement about it one way or another—what *did* the man believe? *Good question,* Sameera thought, even as she resented this intrusion into her father's private life. All the sources, however, agreed on one thing: Dad was neck and neck in the race against the Democrat who had finally clinched her own party's nomination: Senator Victoria Banforth.

There wasn't much online about Sameera herself; obviously SammySez.com hadn't morphed her magically into the most popular teen in America. Nobody was commenting on her disappearance from the campaign trail or hinting that they wanted to find her, and Sameera found herself feeling strangely disappointed. She did find one or two articles that mentioned her existence: 'Candidate and Wife Called to Adopt Orphan,' insisted a popular national entertainment magazine, making up some ridiculous, tear-jerker tale about Mom and Dad finding 'Sammy' on their doorstep. Another one announced again: 'Righton's Daughter Adopted from Pakistan'. But there was nothing about her current presence in Maryfield or about the fact that she wasn't by her parents' side.

Sameera didn't spend too much time at SammySez.com. Wilder, she discovered, had taken her advice on the 'country' spin and was generating boring variations on a patriotic theme:

> i'm heading back to the family farm while Mom and Dad travel... i adore spending time with my grandparents... i've been there every summer, and

> the Heartland of America is the most beautiful place on earth… I'm a country girl, just like my mom, and every day, we thank God for the privilege of being Americans… it's in small towns like Maryfield where you discover who you really are.

She noticed that there was no place for visitors to leave comments. *Definitely not a REAL blog,* she thought scornfully. No wonder I'm back to being invisible. She headed to her myplace.com site to read her own friends' comments and to dash off a quick post:

> Hi, guys. As you know, my grandfather's cut off Internet access on the farm, so I'm having a hard time blogging this summer. I don't have much to say anyway. I could write details about which cows are having trouble producing their daily quota of milk and theories about why that's happening, but if you're not a dairy farmer's granddaughter, you might not be into that. I'll check in with another post when and if things get more interesting. And just before the convention, I'll be back for sure, reporting on life again as 'Sammy', the ditzy, glam-wannabe candidate's daughter. For now, though, during long summer days in Maryfield, Ohio, I'm just Sparrow. Enjoy your holidays, and send many snail mail postcards. Remember: keep your comments short, clean, and to the point. Peace be with you. Sparrow.

# Nineteen

Sameera passed her driving test with flying colours after only a month of lessons. 'The examiner said she was a natural,' Poppa told the family when they returned with her licence in hand. 'Steady, safe, and quick on her feet in a crisis.'

'We knew that already,' Gran said proudly. 'Did you tell James and Liz?'

'Sparrow called them on the way home; they were thrilled.'

Miranda had failed the test twice before passing, but there was no sign of envy on her face. 'That's so great, Sparrow! I'll let you drive the Jeep anytime you want.'

'Thanks, Ran. Thanks, everybody.'

She really did enjoy driving; it was a bit like coxing and downloading music and recording TV shows and blogging—all of which she relished because they made her feel in charge of her life. She loved rolling down the windows of the Jeep, cranking up the tunes, and driving through the country roads around Maryfield. And she was careful; she always pulled over into a shady spot before checking in with Mom or Dad via cell. After a while, when Sameera and Miranda were together, Sameera always drove, leaving her cousin in charge of finding a good song that the two girls could sing at the top of their lungs.

Dad told Sameera to use her credit card to fill the tank regularly with gas, and the Rightons were going to surprise Miranda by installing a new stereo system in the car at the end of the summer. In the meantime, the drives were turning out to be a grand diversion from Sameera's campaign obsession.

Meanwhile, Gran didn't have any distractions. That meant *she* was checking in on the campaign now almost constantly and getting worked up over any negative comment made about her favourite (and only) son-in-law. Poppa responded by making everybody, including Gran, promise not to turn on the television in the daytime. 'We'll watch together in the evenings,' he said. 'I care about the campaign, too. But we've gotten into a terrible habit lately. Sparrow will be gone before we know it, and she'll have spent her entire vacation mucking out stalls, driving, and sitting in front of the television.'

Reluctantly, everybody agreed to a daytime television fast. But one midsummer Saturday morning, Sameera joined her grandmother at the kitchen counter, knowing they were both fighting temptation. Miranda, Aunt Bev, Poppa, and Uncle Jake were shopping in Canobie for the day. Sameera had opted to stay in Maryfield, even though Miranda had begged her to join them.

'Gran needs company,' Sameera had explained, and with a suspicious look on her face, Miranda left with her parents and grandfather.

Sameera fended off a growing desire to check the news by pouring herself some coffee and opening a magazine on the counter. *Maryfield Today* was published only four times a year, and the editorial focus was definitely local, so there was no coverage of the presidential election. This was still a hot-off-the-press issue, and the big story was a collapsed silo on the Seward farm and the new flowerpots along Main Street. There were also photos of a fierce competition that had taken place during the first annual all-Maryfield Xbox Games hosted in the town library. Sparrow smiled at the shot of Mrs Graves gripping a controller with an expression of intense concentration just before clinching the tournament.

Gran grinned, too; she was looking over Sameera's shoulder. 'Those middle school boys were so ticked off when Abigail won,' she said.

The centrespread was called 'Summer's Here!' and featured a collage of kids setting up lemonade stands, swimming in the ponds, helping with the haying, and riding their bikes. There was even a photo of Miranda and Sameera enjoying ice-cream cones at the Fourth of July picnic—with the Jeep in the background, of course.

'Let's go,' Gran said suddenly. 'I know we promised your Poppa, but I can't stand this. We'll confess our sins when they get back.'

The two of them slunk into the family room, pulled down the blinds, and settled themselves in front of the screen. Gran wielded the remote and found a twenty-four-hour news station. There was Dad, giving a speech to a Restaurant Workers' Union in fluent Spanish. Mom was visiting an inner-city pre-school where (Sameera couldn't believe her ears) she introduced the four-year-olds to the plight of internally displaced people. She wasn't surprised when a reporter confronted her mother after the speech.

'Are you really a Republican, Mrs Righton? You don't advocate for any of the traditional conservative or religious causes.'

That riled Mom up; Sameera could tell. 'You prove to me that Jesus wouldn't care about homeless people hiding in the jungle,' Elizabeth Campbell replied, 'and I'll find a more "religious" cause.'

Gran flipped to another channel. 'Even *I'm* not sure she's a Republican, Sparrow, and I'm her mother. She was always reacting to my political position growing up. To me she's sounded like a Democrat for years.'

'Only around you. She's with Dad on most of the issues; she just likes to focus on the poor. She's good for him, Gran, don't worry. And for his image.'

'*He* doesn't need help with his image,' Gran said, gazing admiringly at the screen as Dad continued pontificating in Spanish.

She was right. Dad came across as charming, handsome, and suave as ever. The problem was that his opponent, Senator Victoria Banforth, was getting just as much positive coverage, if not more. Her success in rising to the top as a single mother was lauded, she was graceful and intelligent, and cameramen seemed to enjoy zooming in on her brilliant, handsome, politician-in-the-making son, who had taken a leave of absence from law school to make speeches on his mother's behalf.

As images of the campaign blurred like a movie stuck perpetually on fast-forward, Sameera found herself feeling… invisible again. She didn't want America to *forget* that James and Elizabeth Righton had a daughter. *I guess three days in the limelight and Wilder's SammySez.com just aren't enough to keep me in the public eye.*

The coverage switched to an event that had taken place the night before at the closing banquet of a national teachers' conference. For this appearance, Vanessa had outfitted Mrs James Righton in a stylish white suit with gold trim, diamond earrings, a bouffant hairdo, long, oval (fake) fingernails, burgundy lips, and high-heeled sling-back white pumps. *Liz CampbelL—The Extended Version,* Sameera thought. *Or is it The Director's Cut? Directed, of course, by Tara. Produced by Vanessa, Constance, and Manuel.* In every close-up, Mom was smiling like a vintage version of Mrs America, but Sameera had never seen her eyes look so miserable.

'She looks absolutely exhausted,' Gran said.

'She told me yesterday that she *still* wasn't done with that—er—report.' It wouldn't do to remind Gran of the adjective Mom always put in front of the noun.

'To whom much is entrusted, of them much will be required,' Gran said. 'Liz and I may have our issues, but I'll always be proud of the way she's living out that Bible verse.'

'But what does that *mean,* Gran?' Sameera asked. One of her rare, secret peeves about Maryfield was how the older generation quoted Bible verses as though everybody on the planet understood them.

'Take a look at your mom's life, Sparrow. She's doing so much good in the world. And your dad's always fighting to do what's right.'

'You, too,' Sameera added quickly.

'I used to be of some use here in Maryfield.' Gran sighed.

'It's hard when you feel like things are being taken away from you instead of being entrusted to you.'

*Poor Gran,* Sameera thought. Her once-busy, bossy, hyper-involved grandmother had been forced into the role of resident couch potato. 'Take care of yourself, Gran, and you'll be back to all your good deeds in no time.'

Gran smiled. 'It's a beautiful day, Sparrow,' she said, obviously changing the subject. 'Let's take Jingle for a stroll over to the pond before your poppa catches us in here red-handed.'

'Remote-handed, you mean,' Sameera said, switching off the television.

# Twenty

Sameera had underestimated the public's fickle, unpredictable appetite for news. The Sparrow Hunt, as Uncle Jake dubbed it, started in early August.

One evening after supper, she squeezed herself into the small space still available on a sofa that was already crowded with one grandmother, one aunt, and one cousin. Uncle Jake and Poppa were settled in the recliners. Since Poppa's no-daytime-television rule was now being even more strictly enforced, the family had been staying up later and later to get their campaign fix. They were all starting to look positively bleary-eyed.

Poppa stood up, yawning. 'We need some coffee. I'll put on a pot. How many takers?'

Everybody raised a hand, including Gran, who added an imploring look. Poppa shook his head, but he ended up bringing her half a mug along with the others. Sameera had just taken a big sip of Poppa's black, bracing concoction when the evening news came on. The first shot was of a small, white-steepled country church basking in the sunshine, surrounded by a grove of maple trees. 'Oh, my goodness!' Gran said. 'That's our church! How'd they get that photo?'

'Welcome to Maryfield, Ohio. A small dairy-farming town like so many others across America,' the voice-over was saying. Poppa used the remote to turn the volume up. In the background, the tune 'America the Beautiful' was playing, and photographs of Maryfield's scenery kept appearing and fading. 'And yet, this summer, something happened to set this town apart. A young woman named Sammy Righton moved in with her grandparents, Matthew and Sarah Campbell, third-generation dairy farmers who live in this quiet community.'

They'd found her! *Well, it's about time,* she thought. Aunt Bev was gripping Sameera's arms so tightly that Sameera almost spilled her coffee.

'Sammy is James Righton's one and only child, adopted from Pakistan when she was only three years old. Tomorrow, travel with us to Maryfield to meet this adorable young lady face-to-face. And now, back to you, Dave.'

The family watched and flipped, and watched and nipped, locked in a channel-surfing trance. By ten o'clock, aerial photos of the Campbell farm had been added to the coverage. At eleven, they saw childhood photos of Elizabeth Campbell with her brother and parents, and even a shot of Miranda as a ten-year-old Girl Scout.

Miranda shrieked at the sight of her pre-teen face on national television. 'Why couldn't they have picked my junior class photo?' she wailed. 'The photographer in Canobie still has *that* one up in his store window.'

Next, Sammy Righton's yearbook photo from the International School in Brussels appeared on screen. As the enormous, smiling face lingered in front of the nation, a chipper, perfectly coiffed anchorwoman asked: 'Why is the popular Republican candidate rarely seen with his adopted black daughter? Tune in tomorrow when Channel Thirty-four reveals the whole story.'

This must have been the last straw for Poppa, who turned off the television. 'Come to bed soon, darling,' he said to Gran. Dropping a kiss on Sameera's head just like her father often did, he trudged into his room.

Aunt Bev stood up, too. 'Dad's right to turn it off. Watching so much television makes me queasy. Jake, are you coming? Miranda, don't forget to clean the kitchen.'

Uncle Jake left with her. 'Don't stay up too long, Sparrow,' he said. 'Number 137 is looking a bit under the weather, so you might have to do some of my work while I spend time washing her down.'

*Hello? Your life's about to change here,* Sameera thought. *Get ready, brace yourselves, it's going to get intense.* But her uncle's calm, everyday words reassured her even more than Poppa's kiss of solidarity. Even if the planet started spinning in reverse and the oceans spilled out into the galaxy, her grandfather and uncle would be up at three o'clock in the morning, taking care of their Holsteins.

Meanwhile, Gran was scowling and muttering under her breath, 'They don't get their FACTS straight. She's not BLACK; she's PAKISTANI. Terrible journalism. Scandalous. Someone needs to do something about it.'

*All that muttering and grumbling can't be good for the heart,* Sameera thought as Gran poured another cup of coffee and took it out to the sunroom—even though it was midnight.

Miranda was still gazing at the now-blank screen. 'Oh, wow, Sparrow. I… I was on *television.* Can you believe it?'

'Yeah, and it's going to happen again, Ran. They'll be here by tomorrow.'

'Who? Uncle James and Aunt Liz?'

'No. The reporters.'

'Oh,' said Miranda, her face lighting up. 'Oh! *Paparazzi!* That's awesome! Here I've been secretly envying you, and now things are finally going to get interesting around here for all of us.'

'You've been envying... *me?' I thought we were a mutual admiration society.*

'Yeah, Sparrow. I mean I love having you as my cousin, but sometimes it's hard. Think about it. Here I am, stuck on this boring farm in this boring town, while you've been jet-setting around the planet your whole life.'

'Maryfield isn't boring, Miranda. Plus, you're the shining star around here. You *make* things happen. And you've visited me in every place we've lived, and then I have to fend off the hordes of guys who want to contact you after you leave.' Members of her crew team still left love notes for Miranda as comments on Sameera's blog.

'It's not the same visiting a place,' Miranda protested. 'And then your dad decides to run for president, you get an *awesome* makeover, look *hot* on the tube, and handle questions so well, and start turning into... an actual *celebrity.*'

'But Ran, I'm still Sparrow, your little cow-milking cousin. I love the farm, my family, Jingle, and my circle of blogger buddies. I don't care what strangers think of me—I've been doing an experiment to see What It's Like to Be a Celebrity. I don't actually want to become one myself.'

*It's people who* want *to become celebrities who get trashed by the popularity machine,* she realized. She hadn't needed to bone up before leaving Brussels, watching movies about presidents' daughters and browsing celebrity websites. Maybe because she'd done so much soul-searching about being adopted, or maybe because she'd moved around so much, she already had what she needed to survive life in the limelight—that secret something that let her be Sparrow when she needed to be, stay Sameera when she wanted, and even morph into Sammy without losing her sense of self… or her sense of humour.

'… you looked and sounded so different, Sparrow,' Miranda was saying. 'The one thing that helped me remember that you were still the same *you* was reading your blog.'

'Well, it looks like I should get back to writing "My Life As a Celeb", because things are going to start getting interesting. I'm going to have to open that makeup case and extra suitcase after all. How about you? How are you going to handle the reporters?'

'I can't wait till they get here. I think this might turn out to be the big break I've been waiting for. What do you think?'

'Maybe. But aren't the reporters going to make things stressful for Gran? Remember what the doctor said?'

Miranda shrugged. 'Well, she'd better get used to it. If Uncle James wins this election, she's going to be the mother of the first lady. Which means *you* get to be the first daughter, and I get to be the first niece! How fun is *that* going to be?'

'Yeah, fun for me, fun for you, tough on Gran.'

They could hear their grandmother still muttering to herself in the sunroom. 'She needs some kind of major stress-releaser,'

Miranda said, shaking her head as she left the room to wash the coffee mugs.

*A stress-releaser. Hmmmm…* Sameera climbed the stairs to her room, found the blank book from her English teacher, and brought it down to her grandmother. 'I don't want to interrupt your prayer time, Gran, but I have something for you.'

'It's okay, Sparrow,' Gran said. 'I wasn't praying. I was just… grumbling out loud. I've never been as good at talking to God as your poppa is. Or your mother, for that matter.'

Sameera handed her the journal. 'Why don't you try writing to God? When I feel far away from someone, it helps a ton to write to them.'

Gran looked thoughtful. 'Okay, Sparrow,' she said. 'I just might give it a try.'

*Gran's blog with God,* Sameera thought. *Now THAT should be interesting.*

# Twenty-one

Sameera sat up with a jolt and stifled a scream. Aunt Bev and Jingle were both leaning over her, their faces inches from her own.

'I hate to wake you up, Sparrow, but it's time for the morning milking and they're asking for you.'

Despite the comforting presence of Jingle's body beside her, Sameera hadn't slept well. She squinted at the alarm clock. It was almost five-thirty—she was usually outside working by now. They'd stayed up so late the night before that she'd overslept.

'Sorry, Aunt Bev. I'll be ready in a minute. Who's asking for me?'

'Reporters. They've surrounded the house. I've only been up about ten minutes myself, but I called your uncle in the barn, and at least a dozen of them are waiting for you over there. Of course, they're trespassing on private property, but they don't seem to care, and Jake doesn't think it would be good PR to chase them off with his rifle. Not yet, at least.'

*Bang! Bang!* 'What's that?' Sparrow asked, alarmed.

Aunt Bev opened the door and Jingle shot out like a defensive missile. 'That must be your grandmother nailing the doggie door shut. I ran down to see how she was doing and almost got my head snapped off. She's furious—one of them poked a camera through Jingle's flap exit and took a picture of her sitting at the kitchen table, writing in some book.'

Sparrow threw off the covers and hurried over to the window. It was still dark, but sensor-activated floodlights were lit all over the property. Sure enough, a semicircle of parked cars, most of them with out-of-state plates, had taken over the driveway. Reporters and photographers were milling around the house and the barn, apparently waiting to pounce on any sign of human life.

'When did they get here?' she asked, pulling the curtains closed as one of them glanced up in her direction.

'No idea. Your uncle said they were here when he went out at 3 a.m. We should have locked and bolted the gate last night, but we were all too exhausted to think straight.'

The Campbells never locked the entrance gate to the property; it was too much trouble to drive the five miles back and forth every night. Besides, the only evidence of crime in Maryfield were the tools, casserole dishes, books, and countless other items that neighbours borrowed and forgot to return.

Sameera went into the adjoining bathroom to get dressed, where the outfit she'd worn that day in California was waiting for her. She'd taken it out of the unopened suitcase before going to sleep, along with some of Constance's tubes and vials. 'Where's Ran?' she called through the door.

'Don't ask. I'm so mad at that girl I could explode.'

'Why?' Sameera asked, running a brush through her hair quickly and putting on some lipstick.

'Your grandmother's irate about what she's wearing,' Aunt Bev said. 'Apparently I need to get her inside ASAP. Let's go.'

In the kitchen, Gran was trying to control Jingle, who desperately needed to pee. Since the doggie door wasn't an option, he was racing around the house, trying to find another way out.

'Take him with you, girls,' Gran said. 'Sparrow, stick close to Bev, okay? Your grandfather and uncle are both out there, so there's no need for me to come. And Bev, tell that daughter of yours to come in at once.' Her voice sounded strained and unnatural.

Taking a deep breath, Sameera followed Aunt Bev out the kitchen door. Jingle sped off toward the rosy eastern horizon like a golden blur. He'd deal with the visitors later, after he found a private place to relieve his own anxiety.

'There she is! Sammy Righton! With some farm woman! They're gonna milk!'

Sameera dragged herself into Sammy mode as the reporters surrounded them. 'Welcome to Maryfield,' she said, smiling and giving a Wilder-approved wave.

'Sammy! Why are you living out here on a farm with your grandparents? Sammy! Did your parents send you here? Do you actually milk? Do you like it? Do they make you work, Sammy?'

The now-familiar mikes were shoved at her mouth as Sameera followed her aunt along the path to the barn. 'I come every summer. Yes, I love working on the farm. No, they don't make me. But I'm glad to help out.'

Suddenly, the reporters' eyeballs shifted in one, unified

motion to goggle at something just behind Aunt Bev and Sameera. The questioning came to an abrupt halt; mikes were lowered and Sameera turned to see what had distracted her audience.

It was Miranda. Or was it? The person walking toward them looked like she'd escaped right out of a racy music video. She was wearing sunglasses, scarlet lipstick, and a pair of thigh-length leopard-skin boots. Although the boots were high, the miniskirt was so short that everybody could clearly see the crisscross pattern on the fishnet hose.

Sameera gulped. Aunt Bev had warned her before she'd come out here, but she had no idea that Ran could look so… trashy. Her cousin's silky, waist-length, strawberry blonde hair swayed behind her like a veil, and for some reason, Miranda's curves were jiggling and bouncing even more than usual.

'Oh good, Sparrow's come outside,' Miranda said when she finally made it over. 'You can take some pictures of the three of us doing the milking. "Farm Girls at Work" or something like that.'

Aunt Bev and Sparrow exchanged looks. Miranda hadn't helped with the morning milking in weeks. 'Miranda Campbell,' Aunt Bev muttered in a low, angry voice. 'Get a grip on your sanity, go inside right now, and take off that ridiculous outfit.'

'In a minute, Mom,' Miranda whispered back. 'Please?'

One of the reporters, a youngish guy, checked out Miranda's alligator-skin miniskirt and the plunging neckline of the flesh-coloured camisole she was wearing. 'You milk cows in *that?*' he asked. 'Wow. I'll bet the bulls want to be milked, too.'

Miranda giggled *(She does that perfectly,* Sameera thought), and reached down to re-zip one of the boots that had come slightly undone. Once again, every eye followed her movements. 'There now. A farmer's daughter *has* to take care of her boots. I'll see all of you later, I hope.'

After she sashayed into the house, the bevy of journalists followed Sameera and a still-fuming Aunt Bev into the milking parlour, where Poppa and Uncle Jake were hard at work. Jingle followed them, growling and barking when any reporter came too near Sameera.

'What was that daughter of yours thinking, coming out here dressed like that?' Aunt Bev asked her husband in a fierce whisper. 'Why didn't you send her inside immediately?'

Uncle Jake grunted. 'I figured I'd let her make a fool of herself and then let her read about it in the papers. It's a good way to break a habit from the start.'

'Sorry, Sparrow,' Poppa said to Sameera, his voice low, too. 'I'll lock these trespassers outside as soon as they leave.'

Sameera smiled at his concern. She was more worried about her family than herself; facing this kind of attention felt almost *normal* to her now. 'It's okay,' she whispered underneath the cover of Jingle's yipping and barking. 'Are they getting in the way?'

'Not till you got here,' Uncle Jake grunted, ignoring Aunt Bev's elbow in the ribs. He was trying to shield number 137 with his body.

Reporters were everywhere, swarming the stalls, poking the frightened-looking cows, even dipping dirty fingers into the fresh milk for free tastes. Uncle Jake managed to get number 137 into the safety of a stall, where he started washing her down gently.

It was hard to prod the cows into place with a crowd watching every move. Sameera's faux-jewel-encrusted sandals kept getting stuck in the muck and slipping off. Soon, the pink T-shirt and jeans that had looked so perfect in L.A. were splattered thoroughly with cow grime. She tried to keep working steadily beside her aunt, washing udders, scraping the parlour, hosing it down, all the while answering countless questions that were being shouted at her from every side. She could hardly hear them because of Jingle's continued expression of discontent, but at least he was keeping them at a distance.

'Call it a day, Sparrow,' Poppa called out finally. 'And take that dog with you.'

'But you need my help, don't you?' Sameera asked. 'Uncle Jake's still in there with 137.'

'We can manage, sweetheart,' Aunt Bev said consolingly. 'We're almost done.'

Photographers and reporters followed her like wasps, the zoom of their lenses droning at Sameera from every side. Jingle's ferocious bark was the only thing that kept them from touching her. Sameera headed back to the house, remembering to wave and blow a kiss at her entourage before closing the kitchen door firmly in their faces.

# Twenty-two

The paparazzi stayed around the farm and house all day. Gran and Aunt Bev made Miranda change into jeans and sneakers, even though Miranda begged to stay in her ZTV clothes. 'I want to look like I *belong* in the news,' she said pleadingly.

'When did you manage to buy that outfit anyway?' Gran asked, rubbing her temples. 'I thought your mother had to approve your Toledo purchases. Those boots! Let's send them to one of those brothels in Las. Vegas, why don't we?'

Undaunted, a now more modestly clad Miranda kept running in and out to give interviews and hand out freshly baked banana bread with glasses of Campbell milk. Uncle Jake and Poppa were still working, but Sameera, Gran, and Aunt Bev hunkered in front of the television, where the coverage had already started. Most of it was positive, lauding Sameera's hard work, commending the family's eco-friendly farm, and to Miranda's delight, showing clips of Sameera's 'lovely cousin, Miranda Campbell'. Sameera kept an eye on Gran, who was watching everything intently and grabbing her oldest grandchild every now and then by the back of her jeans to keep Miranda from going out too soon.

At around noon, Mrs Graves turned up, carrying a sheaf of

papers and clippings. 'Sparrow. I need to see you. Alone.' She sounded like a CEO calling a private meeting.

Sameera followed the librarian into the empty kitchen. Mrs Graves had printed out today's SammySez.com entry, with Wilder still waxing rhapsodic about country living and making product endorsements:

> maryfield is a lovely town, with hills and pastures... a little too quiet, but my cousin and i go into toledo to the **great springs mall** and to the **heartland amusement park**... My great-grandpa built our house with his bare hands, and my own grandfather built a wooden bridge across the stream... i always wear my **greenacre jeans** when I help milk the cows...

*Blah, blah, blah,* Sameera thought. *You're no help at all, Wilder.* 'I hate that fake blog,' Mrs Graves said, scowling. 'I wish you'd tell them to get rid of it.'

'I can't,' Sameera said. 'They're the *professionals.* They think that Americans are going to respond to that kind of stuff.'

'Well, if you can't get rid of it on your own, we the people may have to do something drastic. Check out these articles, Sparrow. I didn't want your grandmother to see them, but I think you should.'

'Righton's Niece Tells All,' said a caption underneath a ravishing shot of Miranda. And: 'Sammy Righton Hard at Work.' The photo accompanying this article was the same one of Miranda, only this time the photographer had zoomed out to include more background—a scene that included a thin, short, Pakistani girl mucking out a stall. The headline to the accompanying story read: 'Righton's Adopted Daughter Sent to Work on Family Farm'.

'But Aunt Bev was right beside me when I was doing that job,' Sameera protested. 'And so was Jingle.'

'Someone must have snipped the two of them right out,' said Mrs Graves. 'They've got the technology to do that now, you know.'

'Slave Labour?' wondered another caption underneath a close-up of Sameera washing her hands at the tap. The article next to it was brutal, and Sameera caught her breath as she read it silently:

> Righton's niece chatted freely, telling one and all what a blessing her adopted cousin has been to the family. Especially for her, it turns out.
>
> 'Does Sammy do the milking?' we asked. Every morning and evening, we were told.
>
> 'Do you?'
>
> 'Oh, no. I get to stay inside,' answered the gorgeous, leggy strawberry blonde, giggling happily.
>
> Mrs Elizabeth Righton, Sammy's mother, has been outspoken about outlawing the international trafficking of children for the purposes of labour. Why, then, did she and her husband send their own adopted daughter to live and work on the family farm? Mrs Righton's mother, who recently suffered from a heart attack, is no longer able to help with the cows. An imported Pakistani worker seems to have taken over those duties.

The sting of it, the unfairness, filled Sameera with fury.

She couldn't just shrug this one off; she was already forming a fiery rebuttal in her head. Just because a girl didn't *look* like she belonged in the family didn't mean that her family members were *using* her. And how could they lead poor Miranda astray like that? She'd be mortified. And what about Gran? Thankfully, the stuff they'd been watching that morning hadn't been negative, but Gran could stumble across something like this in her channel surfing at any moment.

'Is this what most of the web coverage is like?' Sameera asked. 'Because the television people have been pretty kind so far.'

'No. Not all of it. Most of it's fairly positive, but I thought you'd want to see the worst. We're so worried about your grandmother, Sparrow. She's been immersing herself constantly in this campaign, and she has absolutely no control over any of it. We want your grandfather to let her take back some of her responsibilities. Work that she loves—that's what Sarah needs.'

'I know. It was my idea to take over Miranda's chores this summer so that she could do Gran's work, but now I think that was a big mistake. Thanks, Mrs Graves. I'm so glad you're around.'

Mrs Graves punched her shoulder lightly. 'I'm in your circle, remember? And show your grandfather the articles. Men in love need all the help they can get.'

After the librarian left, Sameera raced into the family room, where Poppa, Uncle Jake, Miranda, and Aunt Bev were eating peanut butter and jelly sandwiches in silence, chewing and watching themselves appear again and again on national television. *Like a* Twilight Zone *episode,* Sameera thought. *Zombies watching zombies.* 'Where's Gran?' she asked.

'I may have to take her into town later,' Poppa said. 'She's not feeling too well.'

'Check these out, Poppa,' Sameera said, handing him the articles. 'I'm warning you, though, they're bad, so don't let Gran see them.'

Poppa didn't answer; he was frowning over the articles. Sameera tiptoed down the hall and peered into the darkened bedroom. Sure enough, Gran was prone on the bed with a washcloth over her eyes. *She may have seen something troubling already,* Sameera thought.

All day, the atmosphere in the house felt disrupted. Even Jingle found a hiding place and disappeared. The cows were mooing mournfully out in the pasture; soon it would be time to head out again to milk and feed them. *If* they could do it while reporters tripped over each other to get a better shot of Sameera in action.

Poppa must have been thinking along the same lines. 'Why don't you skip the chores this afternoon, Sparrow? I'm going to lock the gates tonight once all these guys leave.'

'Okay, I'll stay inside,' Sameera said. She'd do anything to make things easier for her Maryfield family. But her father's campaign had already changed the fabric of their lives; there was nothing she could do about that.

Gran was still absent when the family gathered for supper; the doctor in town had prescribed some relaxants, and she'd gone to bed early. Aunt Bev vented her anxiety by lecturing Miranda about her outrageous behaviour that morning. 'Cut the Dairy Queen act. And quit dressing like you're some kind of—I can't even say the word. It's demeaning.' She took Mrs

Graves's copy of one of the worst articles and thrust it in front of her daughter's face. 'Here. Read this.'

Miranda took stock of the pictures before reading the captions and the article. 'I… didn't say it like that, did I, Sparrow?' Her voice sounded small, deflated. 'I'm so sorry. I'll stay out of the photos from now on.'

'No, Ran. Just be yourself,' Sameera said fiercely. 'And besides, there isn't going to be a "from now on", at least not here in Maryfield.'

Poppa looked up. 'What?'

'I'm heading to D.C. as soon as I can book a flight.'

Miranda didn't meet her cousin's eyes. 'It's my fault, isn't it? I'm not proud of this morning, Sparrow. Mom's right—I ruined it for you, didn't I? That's why you're leaving.'

'No, Ran, that's not it at all.' *It's partly because I don't want YOU to get ruined.*

'Now, I don't know about leaving, Sparrow—' Poppa began, but Sameera interrupted him.

'I have to leave, Poppa. Those reporters are causing way too much stress for Gran. Not to mention the poor Holsteins.'

'Your grandmother would be the first to protest,' Poppa said. 'She'd do anything to keep you safe, Sparrow.'

'I know. That's why I have to do the same for her.' Sameera took the newspaper article out of Miranda's hands, ripped it to shreds, and tossed it into the recycling bin. 'Besides, Dad's opponent has her son on her side, and I'm sort of looking forward to re-entering the fight. Keep your eyes open for the return of the most amazing president's-kid-wannabe ever born in a Pakistani village.'

'We won't be able to do that, Sparrow,' Poppa announced. 'I cut off our satellite connection today.'

'Oh MY GOSH!' Miranda shrieked. 'This is the most RETRO house on the planet. What are we—*Little House on the Prairie?* No Internet, and now no television, either?!'

'Settle down,' Uncle Jake said. 'It's only for a while. I'll pick up the *Toledo Times* in town, and we can listen to the news on the radio every now and then when Mom's not around. Besides, we have Internet access at the library.'

Sameera frowned. Didn't Poppa get it? Narrowing down Gran's life even more wasn't the way forward. Why couldn't he see that she was chafing at the bit to get back to some of her normal routine? There *was* one solution, though. If Sameera got out of the way, Miranda would have to get back to milking, and Gran could return to doing some of what she loved—preparing hearty, healthy meals, cleaning the house, and making things cozy for her family.

Quietly, Sameera climbed the stairs to her room to call her parents. She left messages on each of their phones telling them that she was going to come to D.C. early, encouraging them *not to worry because everything was fine.* Then she dialed the Bench's cell phone and sent a text message: 'Am coming to D.C. Will send flight info. Sameera.'

A reply from Tara came to her phone in two minutes: 'NW. CU on farm w/tikets tomorrow. TC.'

*Hmmmm...* Sameera thought. *She's a savvy text-messager. And it's nice of her to keep her promise and make the flight arrangements, but why do I wonder if there's an ulterior motive behind this sudden trip to Ohio?*

When the last of the reporters' cars finally drove away, she went downstairs again and found her grandfather sitting alone in the kitchen with his head in his hands. 'Poppa, what would happen to the cows if you kept them in a narrow stall all day?' she asked, not bothering with any preamble.

He looked up, startled. 'You know we don't do that here, Sparrow. We let them graze.'

'And why do you do that?'

'You know that, too—they seem much happier. And we're convinced they produce better-tasting milk as a result.'

'What about their health?'

'Oh, there's no question that cows who roam freely are more healthy.'

Sameera sat down opposite him. 'Then wouldn't that hold true for a sixty-something woman, too?' she asked in a gentle voice.

He was quiet. 'I… I don't want to lose her, Sparrow,' he said, his voice breaking.

'I know, Poppa. I know.' She stood up and kissed him on the top of his head, just like he always did to her. 'Now let's go lock that gate. I'll drive. We need to talk about the stereo system Dad wants to put in Ran's Jeep.'

# Twenty-three

Sameera's family spent every waking hour the next day trying to convince her to stay through August. 'We can handle the paparazzi,' Gran insisted, popping another relaxant into her mouth. 'Your Poppa's keeping them off the property now.'

But Sameera didn't budge. She packed and got ready, Jingle watching her every move with a concerned look on his face.

'Sparrow!' Aunt Bev called. 'They're here!'

Sameera walked carefully downstairs in her high heels as Jingle barked out a ferocious warning. 'It's okay,' she told him. 'It's not a reporter this time. They're all outside the gate.'

Tara Colby looked crisp, polished, and completely out of place in the Campbell living room with its wood-paneled, book-lined walls, big fireplace, rag rugs, chintz couches, and matching curtains. An enormous woman with metal grey hair stood behind Tara, clutching a large briefcase.

'Hi, Tara. Thanks for coming.'

'Sammy!' Tara said, coming over with both hands outstretched. 'You look terrific. Wow. And that's without any help from Constance.' She sounded genuinely impressed.

*Yes, what do you think I am, a dunderhead? Anybody can learn how to put makeup on once someone else shows you what looks good on you. And anybody can learn how to wear the right clothes—especially when you've got a suitcase full of expensive stuff that an expert stylist chose just for you.* She was wearing a long denim skirt and a flowery white silk shirt with an Empire waist, along with the strappy white sandals she'd worn the night of the dance. She'd blown her hair dry for the first time all summer, and her foundation-covered skin was back to feeling like plastic.

Gran, Miranda, Aunt Bev, and Jingle came over to flank Sameera like three warrior women and one wolf who intended to keep her where she belonged—with them.

*My tribe,* Sameera thought fondly. 'This is my cousin, Miranda,' she said. 'My grandmother, Sarah Campbell, and my aunt, Beverly Campbell. This is Tara Colby, everyone.'

'Lovely to meet you all,' answered Tara. 'And this is Westfield, the finest tutor in D.C. She knows exactly how to juggle a good education with the pressures of a campaign. She was *my* tutor twenty years ago, believe it or not, and we're still good friends. I brought her along so that all of you can get acquainted.'

The large woman thrust out a hand, and Sameera's knuckles were crushed inside it. *Yow!* Sameera thought. *What kind of a name is 'Westfield'? No first name? Sounds like some kind of butler. And why did she REALLY get dragged along on this trip?*

'Who's Sammy?' Miranda asked, purposely sounding naive, even though the whole family knew the history behind Sameera's fake identity.

'Sammy Righton—America's next first daughter,' Tara answered, gesturing dramatically at Sameera.

Nobody said anything.

'Would you like some tea?' Gran asked finally, breaking the awkward silence. 'Miranda just put some oatmeal scotchies in the oven.'

The big woman made a guttural sound of appreciation but still didn't speak. *The strong, silent type,* Sameera thought.

'I don't eat sugar,' Tara said. 'Or white flour.'

'Figures,' Sameera heard Gran mutter as she herded Jingle and Miranda out of the room. Aunt Bev followed them.

'Now, Sammy, mind telling me what made you change your mind?' Tara asked.

'Oh, I started to miss the excitement of the campaign. It was kind of fun being there, at least when I wasn't exhausted.' That was true. She didn't need to go into complicated details about keeping Gran and Miranda safe.

'You think getting nasty coverage in the press is fun?' Tara asked, with that tinkly, discordant noise that was supposed to be a laugh. 'Maybe you *are* designed to be a "political progeny", Sammy.'

*Maybe I am,* Sameera thought. *It takes a person with both feet on the ground to enjoy this ride. And ten fingers firmly on her keyboard.* 'I'm ready for anything,' she said out loud.

'Since you're coming back early, we thought Westfield could get started early on the tutoring.'

'Now? But it's only the beginning of August.'

'I know. But three or four hours a day starting right now would make up for time you're bound to lose in October when the campaign really heats up.'

Miranda came in, carrying a loaded tray, and Westfield immediately reached for a still-steaming oatmeal scotchie. She took a big bite. 'Wow,' she said with her mouth full, speaking for the first time. 'These taste just like my grandmother's. I need this recipe. Could you make me a copy?'

Miranda smiled. 'We don't use recipes. Campbell bakers just… go with the flow. But we're about to mix up another batch of dough right now. Want to come watch?'

'Oh, yes,' the woman said eagerly. 'Then I can write down every step. Do you mind, Tara?'

'Not at all. I'll come with you, too, while Sammy packs,' Tara said. 'I actually have been wanting to talk to you particularly, Miranda. And your parents.'

*Aha! The first clue to the ulterior motive.* 'I'm packed already,' Sameera said. She didn't want to miss anything the Bench was planning to accomplish during this unexpected trip. Especially when it came to her precious Maryfield relatives.

'Gran wants to know if the two of you would like to join us for supper,' Miranda said. 'You can meet my father and grandfather, and there's plenty of food.'

Westfield glanced hopefully at Tara.

'Our flight leaves at nine,' Tara answered. 'And the ride to the airport only takes two hours. We should be able to stay.'

'It takes three, usually,' Sameera corrected.

'Not in my car.'

Inside the kitchen, Westfield immediately donned an apron and started mixing dough with Aunt Bev. Under Gran's watchful eye, of course.

'Sammy's going to miss this home cooking,' Tara said, shaking her head. 'She's going to miss all of you. I know how important her relatives are to her.'

Miranda, Aunt Bev, and Gran looked so sad when they heard this that Sameera chose the first thing that popped into her head to change the subject. 'I need something to say to the reporters at the airport,' she told Tara. 'Does Wilder have anything for me?'

Tara took the bait, flipped open her cell phone, and dialled a number. 'Marcus? Hi. Sammy needs a phrase to explain the Maryfield exit.' She listened, nodded, and scribbled a few words on a piece of paper.

'Try that,' she ordered, handing the paper to Sameera after she hung up.

'I'm sort of a daddy's girl. He likes to keep an eye on me.' Sameera tried to make the words seem natural, but they sounded stilted and awkward.

'That's good, Sparrow,' Miranda said. 'But add a little attitude. "I'm sort of a daddy's girl, I guess."' She giggled and flipped a wrist. 'He likes to keep an eye on me. You know how it is.'

'That's perfect!' Tara crowed. '*You're* perfect. In fact, that's one of the reasons why I came; I wanted to meet you.'

'You did?' Miranda asked.

'Definitely. I think you could be a huge asset to your uncle, with your zest and sparkle. Besides, your friendship with Sammy is so sweet that it makes her seem even more like the girl next door.'

So that was it. She wanted to use Miranda's all-American appeal.

Aunt Bev, Gran, and Miranda were staring wide-eyed at Tara, who kept going. 'Westfield could tutor both of you; that's why I brought her along. I figured that after meeting her—and me—your family might agree to send you to us this fall.'

Miranda gasped. 'Really? You mean *I* could be part of Uncle James's campaign? AND GET ONE OF THOSE AWESOME MAKEOVERS MYSELF?'

'Of course, although with your natural beauty and grace, Constance and Vanessa won't need to do much. We'd work out the timing, pay for your tickets, and give you firsthand exposure to good campaigning that would equip you in the future for all kinds of things.'

Aunt Bev didn't look convinced. 'You've got chores to do around here, young lady,' she said, giving her daughter a significant look that meant 'remember your grandmother's condition'.

Miranda's face fell.

'Her uncle and aunt have offered to cover the costs of a housekeeper,' Tara said quickly. 'Liz even suggested flying Mrs Mathews from the Residence out here to the farm to help out. What do you think, Sammy?'

*It might be good for Mrs Mathews,* Sameera thought, *but Gran needs to get back to work. And Miranda needs to get back to the Holsteins, who don't get the word exploitation.* 'I'd love Miranda's company, of course,' she said out loud. 'But Mom and I will figure things out, okay?'

That laugh again. 'Of course. But your mother's the one who convinced me that your cousin could be great company for you.'

Mom was right; it would be wonderful to have Miranda around! But as Sameera took stock of Miranda's glowing, eager expression, she knew she had to think of her cousin first. *I won't let you use my cousin. Ever.*

When it was time to eat, they gathered around the dining table. Candlelight sparkled on the silverware and crystal. The antique grandfather clock that had accompanied one of their ancestors from Scotland was ticking out the minutes as precisely as usual. Jingle was sleeping across Sameera's feet like he always did, and she reached down every minute or two to pat him. She was going to miss him; she was going to miss them all.

Poppa bowed his head to say grace, and they all followed suit, even Tara and Westfield. 'Bless our small Sparrow, Lord—' he started, but he couldn't finish before his voice got choky.

'She's coming back soon, for goodness' sake,' Gran said briskly, but Sameera noticed she'd wiped her nose on her napkin before speaking. Gran usually hated it when people used her good cloth napkins to blow their noses. Get a tissue, she'd admonish, and now she herself had become a culprit.

'The way things are going, James might lose this election big-time and have to figure out what to do with his life,' Uncle Jake said. 'Maybe he'll consider joining us on the farm.'

'You tell your dad to get on his knees when things get tough,' Poppa told Sameera, his voice still gruff. 'Most of our presidents had a deep faith, even if they weren't churchgoers when they moved into the White House. Abe Lincoln didn't start out as a praying president, but that's how he ended up. The same with Ronald Reagan.'

'I'll have to talk to James again about going to church,' Gran added. 'Liz told me to stop going on and on about it, but I think he needs some kind of encouragement now that his own mother's gone.'

'You don't have to worry about that; we're on top of it,' Tara said. 'The American people want a churchgoing president. James and Liz have been attending a service every Sunday in D.C.'

'Well, I'm not sure about *those* motives,' Gran answered. 'But I know that his parents were devout, and that they liked to see their son attending church.'

'It's always sounded to me like they put a lot of pressure on him about it,' Poppa said slowly.

Westfield reached for another huge helping of the taco salad. 'The onions just make this salad, don't they?' She'd cubed the onions carefully, following Gran's instructions.

'Come along, Sparr—I mean, Sammy,' Tara said. 'Let's go, Westfield. We have to hit the road.'

Sameera knew that her cousin had caught Tara's slip of the tongue. Apart from making eye contact with each other, though, neither cousin let her expression get anywhere near triumphant.

Tara's rental car was a brand-new sapphire blue BMW. 'Figures,' Sameera muttered, and then was struck by how much she sounded like her grandmother.

She kept the goodbyes short and crisp.

'I'll be back soon,' she promised her aunt and uncle. *Take care of Miranda. And Gran. And number 137.*

'I'll blog,' she told her cousin. *Stay focused on what's real, Ran.*

'I'll be fine,' she assured her grandparents. *Set Gran free, Poppa. Keep writing in that journal, Gran.*

When she went to get in the car, she realized that Westfield was in the backseat and that Tara had climbed in the passenger seat.

'Can you get us to the airport in two hours, Sammy?' Tara asked, tossing her the keys.

'I'll try,' Sameera said, climbing in the driver's seat. There were times when Tara Colby's shrewd people skills were easy to appreciate, and this was definitely one of them.

Jingle followed the car, barking his confusion and distress over her leave-taking, and Sameera glanced at the rearview mirror until he became a small golden fleck in the distance. It took the five miles on the property to get used to the BMW, which handled like a dream compared to the second-hand Jeep. She counted off the familiar landmarks of the farm one by one until they reached the gate, where a dozen cars were waiting with engines running. The posse of reporters followed them to Toledo and into the airport.

'I'm sort of a daddy's girl,' Sameera said at least a dozen times, smiling widely. She felt obligated to use the phrase, since she'd asked for it, even though it was so ridiculous. 'He likes to keep an eye on me.'

'Of course, I love it there,' she answered, when they asked if she was going to miss her life in Maryfield. *At least I'm telling the truth,* she thought, accidentally flipping her wrist so hard she heard a joint crack.

# Twenty-four

'Constance and Vanessa are in town, and I've lined them up for another session before the convention,' Tara said as the limo took them from Dulles Airport toward the District of Columbia.

'I have a lot of clothes I haven't worn yet,' Sameera protested. 'And I'm starting to get the basics of how to put makeup on for the cameras.'

'You did a nice job on your own, Sammy, but you're still open to learning, aren't you?' Tara asked. 'Besides, you have to look absolutely perfect for the convention.'

Westfield frowned at Tara. 'What's the matter with the way she looked before your people did that makeover? I watched the coverage of her arrival at LAX in June. She looked modest and sweet, like a girl her age ought to look. And I loved that poncho.'

Tara ignored the comment. *Considering the source, I think I will, too,* Sameera thought. Westfield was wearing a boxy, outdated suit that didn't fit her too well.

'What am I doing until the convention?' Sameera asked Tara. 'It's three weeks away, isn't it?'

'Yes, but we didn't know you were coming back early, now did we? Your parents thought it would be good for Westfield to get started with some math tutoring while you have a little time on your hands.'

*Oh. So I came back early to do geometry. How fun.*

'I've already emailed your teachers in Brussels to find out where you are,' Westfield added. 'We'll get you up to speed, Sparrow. Don't you worry. First session tomorrow at ten?'

'But tomorrow's Friday,' Sameera said.

'No use putting off till Monday what you can start on Friday,' Westfield said heartily. 'Are we set, then?'

Sameera nodded reluctantly, thinking of all the terrible grades she'd gotten in math through the years. Westfield was used to tutoring the brilliant offspring of other political candidates; she was in for a rude surprise when it came to the combo of James Righton's daughter and math.

The limo stopped in front of one of those familiar-but-impersonal State Department apartment buildings that overlooked the green lawns of the Mall. 'Do you want us to walk you up?' Tara asked as she and Westfield walked Sameera into the lobby. 'It's apartment eight-oh-nine.'

'No, thanks. Mom and Dad are there waiting for me.' She'd called from the airport, so she knew it was true.

'Oh, and Sammy, try and avoid being interviewed or photographed until the convention, will you?' Tara added, almost as an afterthought.

'Why?' Sameera asked. 'I thought that the more press coverage we get before the election, the better.'

'Yes, but it has to be the right kind of press coverage. We don't want any more shots of you covered in cow manure from head to toe.'

'You mean muck.'

'Muck, manure, same thing.'

'Did Wilder manage to get me out of the muck? I haven't read his posts lately.'

That averted glance again. 'He… posted something about how you get cleaned up after milking the cows, I think.'

*Oh. With lots of product endorsements, I'll bet. I wonder what the campaign's getting in return.*

'Marcus is heading out to some top secret destination for a couple of weeks,' Westfield added helpfully, ignoring Tara's glare.

'He is? Right before the convention? Now *that's* interesting,' Sameera said.

'The campaign's heating up,' Tara said. 'We're all under stress. For your father's sake, stay out of the news for now. I'll be in touch.'

After asking the doorman to bring Sameera's suitcases upstairs, Tara and Westfield climbed back into the limo and disappeared into the dark D.C. night.

Sameera rode the elevator to the top floor, but as she walked closer to the door of the apartment, it flew open, and her parents came barrelling down the hall.

'Sparrow! You're here. We couldn't believe it when we heard you were coming back!'

Wrapped in her parents' embrace, Sameera took a deep breath—and immediately started coughing. What *was* that fierce, musky smell? It was a new perfume emanating from Mom, and Sameera was definitely allergic to it.

They walked into the apartment, Sameera still hacking away, and Dad brought her a bottle of purified water and a box of tissues. She checked out her parents as she dabbed at her eyes. Dad looked the same in one of his classic navy blue jackets, white shirt, and red tie. Mom was wearing an ivory linen sheath with matching heels and stockings that were almost the exact colour of her skin. The all-of-a-colour ensemble made her blue eyes stand out like sapphires, and her figure looked sleek, as though she'd lost ten pounds during the weeks Sameera had been away. Her hair was styled into a bun, with a few loose blonde tendrils cascading in a calculated-but-casual way to her shoulders. She seemed polished and perfect at first glance, but when Sameera looked a bit closer, she saw that the dark circles under Mom's eyes were camouflaged with ivory-coloured makeup.

'We spent the whole day up in Baltimore, Sparrow,' her mother said wearily. 'It's a miracle we're actually back in time to greet you. I read aloud to three hundred kids, your father handled questions at a televised town hall meeting where calls came in from around the country, and we took a dinner cruise on the harbour with a gang of Maryland power players. I've had four hours of sleep for three nights in a row, and my feet are killing me. And… I'm still not done with that freakin'…'

Her voice trailed off. She slipped out of her pumps and collapsed into one of the apartment's uncomfortable armchairs, which was upholstered in exactly the same ivory as her dress… and her skin. *SHE looks invisible now,* Sameera thought, as Mom shut her eyes and propped her feet on the brocade ottoman. Within minutes, her mother was breathing deeply.

'Wow,' Sameera said. 'I had no idea someone could plunge into REM sleep so quickly.'

Dad perched on the sofa, yawning and loosening his tie.

'We're so glad you joined us early, Sameera. Turns out there's no way your mother and I could have visited Maryfield this summer. The three of us will campaign throughout the country starting in September, after the convention, but for now, we'll stay based in D.C.'

'Will we travel by plane?'

'Some of the time. But the rest of the time we take buses. It could be fun, if we don't drop dead of exhaustion before then. Sometimes I wonder if this is what I should be doing with my life.'

Dad leaned back in his chair. He looked so despondent that Sameera remembered the message her grandfather had wanted her to relay. Although the topic was tough to broach, she made herself say it: 'Poppa told me to tell you, Dad, that—that a lot of presidents started praying during their terms, even though they didn't pray much before. Like Lincoln. And Reagan.'

Dad was quiet. Then: 'Your grandfather's a wise man,' he said. 'I'll give that some thought.'

'You don't have to know all the answers about religion, Dad. I've got tons of questions myself.'

'You're right about that, Sparrow. People of faith *have* to keep asking questions. That's one of the reasons I didn't talk about it with my own parents—they were so sure they had all the answers. Everything was black and white.' He yawned again and closed his eyes, as though the conversation had now totally exhausted him.

*Great,* Sameera thought. *I haven't seen them in weeks, and they're comatose. But at least Dad and I had our first real 'religion' talk. It was short, but I think he heard me.*

She looked around at the immaculate, sterile apartment that was supposed to be their home, trying not to think of the cozy family room in Maryfield. Her parents had been based here for months, and they hadn't done anything to personalize the place.

Somebody knocked, and Dad leaped to his feet. 'I'm awake! I'm awake,' he insisted, still in a daze. 'Did they get that on camera?'

'Dad. It's okay. You're just here with me and Mom.'

It was the doorman, bringing up Sameera's suitcases. Mom hadn't even heard the knock; she was actually snoring now. Dad, who had managed to wake up all the way, tipped the doorman and picked up the suitcases.

Sameera followed her father into yet another colour-free cream-and-glass room, picturing the bright, homemade quilt on her four-poster bed in Maryfield. Not to mention the golden warmth that Jingle's fur added to the scene. *Can you overnight express a live animal?* she wondered wistfully.

# Twenty-five

The next morning, she found a note in Mom's large, sprawling handwriting on the kitchen counter: 'We're in Delaware all day, and we'll be back quite late—after midnight, probably. Stay safe. Call my cell if you need me.' Dad had added a few words in his neat, upright printing: 'Don't go out on your own. D.C.'s a dangerous city. Love you. Dad.'

Sameera sighed. Obviously her parents weren't done with being overprotective.

She showered and slipped into comfortable jeans, a T-shirt, and the fleece from Poppa that she'd rescued from annihilation in L.A. Then she pulled back the curtains and watched countless Starbucks-cup-clutchers walk their dogs around the Mall. *Poor pooches,* she thought, thinking of Jingle roaming freely through the woods, jumping into the pond for a swim anytime he wanted, not knowing that terrible things like leashes existed.

The apartment felt quiet. Too quiet. *I need to blog,* she thought suddenly.

Without any new posts from Sameera, her circle of twenty-nine had been comparing summer jobs and complaining about how boring vacation always got by the end. The most recent comment had come from Miranda, telling everybody how *awesome* it was to be *almost famous,* and how much she was going to miss Sameera. 'Now I'm back to the cows,' she wrote. 'And our grandmother's bustling around the kitchen again. When she isn't writing in that journal Sparrow gave her.' This last sentence cheered Sameera up immensely.

Then she started typing.

> Here I am, immersed once again into the excitement of my father's campaign! This time, though, my main job is to... CATCH UP ON MY MATH! Wahoo! I'll be making my official appearance at the convention in three weeks. Until then I've been commanded to stay OUT OF THE NEWS because Wilder's mysteriously disappeared, and hence there can't be any new SammySez.com posts to do damage control if I blow it. So once again, I must be invisible. I WILL challenge this decision, as I'm feeling more and more confident about handling tricky questions on my own. In the meantime, I'm going to have to figure out a way to go out incog or else I'll go nuts. Are any of you going to be in D.C. anytime soon? Wanna meet for a cappuccino? Remember: keep your comments short, clean, and to the point. Peace be with you. Sparrow.

Short, clean comments came pouring in from the four corners of the globe, making her feel much less lonely.

'Jingle howled at the moon all night,' Miranda wrote. 'And so did I. I'm working on Mom and Dad to let me join you, Sparrow. What do the rest of you think? Should I come before or after the convention?'

The consensus of the circle seemed to be afterward, when the campaign would ramp up considerably and get even more interesting. Sameera waited for someone to ask if it wouldn't be hard on her small-town cousin to handle the stress and attention of being in the public eye, but nobody did.

Promptly at ten Westfield arrived, equipped with sharpened pencils, notebooks, textbooks, and a calculator. And a grocery bag full of food. 'Let's start with algebra,' she said brightly, putting out bagels, cream cheese, and a bowl of pistachio nuts along with two bottles of icy diet soda.

Sameera's math teachers had always been the kind who droned on for a whole hour without pausing for breath; she'd escaped into Ahmed or Matteo fantasies to survive the excruciating boredom. She especially hated algebra and had barely gotten a C-minus last year when they'd covered it, just like the C-double-minus-almost-a-D she'd scraped out this year in geometry. But as Westfield started the session, Sameera discovered that it was impossible to zone out when you were one-on-one with a top-notch teacher. Westfield patiently broke the problems down into such small steps that even a self-labelled math dummy could grasp them.

After an hour, Westfield announced that it was time for a 'refreshment break'. Are those oatmeal scotchies from Maryfield that I see on the kitchen counter?' she asked, eyeing the packet that Miranda had sent along for Sameera's parents.

'Yes. Help yourself. Westfield, what do you know about Victoria Banforth?' Sameera munched on another half a bagel. They were *good.* Westfield, meanwhile, her eyes closed as she slowly chewed, was savouring a scotchie. *Note to self,* Sameera thought. *Tell Ran to send Westfield one dozen scotchies.*

'Funny you should ask,' Westfield said when she'd swallowed her bite. 'I tutored Thomas Banforth about ten years ago, when he was in high school, and Victoria was running for a second term. They're lovely people; we still stay in touch.'

Sameera groaned. 'You've tutored *everybody*. Don't you feel like a traitor, party-hopping like that?'

'Not really. You're all good people. In fact, you'd love Thomas. He's a gem.'

'Let me guess—he was a whiz kid even back then, right?'

'He has his strengths, Sparrow. And so do you. Which reminds me: let's get back to math, shall we?'

Sameera couldn't believe how much she learned in her first tutoring session. Westfield went back to review stuff that should have been learned in elementary school, slowing everything down—way down—until she was sure her pupil got it. Sameera actually understood the concepts of 'majorities' and 'percentages' for the first time in her life. She felt like she'd started climbing a mountain range and reached a couple of minor peaks. *I claim you, Mount Percentage,* she thought jubilantly, remembering how she used to dread even hearing the word. *You're mine forever, Majority!*

When the session was over, Sameera stretched and wandered over to the window while Westfield packed up. Lines of summer camp kids were snaking into museums, and people endured the August heat by eating ice-cream cones and sunbathing facedown, wearing tiny bikinis. Suddenly, Sameera noticed half a dozen people with cameras around their necks loitering across the street. Paparazzi! Were they waiting for her, or for someone else?

'Do the reporters know we're here, Westfield?'

'You bet. They've been keeping track of your parents' whereabouts 24/7. Well, I'll see you on Monday, Sparrow. Got anything planned for the weekend?'

'Not really. I don't know a soul in D.C.'

'If Tara hadn't told you to sit tight, you could head over to one of the colleges or take a walk along the Potomac. There's a lot to see and do in this city, especially on the weekends.'

Something clicked in Sameera's mind. As soon as Westfield left, she ran into her room to find the white beaded clutch purse she'd been carrying that evening at UCLA. Ah! There it was, and the card was still safely inside. It was time for some quick online research.

# Twenty-six

She entered 'SARSA' and 'George Washington University' and 'students' into the search engine, and bingo—she found it. 'SARSA@GW: South Asian Republican Students' Association'. So that was it! When she browsed the site, she found the same cryptic information that was on the card with a bit more information: Fridays. 4-6 p.m. Revolutionary Cafe. Foggy Bottom, District of Columbia. A small line of print did say 'Meetings resume in the fall'. It was only the third week of August, and according to the George Washington University website, school didn't start until the first of September. Would they be meeting today? Brief but well-written directions at the bottom of the page informed interested visitors how to get to the coffee shop by Metro.

Sameera glanced at her watch. It was two o'clock now; the SARSA meeting, if there was one, started at four. She might make it in time if she could figure out a way to avoid the paparazzi. Besides, even if there wasn't a meeting, it would be nice to enjoy a cup of good coffee after drinking Poppa's instant stuff all summer.

*A disguise, I need a disguise.*

Suddenly, she remembered the salwar kameez she'd brought with her from Brussels. Where was it? She rummaged through her suitcase. Yes! Blessed Mrs Mathews had folded the cotton knee-length top, loose-fitting pants, and matching scarf carefully in Ziploc bags at the bottom of the suitcase.

After putting on the pants and tunic, Sameera took the long scarf and wrapped it completely around her head the way she'd seen Muslim women wear it. She gazed into the mirror. No, something still wasn't right. Quickly, she grabbed the dark eyeliner pencil out of Constance's makeup supply and outlined her eyelids heavily with it, both top and bottom. Then she wrapped the scarf again until it covered her head *and* most of the lower half of her face, and pinned it into place. There. That was much better, even though she could hardly breathe.

Quietly, Sameera headed down the back staircase at the end of the hall. The photographers and reporters waiting outside the building didn't even glance her way. They'd heard that a giggly, kiss-blowing hottie named 'Sammy' had entered the hotel the night before, and they were waiting for any sign of *her* to appear. Why would they notice a devout Muslim girl exiting a staff-only door that opened into a side alley?

The Metro station was starting to get crowded with people heading home for the weekend. Sameera had ridden the train before when she and her parents came to D.C. for brief visits, but it still took her a while to figure out how to pay the fare. The blue train was arriving just as she reached the platform, so she boarded it. To her dismay, a woman on the train gave her a suspicious look. *What's up with her?* Sameera thought. *Does she recognize me?* Oh, well. She'd have to worry about that later. Right now, she had to concentrate on getting off at the right stop and finding the Revolutionary Cafe.

The streets around George Washington University were bustling with Friday afternoon activity, and a still-sweating Sameera stopped an elderly woman and showed her the card. 'You go straight down the street for three blocks, love,' the woman said, clutching Sameera's hands. 'And please, let me welcome you to America. We're so glad you're here and hope you'll consider becoming a citizen of this country.' She beamed, peering over the reading glasses she must have forgotten to take off.

*An ancient, real-life Statue of Liberty,* Sameera thought.

'Thanks, but I'm an American already,' she said, hating to disillusion this hospitable stranger.

Sure enough, the woman's face fell, and she released Sameera's hands. 'Really? I thought you *must* be a newcomer, and I vowed, after 9/11 happened back in 2001, always to welcome newcomers, because those terrorists might have thought about what they were about to do if *someone* had been kind to them in this country. What do you think?'

So *that* was it. Sameera's veiled head was reminding people of all sorts of strange things. 'Er... maybe. I don't know. Thanks for your help.'

She looked around furtively—not a reporter in sight. With a sigh of relief, she headed for the Revolutionary Cafe.

# Twenty-seven

Sameera had hoped to find the place swarming with Indian, Pakistani, Bangladeshi, Nepali, Burmese, and Sri Lankan SARSA@GW members, but most of the students inside weren't South Asian at all. Sameera stood to the side, scanning the room for any sign of the robust, friendly girl she'd met so briefly all those weeks ago. There she was! So they *were* meeting! Sangita Singh and three South-Asian-ish companions were clustered around a small, round table. One was a girl with waist-length hair; she had her back to Sameera along with one of the guys.

Sameera hesitated at first. They looked like such a cosy circle that she hated to interrupt. But as she watched, the four of them burst into laughter, and she couldn't bring herself to turn around and go back to an empty apartment. She edged a bit closer.

'It didn't hurt to give fund-raising a try, Bobby,' Sangi was saying. 'But nobody's giving us anything, that's for sure.'

'We're not about raising money for Righton's campaign,' the guy with his back to her said. 'What happened at your booth last spring, Nadia?' *Sweet Southern accent,* Sameera thought.

The girl with the shiny long hair sitting next to him answered; Sameera couldn't see *her* face, either. 'When I set up my "Righton for President" table at the student centre, someone actually snatched the three dollars I'd put in the can myself.'

'Let's face it,' the other guy said, sighing. He was tall and skinny, and wore glasses rimmed with rhinestones. 'We might be the only Republican South Asian students at George Washington University.'

'That can't be true.' It was Delicious Southern Voice again. 'There are a lot of closet conservatives around here. But let's leave the fund-raising to Righton's middle-aged staffers. This group's about convincing the under-twenty-five crowd that he's exactly the kind of global leader our generation needs.'

'We have to revamp our site,' Sangi said. 'George, you're our token web-savvy geek. I'm sure you could morph it into a state-of-the-art portal for us.'

Rhinestone Rims shook his head. 'I could make it look sharp and hum along, but good sites need content. What could we add that Righton's official site doesn't have already?'

Just then, Sangi caught sight of Sameera, who quickly sidestepped away until she was standing in the line of people waiting to order coffee.

Sangi stood up and marched over. 'Can I help you?'

'I'm waiting in line,' Sameera answered.

'Did you want to join us? You're welcome if you do.'

Sameera shook her head.

'Then why were you listening in on our conversation?' Sangi's voice was getting more strident, and people were turning to stare.

'It's me, Sameera Righton,' Sameera whispered, standing on tiptoe to get the crucial words into this girl's ears. 'You invited me to come, remember? But keep it down. I'm not supposed to be out alone; I snuck out of the apartment.'

The girl took a step back in surprise. Then she moved closer again, bent down, and squinted into Sameera's eyes. 'Get your drink and come join us,' she said finally, but this time her voice was low, too. The onlookers turned back to their own coffees and conversations.

Sameera watched Sangi whisper something to her SARSA companions. Rhinestone Rims stared at Sameera over the top of his sparkly glasses, his mouth open, but neither the girl nor the guy with the Southern accent turned around. Sangi had obviously warned them to play it cool for Sameera's sake.

She walked over to the group clutching a cappuccino, wondering why her heart was racing. She felt more nervous about this meeting than she had about facing hordes of reporters.

'Hello and welcome,' that mega-attractive voice drawled as the owner of it stood up to give her his stool. He turned to face her, and Sameera's mouth felt as though it had been wiped clean with an extra thick paper towel. Long legs covered in faded blue denim, black T-shirt with a V-neck, a silver bangle on his wrist, great hands, curly black hair... this guy could definitely erase any lingering images of her crewmates from her late-night fantasies.

'Here, Bobby, there's space here,' said the girl sitting next to him, shifting her body to make room on her stool. She was slim-hipped and beautiful, of course. Tall, elegant, wearing a tight black sweater, jeans, and sequined sandals. And that long, thick, shampoo-commercial curtain of hair! Even Sameera's fingers wanted to touch it.

The bangle-wearing hunk rested his butt partly against the girl's stool, but Sameera noticed that he leaned forward against the table so they didn't actually touch. 'I'm Bobby,' he said to Sameera. 'And this is Nadia and George. You've already met Sangi, right?'

'We're the founding members of SARSA@GW,' George added.

'The only members, actually,' Sangi added. 'We're affiliated with a nationwide organization that links together all the South Asian Republican Student Associations. Great outfit, by the way.'

Sameera set her coffee on the table. 'Yes. Well. I was going bonkers in my hotel room, and I remembered that when I met her in L.A., Sangi asked me to come if I was ever in D.C. So I thought I'd ditch the paparazzi by wearing this.'

'You look terrific, Sammy,' Sangi said. 'That head covering looks really authentic. Of course, what do I know?'

'Call me Sameera, okay? I don't really like "Sammy".'

'*I* certainly will,' Nadia said, smiling for the first time. 'I get so tired of people calling me "Noddy", I could scream.' Sameera noticed that she'd shifted a bit closer to beautiful Bobby.

*They must be a couple,* Sameera thought. But then he leaned away even more, and she wondered if she'd gotten it right. It looked more like a girl-predator, boy-prey situation; her crewmates had often been the targets of girls on the hunt, so she knew the body language.

'I didn't think you'd be meeting in August,' she said.

'We came back early to help out with orientation. And to brainstorm ways to help your father's campaign,' Bobby said. 'Got any suggestions?'

Sameera took a big swig of cappuccino and made sure to wipe away any traces of a coffee mustache. 'I'm still looking for the best way to help him myself,' she said.

'I'm hungry,' George said suddenly. 'I need fuel for tonight.'

'Okay, we'll eat,' Sangi told him. 'Hey, Sameera, you want to join us? Or do you have to be somewhere?'

She thought of the empty apartment; her parents weren't going to be back for hours. 'No,' she said. 'I've got nowhere to be.'

'We're going to a party,' George said. 'We're all dying to see Bobby bhangra for the first time... '

'Hey, wait a minute,' Bobby said. 'I didn't say I was going to dance. I'm coming along to watch. That's a big enough concession.'

Sameera knew what bhangra was, thanks to the Bollywood films she and Mom rented every now and then, but she'd never actually tried it herself. 'I've never danced bhangra, either,' she said. 'And, I'm not sure I'm dressed right.' *Besides, my parents don't even know I'm out on my own,* she thought, but she certainly wasn't about to confess that to a group of college students.

'You'll be fine,' Nadia said confidently. 'A dozen or so girls always dance the night away with their heads covered.'

'Yeah,' Sangi added, shaking her head. 'Everybody calls them the Covered Girls. Tight jeans and head coverings—it's the new all-American look.'

'I didn't notice the tight jeans,' Nadia said.

'I sure did,' George said, and Sangi pretended to punch him.

A crowd of college-age brown-skinned party animals? This she had to see. 'Why not?' Sameera said, grinning. 'Maybe I can learn, too.'

'Oh, good,' Bobby said, a slow smile lighting up his face. 'You know what they say—misery loves company.'

*If you're Company, then I'm definitely Misery*, Sameera thought.

# Twenty-eight

The five of them stopped to eat samosas at a hole-in-the-wall Indian restaurant near the campus before heading over to the student centre. Sameera listened to her companions bantering and making jokes about one another's heritages that she didn't quite get. They were definitely all South Asian, but their parents were from different places. George was a Christian with roots in South India, Bobby's parents spoke Bengali, Nadia's parents were from Pakistan, and Sangi's heritage was Punjabi.

'The land that brought the rest of you bhangra,' Sangi bragged as they made their way through the streets of Foggy Bottom. 'Punjabis know how to party.'

Sameera knew that several different languages were spoken in Pakistan, including Punjabi. Had her birth parents spoken it, or were they Urdu speakers? Mom and Dad hadn't kept any secrets from her; they didn't know either.

She could hear the beat of Bollywood-sounding music now, even though they were still walking across the wide lawn on the campus, and she felt like she was dreaming. What would Tara say if she knew that Sameera was heading to a bhangra party in Washington, D.C., on a Friday night? And what about her parents?

She followed the four founding members of SARSA@GW into the big darkened room. The dance floor was packed with bodies rising and falling to a fusion of what sounded like pop, Bollywood, and reggae. Sweaty dark skin gleamed under strobe lights and near glitter balls. Most of the dancers were wearing western clothes, but several of the girls were in salwar kameez outfits, and some guys and girls were wearing long, cotton kurta shirts over their jeans.

'WHEE!' Sangi screamed, racing for the throng and throwing her body into it as though she were leaping into a pool on a hot day. George grinned, pulled a red bandanna out of his pocket, and followed her, waving the bandanna in the air in time to the music. Their bodies disappeared from sight, but Sameera watched the red bandanna's frenzied dance move through the field of raised hands. A few other kerchiefs and bandannas were waving in the air, too.

Bobby stayed by Sameera on the periphery of the moving, heaving crowd, and Nadia glanced back at them. 'Coming?' she yelled. 'I'll teach you.'

'I'm going to wait,' Bobby shouted. 'You go ahead.'

Nadia shrugged and began curving her body—and hair—to the music, twisting herself into the crowd's syncopated movement as though she'd planned her entry perfectly.

Bobby turned to Sameera. 'I don't think I'll be good at this,' he yelled in her ear. 'They don't bhangra much where I'm from.'

They watched for a while. Sameera's eyes followed the roving, multicoloured searchlight that swept across the dance floor every now and then. She squinted into the crowd. 'There they are!' she yelled.

'Who?' Bobby demanded.

'The Covered Girls!'

Sure enough, a group of heads draped in black were bobbing up and down at the far end of the room. She couldn't see the tight jeans from where she was standing.

'They're good,' she said. 'They're moving right to the beat.'

'SAMEERA!' a voice behind her shrieked suddenly.

Sameera couldn't believe that someone had recognized her in this outfit, in this loud, swarming crowd, in a place where nobody could have anticipated her presence—least of all herself. But when she turned, she saw two girls she'd never seen before kissing each other's cheeks. 'Looks like you're not the only Sameera on the planet,' Bobby said in her ear.

Sameera turned back to the dance floor, relieved that she was still incognito. It was too hard to talk, and the music and energy of the dancers seemed to be inviting her to join them. Even Bobby's feet were starting to tap.

'Let's try this!' she said. Before he could protest, she took his hand and pulled him into the mass of dancers. His fingers felt strong and clean intertwined with hers, but they both let go as soon as they were surrounded by undulating bodies.

'What now?' Bobby shouted, dodging flying elbows and swinging hips.

A girl moved next to Sameera, and a boy came up by Bobby. 'First-timers?' they hollered over the music, still dancing.

Bobby and Sameera nodded.

'Watch and learn,' the girl yelled.

She lifted both hands and cupped the air, twisting her wrists, and Sameera tried to imitate her. The girl bounced her knees slightly, keeping her heels on the ground, and Sameera did the same. Bobby was copying the movements of the guy beside him, jumping, swinging his arms in short, circular motions and thrusting them into the air. Sameera tried that, too, feeling at first like she was doing shoulder presses at the gym, but soon she realized that all four of them were actually dancing.

'We're doing it!' she yelled.

'We're great!' Bobby shouted back.

The couple that had given them the lesson smiled and moved along to find the next initiates, leaving Bobby and Sameera to dance, and dance, and dance. *Maybe I AM part Punjabi,* Sameera thought as the movements grew easier.

Eventually, George, Sangi, and Nadia found them. Sameera felt like she was attached to the sinuous, weaving bodies moving around the floor, even though most of them weren't touching her.

Finally, the musicians took a break, and Sameera wiped the sweat off her forehead with the loose end of her scarf. It had stayed around her head nicely; she'd done a good job with the safety pin. *I may never be a cover girl,* she thought. *But I make a semi-decent Covered Girl.*

'Wow! You two sure learned fast,' Sangi said.

'Thanks to Sameera,' Bobby answered. 'I probably would never have tried it if she hadn't pulled me in. But it's fun—you were right.'

'I'd better go,' Sameera said, reluctantly glancing at her watch. It was almost eleven o'clock.

'Already?' George asked. 'We're just getting started.'

'I'll walk you to the station, Sameera,' Bobby said.

'It's Friday night, Bobby,' Nadia said pleadingly. 'Stay just a little longer.'

'I can't,' he said. 'I have to make a phone call.'

Nadia's face fell, and Sameera flashed back to the times that her crew guys had exited a conversation with her at any sign of their girlfriends. *It's strange being on this side of the equation,* she thought, even though she knew that Bobby was probably just being polite.

'Didja check out your fellow Muslim girls gone wild?' George asked her.

'You bet I did,' Sameera answered. 'Their hair was nowhere in sight, but their bellies certainly were.'

'Lots of beautiful belly bling out there tonight,' George said.

'Stop being sexist,' Sangi admonished him.

'How is that sexist? Admiring the female form is—'

'I'll see y'all later,' Bobby interrupted. 'I've got to go make that call.'

'Join us next Friday, Sameera,' Sangi said.

'I'll try,' Sameera answered. 'But... I'm not sure I can.' She couldn't believe how *forlorn* she sounded.

To her surprise, all four SARSA members moved a step closer, almost inadvertently. 'We'll wait for you,' Nadia said, reaching over to straighten Sameera's head cover. Any animosity or suspicion she might have been harbouring seemed to have disappeared.

'Keep in touch,' George said. 'Think about adding some belly bling.'

Sangi said nothing but wrapped her in a huge hug. Then, for once, it was Sameera's turn to walk off with the planet's most perfect guy.

# Twenty-nine

Blues, jazz, and rock music drifted out of various clubs and bars as they walked to the Foggy Bottom Metro stop. Sameera tried desperately to think of something to say. Bobby was a college student; he was used to intellectual, stimulating discussions. 'You're from the South, right?' she asked, and then felt like kicking herself. People probably asked him that ten times a day after hearing him speak.

'How can you tell?' he asked, grinning. 'Must be my good manners, right? My father's a doctor in a small town—Creighton, South Carolina. That's who I'm supposed to call—my parents. They moved to Creighton the year I was born.'

'Really?' She paused. 'And how many years ago was that?'

'Eighteen.'

'You're only eighteen?' she asked, surprised. 'Are you a freshman?'

'No. This is my second year of college. I skipped a grade in elementary school.'

'Oh. How was it growing up in South Carolina?'

'Fine, even though I was the only brown kid for miles around. It was great while I was little; everybody was friendly. But when I got older, I always felt either too visible or invisible.'

*I know what you mean. Seems like there's no happy medium.*

'Weren't there any African Americans in your town?' she asked.

'Nah. That's one of the things I love about being here. Look, nobody's paying the slightest attention to you, even wearing that head covering.'

'I don't know. I think it's different now because I'm walking with you, and you're dressed like an "American".' She described what had happened on the train, and how the older woman had over-responded when she'd asked for directions. 'I didn't think the D.C. area was like that.'

'It's not too bad, usually, so I'm surprised. *My* theory is that people are more suspicious about how you sound than how you look. Strangers warm up instantly in the South as soon as I start talking. But up here, they think I'm stupid.'

'I think your accent sounds great. It fits you perfectly.'

'Thanks,' he said. 'You know what? You could test out my theory. Try using an accent when you're dressed like that, one of those Indian ones that lilt up and down, like my mother's. And then see if people treat you differently.'

'You mean like this? "Are you having any brothers and sisters, Bobby"?' Once again, she applied the Pakistani accent that came so easily to her.

'That's perfect!' Bobby said. 'Wow, you're good at that.'

'My cleft palate was formed around Urdu. So do you have siblings?'

'No, sadly, I'm an only child.'

'Me, too. At least I think I am.' She couldn't believe she was bringing up her adoption with a stranger. Usually, it was the other way around.

'You're close to your cousin, though,' he said, and then seemed embarrassed. 'Sorry. I've been watching the coverage of your family, like everyone else.'

Sameera smiled. 'Yeah. We are close, even though Miranda wasn't quite herself that day.'

He walked her down the stairs into the station. 'Get off at the Smithsonian stop. Do you want me to go with you?'

*Yes. Forever.* 'I'll make it,' she said. 'You have that call to make. Thanks for walking me.'

He gave her one last smile before turning to climb the stairs. She watched until the frayed hems of his jeans disappeared.

Sameera dialled her cousin as soon as there was nobody within listening distance. 'Ran! I think I'm in love.'

'What? Where are you? Who is he?'

She described the whole night in detail, trying to explain the magical combination of bhangra and Bobby.

Miranda sighed. 'That sounds just like that movie you love—you know, when Audrey Hepburn goes off on her own and falls in love with Gregory Peck.'

'It *was* like that, Ran.' *Roman Holiday* was absolutely number one on Sameera's top-ten-most-romantic flicks ever. 'I needed to tell you because I won't be able to blog about this. Mrs Graves is great, but she might freak out if she knew I was roaming around D.C. on my own.'

'Will you see him again?'

'I don't know. I hope so. The four of them are meeting next Friday and going dancing, and they asked me to join them.'

'Are you going out in that disguise thingamajig again?'

'Probably. It actually made me feel kind of free and powerful. Of course, *I* can choose when to wear a head covering and when to take it off. I wonder what it's like for women who have to wear it all the time—whether they like it or not.' And then, because her cousin had gotten so quiet, she said something really stupid: 'Maybe you should try it sometime.'

Silence.

'I've got *freckles,* Sparrow,' Miranda said finally. 'How many veiled Muslim women have *freckles?*'

*I don't know; they're veiled. That's the point.* 'What's wrong, Ran? You sound upset.'

'I guess... I guess I'm sort of scared that I'm going to lose you, Sparrow.' Miranda's voice was shaky. 'You had to leave the farm, and now you're finding all these cool new friends that probably look more like they're related to you than I do.'

'Are you kidding? You're my cousin, Ran, and my *best friend.*'

'Oh. That's good to hear, Sparrow. I'll be working hard on my parents about coming out there. I'll let you know if there's a breakthrough.'

'I'll be waiting,' Sameera promised, trying to sound like bringing Miranda to D.C. was the number one item on her to-do list.

She got off the train and walked to the apartment building and into the lobby, completely forgetting that she still had her head covered.

'Can I help you?' It was the doorman, blocking her way into the elevator; he obviously didn't recognize her. 'Are you visiting someone, madam?'

'I—I... ' She didn't want to reveal her identity to this guy, who might tell her parents and worry them unnecessarily. 'I am so very sorry,' she said, shifting easily into a Pakistani accent.

The doorman escorted her through the lobby and out the front door. Sameera walked around the corner and went in by the staff-only door in the alley, climbing the eight flights of stairs and reliving every moment of the magical evening in her imagination.

# Thirty

The next morning, Sameera emerged to find her parents drinking coffee in silence in the living room. 'We need to talk,' she announced. 'Tara told me I'm not making any appearances until the convention. Is that right?'

'I think so. Why do you ask?'

'I've been noticing that Senator Banforth's son is getting a lot of coverage lately. Don't you think *I* need to get out there and tell America that you're the best father on the planet?'

Dad grinned. 'Okay. What's in it for you?'

'I'll go nuts staying in the apartment for three weeks. Marcus Wilder's disappeared and Tara's scared to let me handle the press on my own. But I think I can come up with more intelligent responses than those canned giggles he thinks are so great.'

'I agree,' Mom said. 'You've always been so good at handling people, Sparrow. I think she's right, James.'

'I haven't forgotten the math grade on your report card, Sparrow,' Dad said. 'You'll be applying for colleges soon, and you won't get into a good one unless you pull your math grade up. Why don't you focus on studying for a few weeks?'

'Oh, I will. Westfield's great. I'll get my grades up, Dad. I promise.' *Maybe I can even get into George Washington University.*

'But why can't I do my tutoring in the mornings, and join you and Mom for afternoon and evening events?'

'You're the one who said the campaign was ten times more fun and relaxing when we had Sparrow around, James,' Mom said.

*He said that?* 'Please, Dad? I won't let you down.'

'Okay. I'll try and arrange it. Tara won't back down easily, though. She's certainly attached to that strange Wilder guy. He strikes *me* as being a little… off.'

'Women in love do strange things, James,' Mom said. 'Take me, for example.'

Sameera shook her head. 'Tara? In love with Wilder? No way. She falls for the JFK Junior type of guy.'

But Dad had lost interest in Tara's love life. 'I'll call her right now.'

Sameera and Mom listened in on Dad's end of the conversation.

'I'd like Sameera to join us for some of our appearances before the convention, Tara.' Pause. 'She can handle it on her own.' Pause. 'She'd never make *that* kind of mistake. She's got her feet on the ground.' Pause. 'Okay. That sounds like a good compromise. Where is Wilder, anyway? Is everything okay?' He listened for a while before saying: 'Send him our best. I hope everything works out.' He hung up. 'She's agreed to let you join us for a week without Wilder's help on a "trial basis". I tell you, it's tough keeping my campaign staff on a short leash without having them quit in a huff.'

'What's up with Wilder, Dad?' Sameera asked.

'Apparently, he had to check himself into one of those stress-detox meditation places for a couple of weeks. He was having a terrible time with insomnia and high blood pressure.'

Mom sighed. 'I wonder if I could join him.'

'So, what's on for this weekend?' Sameera asked.

As she listened to her father describe the busy schedule ahead, she felt confident that she was right. Speaking from her heart would be much more helpful to Dad than using Wilder's falsetto phrases and gestures.

At first the press seemed a bit taken aback by the absence of giggling, waving, and blowing kisses, but they, like Sameera's circle of twenty-nine, responded well to the truth. So that's what Sameera focused on in her answers.

***Q: If your Dad wins, you'll become the president's daughter. Are you excited about that?***

*True Answer: Definitely. But I'm also scared for him; it's a tough job. I don't want him to get hurt.*

***Q: Are you going to look for your birth parents?***

*True Answer: Mom and Dad were told they were dead. But if we have the chance to find out more, we'll definitely take it.*

***Q: What are your career plans?***

*True Answer: First, I have to get my math grades up (laughter). This year I'll take the SATs, and I'll have to start thinking about colleges. Got any suggestions for a girl who loves to write?*

Tara arranged a session with Vanessa and Constance before the evening events, but otherwise, Sameera was managing to use what she'd learned from them to good effect. After the first week, even Tara had to admit that she was doing quite well… for a political novice. 'Of course, August is a slow month,' she said. 'You'll need Marcus's help again at the convention.'

Sameera managed to opt out of any campaign appearances on the two Friday evenings before the convention. After Westfield left, she headed out to Foggy Bottom clad in her salwar kameez. Once again, the combo of South Asian clothes, a head covering, eyeliner, and the staff exit door seemed enough to fool the Sammy-hunting paparazzi congregated outside the building.

The SARSA@GW afternoon coffee or tea was always followed by a bhangra party and a walk to the Metro station with Gregory Peck. *Er… I mean Bobby,* Sameera thought, floating beside him underneath the starry summer sky.

During Sameera's third and last Friday in D.C. before leaving town for the convention, the five of them lingered over their coffee. 'I just had the most brilliant idea!' Sangi said.

'What now? You're always coming up with crazy ideas.' Nadia shook her head slightly, but her hair kept swaying behind her, as though it didn't think she'd expressed herself strongly enough.

'Most of Sangi's ideas work,' George said. 'She's the one who started our SARSA chapter, remember?'

'Don't worry, she's going to tell us about it anyway,' Nadia said. Her hair stopped moving, as though it, too, was resigned to the inevitable.

Sangi started talking so fast she sounded like an auctioneer. 'What about if we feature a column, or a blog, or something like that on our website? From Sameera. About the campaign. You know how we've been wanting an insider's take, something to help our site get a lot of hits from younger voters. Well, this could be it. She can give our visitors the scoop on what it's like to be the first South Asian with a shot at living inside the White House. *We* spread the word through our SARSA contacts; *she* fields questions about what her father's really like, you know, tell the truth about what a great guy he is.'

'How do you know he's a great guy?' Sameera asked.

'Her own website already features a blog,' Nadia said at the same time.

Sangi looked momentarily confused before sorting her answers out. 'I know he's great... well, because he's so globally involved. A real peacemaker. And he cares about South Asian issues. I mean, he adopted you, didn't he? Plus he's married to your mom, who's done such good work—promoting small-scale businesses run by village women, for example.' She grinned at Sameera's surprised expression. 'I'm an econ major. With a global development minor. I've read about Elizabeth Campbell's work.'

'What's this about a blog on your website?' Bobby asked. Sameera felt her cheeks get hot. 'The campaign set up a "custom blog" for me,' she said. 'I don't really have anything to do with it.'

'I could write a "custom blog" for you on our site,' Sangi said earnestly. 'Or maybe we could write it together.'

'I know how to blog,' Sameera said firmly. She wasn't about to authorize yet another fake virtual identity. 'I've been keeping an online journal for a year.'

'You do?'

'You have?'

'That's fantastic!'

'Can we check it out?' That was Nadia. Of course.

'Er. No. It's not accessible to the public; I only let a short list of buddies read it.'

They were quiet, and Sameera suddenly realized how inhospitable she sounded—especially to a group of people who'd made *her* feel so welcome.

'Would you consider making it public?' Sangi asked. 'We could link to your blog from our website and send the link to other SARSA groups; you'd get tons of readers in no time.'

'That's the point. My father's campaign team doesn't want me expressing my own opinions so publicly. They want to stick with my "official" blog.'

'Are they nuts?' Sangi asked. 'Reading personal stuff that his own daughter writes about the campaign could only score major points for your father.'

'How do we know that Sameera can write, anyway?' asked Nadia. 'I mean, no offence, Sameera, but the stuff on your "official" site sounds like it's written by a pre-teen TV addict.'

Sameera sighed. 'I know. It's actually ghostwritten by a thirty-something marketing expert. He's convinced that voters are a bunch of narrow-minded shoppers who hate foreigners.'

Sangi refilled her friends' cups with hot coffee from the carafe they were sharing. 'So here's your chance to prove him wrong, Sameera. If *your* blog—the real blog—gains steam and starts helping your father, they might decide to bag the fake one and let you use your real voice.'

Her words rang like a bell in Sameera's ears. Using her 'real voice' was exactly what she'd been doing lately in front of the cameras, and what she'd *always* done through her blog—writing about what she was learning, thinking, experiencing, and always, always telling the truth. But could she do that when she knew that hundreds, maybe thousands, of people would read her words? 'I—er… I'll think about it, okay? Let's see how it goes after the convention.'

After a couple of hours on the bhangra floor, she said goodbye to the others and Bobby walked her to the Metro station again. Just before they parted, he hesitated, and Sameera glimpsed an unidentifiable emotion in his eyes—it couldn't be *pity,* could it? She certainly hoped not. Then, to her amazement, he leaned over and kissed her softly on the cheek. '*Phir milenge,* Sameera,' he said, and turned to climb the stairs two at a time.

Again, she watched until the soles of his sandals disappeared. Could she count this as her first kiss? Or had it been just another one of those brotherly pecks that her teammates used to give her all the time? It certainly hadn't felt like that. And *phir milenge* meant 'we'll meet again' in both Urdu and Hindi. It was a common way of saying goodbye in the part of the world where both of their ancestors came from, but Sameera hoped with all her heart that Bobby meant it.

# Thirty-one

The four days of the convention went by in a blur. Sameera listened to speechmaker after speechmaker praise and commend her father. She sat onstage beside Mom, smiling and nodding and clapping in the right places, just as Wilder had prepped her to do. Yes, Wilder was back. But the couple of weeks of yoga and therapy or whatever he'd tried hadn't made a dent in his stress level; he was popping beta-blockers as if they were Tic Tacs.

Sameera didn't mind his re-entry into her life, and actually found herself sifting through his barrage of advice to find stuff she could use. She let Constance and Vanessa have carte blanche, too, partly because she knew that Bobby would be tuning in and she wanted to be as gorgeous as possible.

The day that Dad accepted the party's nomination, Sameera wore the red sleeveless dress Wilder had featured on SammySez.com and felt fantastic in it. She actually thought that it looked much better on her body than on the virtual whirling dummy who had modeled it on the website. And so did everybody else, judging by the admiring gazes and words she got all night long. As she stayed up late with the campaign team—big donors, real celebrities, and other bigwigs—celebrating and dancing,

Sameera could have stored up a lifetime's worth of unearned adulation if she'd wanted it.

When they returned to D.C. after the convention, the leased apartment didn't feel as generic anymore. Gran had sent homemade quilts to cover each bed, and Sameera had adorned the mantelpiece and walls with family photos. She'd also ordered some plants and bought a colourful tablecloth, place mats, and napkins for the table. Miranda had mailed a huge stuffed Lab for her bed, and leaning against that made Sameera miss Jingle a little less. The place wasn't home, of course, but at least there were some homey touches now.

'What's the use of unpacking?' Dad asked, dumping his suitcase in the living room. 'We have to leave again the day after tomorrow.'

*For someone who's just won the Republican nomination for the presidency, he sounds pretty grumpy,* Sameera thought, going to the window and checking out the view of the Mall. If only the campaign bus wasn't leaving before Friday! She wouldn't be able to see her SARSA friends again unless she figured out a way to get in touch with them. She'd felt hesitant asking for their cell phone numbers, and they hadn't asked for hers.

'Oh, *man*! I'm so freaking tired of travelling I could scream. Where are we headed first?' Mom asked, setting her tongue free like a lion tamer unlocking a cage. The three Rightons were finally alone for the first time in days, and Elizabeth Campbell Righton had been on extra good behaviour during the convention.

'The bus meanders down to Alabama, and then we fly from Montgomery to Chicago, where I'll do one debate, hit a few key midwestern states, and then we're off to Colorado to do a tour of the western states and the second debate,' Dad said. 'Sounds like torture, doesn't it?'

Sameera had never seen her calm, diplomatic father so edgy.

'Sorry,' he said quickly, catching her surprised look. 'I'm shattered. Shattered. I need a hot shower, a beer, and the chance to watch *Monday Night Football* in peace. Nobody talk to me for a couple of hours.'

'Don't be a drama queen, James. We're all as tired as you are.' Mom was more irritable than Sameera had ever seen her, too—which was scary.

Dad waggled a finger in her face. 'You're just ticked because you STILL haven't finished that report, and you're taking it out on me.'

'Don't you DARE lecture me! You sound EXACTLY like my MOTHER!'

Sameera shouldered her body between her parents like a referee at a boxing match. 'Dad, get in the shower and de-stress yourself. Mom, Dad's right. Go finish that absolutely freaking report so you're not barking at us all the time. You've got a couple of days to work before we leave. You *have* to get it done.'

Grumbling but subsiding, her parents obeyed, and the three Rightons went their separate ways. Sameera dragged her stuff into the bedroom. Her parents hardly ever fought, but then again, they were used to travelling on separate business trips and enjoying passionate reunions, not spending every waking moment together while a zillion eyes watched their every move.

She called Miranda as she unpacked.

'I've got some big news,' her cousin told her. 'My parents have cut a deal. If I focus on schoolwork and chores for a semester, and *if* Uncle James wins, I can move into the White House with you in January! Isn't that great?'

'That's... *wonderful!*' Sameera said, straining so hard to put enthusiasm into her voice that she practically shouted the adjective. She couldn't picture her cousin in the White House, but then again, she couldn't picture herself there, either. The place had been dubbed 'the most luxurious prison in America', though, so it actually might be better for Ran to be safely inside the White House instead of out in the open, facing the pressure of the campaign.

'Now Uncle James really has to win! I'm going to do all I can to get him votes around here, that's for sure.'

'How's Gran doing?' Sameera asked.

'Much better. Poppa's been easing off a lot lately, letting her get back to some of the things she loves. And you know-that notebook you gave her? Well, she's always pulling out a pen and scribbling in it, even if we're right in the middle of dinner, or church, or at the grocery store. It's weird, but she seems a lot less anxious since she started doing that.'

*GranBlog,* Sameera thought. *I wonder if God leaves any comments.*

'I also think she's more relaxed because we don't have television or the Internet at home anymore,' Miranda added. 'But don't tell Poppa or my parents I said that. I had to go over to Mrs Graves's place to see how fabulous you looked in that red dress.'

'Oh no! Mom and Dad are starting to fight again,' Sameera said. 'I'd better order some takeout; I think they're having a calorie meltdown. Talk to you later.'

Her parents did seem to settle down after eating huge helpings of pad thai. Sameera said good night, leaving Mom writing on her laptop in a living room chair, and Dad sprawled on the couch watching an old movie called *Jerry Maguire. He's bagging the football and tuning in to a romantic chick flick for her sake,* Sameera thought. *Good move, Dad. They'll be cuddling again in no time.*

'Join me?' Dad asked Sameera wistfully.

'Er… no thanks, Dad. I want to get some sleep.'

What she really wanted to do was start an email correspondence with Bobby, but how could she? She didn't have his email address, and she didn't want to turn into one of those stalker types by searching for his online identity. She decided to send a short, generic thank you to SARSA@ GW.EDU:

> I had a great time with you guys these last three Fridays. Thanks for your support. I love bhangra! I'll be in touch. Sameera.

She was about to post a new entry on her myplace.com site when the 'you've got mail' icon flashed on the screen. She went back to her inbox, and there it was—a reply from info@ SARSA.GW.EDU.

> Hey, Sameera. Sangi here. The four of us were sitting around brainstorming about revamping the site, when lo and behold we get an email from you. Must mean you're going to blog for us, right? Send us a sample post, will you, to shut Nadia up? I KNOW you're a

great writer. I can tell these things. Here's Bobby; I'm passing the keyboard to him.

B: It was great to see you looking so relaxed during the convention. Stay in touch, Sameera, and keep making your circles.

George: I have no idea what Bobby's talking about. Weirdo English majors, using metaphors the rest of us don't get. If you figure it out, let me know.

Nadia here. There are SARSA chapters everywhere you go, if you need them. Here's the link to the national website. Sangi's right—send that post to us. You need to show America that you have absolutely nothing in common with 'Sammy.'

It's me again—Bobby. Okay, I'll translate. The four of us talked about how we felt like we'd known you forever, even in such a short time. And not the 'Sammy' version of you, either. My guess is that the REAL Sameera has the gift of gathering circles of people around her. You might not even realize it yet, but the people around you do. Like us.

George: Whatever. Still don't get it. Keep dancing, Sameera.

Sangi: WRITE BACK SOON! SEND US THAT SAMPLE BLOG POST!

Sameera reread their message five times, her eyes lingering on Bobby's words. It was funny how he'd used the word *circle*, she thought, because he didn't even know about her myspace.com circle of twenty-nine. And then she thought of Gran and Poppa, Mayor and Mrs Thompson, Uncle Jake and Aunt Bev, Ms Graves, the Ladies' Aid, the church folks, and how she was always welcomed back as one of their own. In fact, the entire town of Maryfield could probably be listed as another circle in the Sameera collection. Plus, she'd always had Mrs Mathews and her parents. And now could she add SARSA@GW to the list? She reread their note again; it seemed like she could. *What a great feeling,* she thought. *I am encircled.*

# Thirty-two

The next morning, Dad was sitting alone at the kitchen counter, drinking coffee and reading the morning paper. 'I won't be back until dinner tonight, Liz,' he announced from behind the paper.

'It's me, Dad.'

'Oh.' Dad put down his paper and poured Sameera a cup of coffee.

Mom breezed in, decked out in the peach-coloured suit again. 'I've got meetings all morning, too,' she said; she'd obviously heard Dad's announcement. Sameera noticed that she was smiling brightly—a genuine smile, the original Elizabeth Campbell version. '*I* won't be home until just before dinner, either, and then I'm taking you both out somewhere nice to celebrate.'

'You finished your report, didn't you, Mom?'

Mom jabbed the air with her fist. 'YES! I wrote the last line of the conclusion just as Jerry Maguire was saying "You complete me". It was perfect timing.'

Dad stood up and threw his arms around her. 'I'm so proud of you, honey. But why didn't you tell me last night?'

'You didn't ask,' Mom said, pulling out of his embrace. 'You just sat there looking glum all night.'

'That's because *you* didn't seem interested in getting close to anything but that laptop of yours.'

'Oh—you say you're supportive, but when it comes to…'

Sameera tiptoed back into her room until round two of the sparring was over. *I'm not getting involved,* she thought. *I've got to get rid of both of them—and cancel my tutoring session with Westfield.* She'd realized that she needed more than one salwar kameez in her closet, and she was planning to use this last day in D.C. to find a shop that sold South Asian clothes.

She called Westfield as soon as her parents left. 'I… I'd like to skip our lesson today, if that's okay with you.'

'Fine, Sparrow. I could use the time myself to get a few things ready. We'll be together a lot on the road trip; we can easily make it up.'

'Gran sent an extra tin of scotchies for you, by the way,' Sameera said.

'Oh, goodie. Bring them along, will you?'

Sameera changed into her disguise quickly this time. Maybe she could find a store that sold real burkas with veils, along with salwar kameez outfits.

She got online, did a search with 'burka', 'salwar', and 'D.C.', and sure enough, there it was: Muhammad's Attire, only about three miles away. Writing down the address, she grabbed her purse and headed out the staff-only exit again.

It was such a beautiful day, she decided to skip the Metro and walk the twenty or so blocks to the store. Every now and then, she'd stop someone and ask for directions, sometimes using a fake Pakistani accent and sometimes not. Most people were friendly; a few weren't. *I'm like a one-woman reality show,* she thought as one disgruntled man shook his head and refused to answer. *Surprise! You're LIVE on 'Foreign in America!'*

She got to an interesting neighbourhood of second-hand shops and inexpensive restaurants. From the names of the stores and the menus posted in the restaurant windows, she realized that the people who lived and worked in this part of town included immigrants from Vietnam, Brazil, and definitely… Pakistan. A few women wearing real burkas passed her, and she could see their eyes measuring her imitation version. Girls wearing small salwar kameez outfits turned to giggle at Sameera, their glossy black braids swinging behind them.

Sameera found herself wishing she were strolling along with Bobby, chatting, reading menus together. The international flavour of the neighbourhood reminded her of the open markets in Europe where immigrants from every corner of the planet sold their wares. All the stores here, though, even the most 'ethnic' ones that used little or no English in their signs, were decorated with American flags.

Ah, there it was—Muhammad's Attire, a small, narrow store wedged between a Brazilian restaurant and a thrift shop. Sameera walked in, feeling like a kid entering a costume store at Halloween. She was the only customer.

A plump, beaming man came around the counter to greet her. '*A-Salaam-Wa-Lek-um,*' he said, nodding. 'I am your Uncle Muhammad.'

'*A-Wa-Lek-um-A-Salaam,*' she replied, bowing slightly. These traditional greetings were the only other phrases in Urdu that she knew, other than the 'we'll meet later' farewell that Bobby had used.

'Shall we get started?' he asked in English.

'How did you know I speak English?' she asked. But of course her fake Pakistani accent would never be able to fool this man. *He* had the real thing.

'I have quite a few good Pakistani-American girls like you coming who are eager to dress modestly again, like our women do back home. Mariana, my own daughter, likes to wear the head covering, even though some hoodlums at her school have teased her. Don't you worry! Uncle Muhammad knows just what you need when it comes to clothing.'

*Hmmmm. You might know how to dress a conservative Pakistani version of me, but you have no idea how to clothe Sammy, or even Sparrow for that matter.* What Sameera really needed was the power to shift from visible to invisible, from elegant to funky, from modest to sexy—and to stay in charge of when, where, how, and why.

He found two burkas that were the right size, and together they chose several salwar kameez outfits with scarves, or dupattas, as Uncle Muhammad called them, that were long and sturdy enough to be used as head coverings. He even sold her a different head covering with a veil that only revealed her eyes.

Sameera reached for her credit card to pay for her purchases. Her parents had always been generous with her monthly limit, probably because she so rarely reached it. 'What's my total?' she asked.

'Sorry,' Muhammad said, his head moving in a figure-eight when he saw the card. 'I take only cash here.'

'Oh. Where can I get cash?' It was better to use cash anyway, she realized. Dad would probably have questions about a purchase from Muhammad's Attire bearing a strange D.C. address.

'There's a cash machine at the market on the next block,' Uncle Muhammad said. 'I shall be here waiting for you.'

Sameera was waiting in line for the ATM inside the store when she heard a scream. 'AY-O!' It was a woman's voice.

Sameera turned. An old woman wearing a burka was trying to wrestle a gallon of milk away from a beefy security guard. She was shouting something that sounded like 'MERRY DUDE! MERRY DUDE!' and pummeling the man with her free hand.

Almost inadvertently, Sameera stepped toward them.

'Lady, I'm about to have you arrested,' the guard was saying, trying to fend off the old woman's punches.

'MERRY DUDE!' the woman shouted again, landing a hard uppercut right on the guard's beer belly.

'OOF,' he grunted, doubling over and dropping the milk.

The woman picked it up and scurried for the door. 'HARRY! GRAB HER!' the guard shouted.

A younger guard was racing over from the other entrance to the store. He caught the old lady, who now looked terrified, and dragged her back to his partner.

'YOU are going to JAIL!' the first man said, snapping his walkie-talkie off his belt with an angry flourish.

Sameera watched the woman's face crumple and the feistiness drain out of her body. She might not understand English, but she definitely knew the word 'jail'. It was high time to intervene. 'What's going on?' she asked, striding toward the three of them.

The guard looked up suspiciously, but he snapped his walkie-talkie back into his belt. 'Thank goodness. One of them speaks English. Can you explain *why* she was strolling out of the store with a gallon of milk that she didn't pay for?'

The woman stumbled and almost fell. 'Can't you see she's about to faint?' Sameera asked, catching the older woman just in time. 'She needs help.'

Sameera walked her charge slowly over to a bench near the newspaper stands. As the woman sat down, still trembling, Sameera noticed that she was clutching some papers in her fist. Sameera held out her hand, and the woman gave them to her. One was a coupon cut out of a newspaper; the other was a completed crossword puzzle. Sameera glanced at them both; the crossword puzzle was a difficult one, but someone had printed the correct answers in neat handwriting.

Sameera marched back to the guards. 'She didn't HAVE to pay for the milk,' she said. 'Your store is offering a free gallon of milk to anybody who completes this puzzle. Don't you know your own promotions?' She thrust the coupon and the puzzle under the big security guard's nose.

The man looked embarrassed. 'She's supposed to go to the checkout counter with that kind of thing, not just walk out with a gallon of milk. How was I supposed to know?'

'She's an *old* woman. You didn't have to grab her like that. You scared her half to death.'

'Okay, okay. Take the milk.' He handed the gallon to Sameera and turned away, but not before she heard him mutter an obscenity and say, 'Stupid foreigners.'

Something snapped inside of Sameera. 'We're not leaving until we get an apology,' she said loudly. 'May I see a manager, please?'

# Thirty-three

When she and the old woman finally exited the store, Sameera was carrying a bag full of groceries that the manager had given the woman for free. Her companion was smiling, stroking Sameera's arm, and asking her something over and over in Urdu—not a word of which Sameera could understand. She could tell it was a question, but that was about it.

'Yes, I'll walk you home,' Sameera said, taking a wild guess, and the woman clapped her hands happily. She definitely understood more English than she could speak.

Sameera lugged the groceries along until they were standing in front of Muhammad's Attire again. 'You live *here?*' she asked.

'OO-PORE!' the woman shouted, pointing at the apartment over the store. She was obviously hoping that if she increased the volume of her voice, Sameera would somehow become fluent in Urdu.

Muhammad came running out of the store. 'AMMA!' he shouted. *Aha!* Sameera thought. *This is Uncle Muhammad's mother.*

The storekeeper let loose a stream of Urdu that Sameera could tell was a combination of scolding, anxiety, and relief.

The old woman spoke again, turning to Sameera and stroking her cheek with her palm. Sameera stood there, clutching the bag of groceries and feeling like a language-less idiot.

Finally, after listening intently to his mother's explanation, Muhammad turned to Sameera, beaming. 'You… you have saved my mother from a bad time. How can I thank you? I have told her a thousand times to stay inside the apartment. A woman of her age should not be walking these unsafe streets alone, but she does not listen to her son. She might have been in jail if not for you.'

'No, really, it was nothing,' Sameera said. 'The manager did give her all these groceries, though.'

Muhammad's eyes opened wide. 'Now I know you are a miracle worker. That man is one cheap SOB.'

Immediately, the older woman punched his arm. Hard. Sameera couldn't help smiling. Her dairy-farming midwestern grandmother and this Pakistani woman in burka had more in common than met the eye.

'Come,' Muhammad said, rubbing his arm. 'You must have lunch with my mother and wife. We want to show you our thanks.'

'No, really,' Sameera said, handing him the bag of groceries. 'I should get back.'

'I insist. My daughter Mariam will escort you to the corner Metro station when she comes home after her school. In the meantime, take my wife's cooking. And have a rest in my home. You would do us a great honour.'

Sameera glanced at her watch. Her parents wouldn't be back at the apartment for a while. 'It would be my pleasure,' she said. She followed Muhammad and the old woman up the narrow flight of stairs.

They both left their shoes outside the door, so Sameera unzipped her boots and walked into the apartment in her socks. The older woman took her hand and gave her a tour, escorting her from room to room and jabbering away in Urdu. It didn't take long.The apartment was as tiny as the shop underneath it—a 'living room' with two beds in it, one bathroom, a bedroom, and a kitchen where a lovely but tired-looking woman was stirring spices into a sizzling pot that looked like a big wok. She listened to her husband's explanation and gazed in wonder at the groceries he was unloading from the bag. Then she wiped her hands on her dupatta, walked over to Sameera, and embraced her, kissing her on both cheeks.

'We are thanking you,' she said. 'I no see our mother leaving. You save her life.'

'No, I didn't. Really.'

'Please, you wait.' She used her head to point to the living room. 'He eat, then we three eat.'

Sameera had been a diplomat's daughter for thirteen years. She knew that different cultures had different ways of doing things; here, obviously, the man of the house ate first. She sat on one of the cots in the living room with the old woman still stroking her hand, watching as Muhammad washed his hands, and then was served rice, lentils, fish, and potatoes by his wife. He ate his lunch, washed again, smiled at Sameera, and headed downstairs.

'Come,' said Muhammad's wife, wiping off her husband's chair with her multipurpose dupatta. 'My no good English, but my Mariam speak like her Abba. So good girl she is. Like you.'

The food was delicious, fresh, spicy, and steaming hot. Afterwards, while the grandmother took a nap on one cot in the living room, Muhammad's wife and Sameera sat together on the other one. The woman showed her five albums full of family photos, trying to explain dozens of different names and relationships in broken English until Sameera's head was spinning.

Sameera peeked at her watch; it was already almost four o'clock! She needed to get back before her parents got home. Just as she stood up to leave, the door flew open. A girl about her age ran across the room, threw her arms around Sameera, and kissed her on both cheeks. She looked exactly like a younger clone of her mother, so Sameera wasn't too surprised by the effusive gesture.

'Thank you so much,' the girl said, and this time Sameera *was* surprised. There was no trace of a Pakistani accent. The girl's head was covered, she wore a green salwar kameez, but she sounded as 'American' as Miranda. Or Sameera herself. 'My father told me what you did for my grandmother. How can we ever thank you? Do you live around here? My father wants to meet your father and thank him personally.'

'Er—no. We're only in town today. We're… leaving first thing in the morning, actually.'

'Oh, that's too bad,' the girl said. 'I'm Mariam. We could have… gotten to know each other. What's your name? How old are you?'

'I'm Sameera. I'm sixteen.'

'I just turned sixteen, too,' the girl said.

Sameera smiled; somehow she, too, could tell that the two of them could be friends. 'Did you do that crossword puzzle?' she asked. 'It was *hard.*'

'Yeah. It was a tough one, but I love doing them.'

'How long have you been in America? Your vocabulary's better than mine.'

'Six years. How about you?'

How did she answer *that* question? 'Thirteen.' No use going into too much detail—everybody didn't need to know everything about you in your first conversation with them. That was something she'd learned years ago when it came to her adoption.

'You've forgotten how to speak Urdu?' The girl looked shocked.

'Yeah. It's sad, isn't it? Mariam, what does "merry dude" mean?'

'Oh. *Meri doodh.* It means "my milk",' Mariam said, smiling. 'Is that what my grandmother was shouting in the store?'

Sameera grinned back. *Merry Dude Dairy Farm,* she thought, remembering her family's ongoing need for a new name. *I'll have to suggest it.*

She glanced at her watch again. 'I have to be getting back,' she said.

'I'll walk you downstairs,' Mariam said.

Mariam waited at the door while her grandmother hugged and kissed Sameera over and over again, and then it was her mother's turn. After a while, Sameera gently disentangled herself and put her boots back on.

The old woman shouted something at her again.

'My grandmother says to come back again,' Mariam translated. 'Our door is always open to you.'

'I'll try,' Sameera promised.

She and Mariam descended the narrow stairs, and Muhammad was standing there, holding a bag full of Sameera's purchases. 'Oh no!' Sameera said. 'I forgot to get cash. I'll have to go back to the ATM.'

'You'll do no such thing,' Mariam said, taking the bag from her smiling father. 'My father is giving you these as a gift from our family to yours.'

'But—but I have the money! It's too expensive! I could just run—'

'No,' Mariam said, dropping the bag over Sameera's shoulder. 'You'll dishonour my father. Besides, it's the least we can do.'

Sameera had to accept the gift, but how could she repay it? Suddenly, she remembered the verse that her grandmother had quoted that day in Maryfield: 'To whom much is entrusted, of them much will be required.' It was time to widen her circle so that someone like Mariam could join it.

# Thirty-four

When she got back to the apartment, Sameera stayed in her salwar kameez and head scarf. She set out some hors d'oeuvres for her parents (she wasn't a diplomat's daughter for nothing). Then she retreated into her room to call Miranda and describe her most recent escapade in burka. '… and then I found the store, Muhammad's Attire, and—'

'That doesn't sound safe to me, Sparrow,' Miranda interrupted, her voice doubtful. 'Going by yourself into some strange neighbourhood in D.C.? Uncle James and Aunt Liz would be completely freaked out if they knew.'

Sameera sighed. She never had a problem getting her cousin to listen when she could write out her thoughts. That was another great thing about blogging—you got to have your say without getting interrupted. 'Hush up and let me finish,' she said.

When she was done with the whole story, Miranda rose to the occasion. 'You did the right thing, Sparrow,' she said indignantly. 'What a bully! Treating an old woman like she was a criminal. That kind of thing would *never* happen here in Maryfield'

'You would have done the same thing if it had, Ran.'

'Your parents would still freak out if they knew. Are you going to tell them?'

'The old version of Mom and Dad would be fine with it, but I'm not sure about the campaign versions. They've been a bit better, though, lately...'

'I overheard Gran the other day giving your mom a big lecture about trusting you to handle yourself. Maybe Aunt Liz got the message.'

*Wow. You go, Gran.* 'I hope so.'

'Oh. My. Gosh. I completely forgot to thank you for the awesome stereo system in the Jeep—Poppa had it installed on the first day of school. I couldn't believe it! Thank you so much, Sparrow.'

'I'm glad you like it, Ran,' Sameera said. 'I can't wait to drive again. Do presidents' daughters *get* to drive?'

'They do if they have a cousin who lives in Maryfield. Now you'd better post something soon. The circle hasn't heard from you in so long, they're starting to get worried.'

'I'm about to, because I have big news. I've decided to make some of my posts open to the public. If that's okay with you guys, of course. The blog sort of belongs to all of us, so I'm going to ask everybody's permission.'

'Can we still comment?' Miranda asked.

'Of course. Only *you* have to promise not to say anything about my disguise, because I may want to use it again down the road. I'm not going to tell the rest of them about it.'

'I won't breathe a word. Now go post that entry.'

> When you're a celeb, you have to care a lot about what strangers think about you. But what really matters is what your buddies think about you. And what you

> think about yourself. That's why I've just purchased a domain name called www.sparrowblog.com and am asking for your help to launch it as a public site. I'll be blogging this week at myplace.com from the road, and I want you to vote on which post I should share with the country at Sparrowblog.com.
>
> Why am I doing this? Well, it's hard to explain. Lately, I've been able to experience a little of what life might be like as a foreigner in America, and I haven't liked everything about it. But I have met some amazing people. So now I want to blog about stuff like that and invite anyone who wants to listen to tune in and anyone who wants to comment to pipe in. Including you. Are you with me? Remember: keep your comments short, clean, and to the point. Peace be with you. Sparrow.

When she came out of her room wearing one of her new burkas, her parents were sitting in the living room enjoying the Brie, crackers, tart, and cold grapes that Sameera had bought on the way home. Dad almost choked on a grape.

'Wha—Wha?' he sputtered.

For the first time in her life, Sameera's mom was speechless.

'Dad, Mom, I want to confess my secret life. Are you ready for the truth?'

'I… think so,' Dad said, groping across the sofa until he found Mom's hand.

They listened intently as Sameera told them about slipping out of the apartment to meet the SARSA group at GW, and heading out to buy the burkas at Muhammad's Attire. '... I knew you'd worry, so I didn't tell you where I was going. But I was perfectly fine. D.C. is a great city to explore, and I used to wander around London and Brussels on my own. In fact, wearing this, I felt extra safe because I'm practically invisible.' No need to burden them with descriptions of some of the more unfriendly responses.

Her parents exchanged glances. 'I know we've been a little over protective, Sparrow—' Mom started.

'A little? Come on. You guys have never treated me like I wasn't worthy of your trust until this campaign.'

'I know. I got a big lecture from my mom the other day.'

'We've been talking about how we need to apologize to you, Sparrow,' Dad said. 'You've always had a good head on your shoulders. We should have known that even something as insane as a presidential campaign wouldn't change that.'

It was good to hear. 'Apology accepted,' she said. 'And I'm sorry I went behind your backs with this burka thing, but I was sort of worried that you'd freak out.'

'We probably would have,' Mom said. 'In fact, I think I still am, sort of.'

'Okay, are we even, then?' Sameera asked. 'I'd like to keep my disguise a secret. Besides you, only Miranda knows about it. Are you okay with that?'

'You bet, Sparrow,' Dad said.

Mom took a deep breath. 'Can you carry your cell phone when you wear one of those things?'

'Of course. It's got pockets.'

'Then I'm okay with it, too.'

'We were going to have dinner at an Indian restaurant and

clink lassi glasses to celebrate your mom's report,' Dad said. 'But now we'll have to toast the emancipation of Sparrow Righton as well.'

'Who would have thought that a burka, of all things, could give our daughter some freedom during this campaign?' Mom asked, shaking her head. 'They've always struck me as being oppressive.'

'Careful, Mom,' Sameera said. 'Some strong, smart Muslim women out there would love to debate you on that one.'

'You're right, Sparrow,' Mom said. 'The head of the orphanage always told me that dressing traditionally was one of the most liberating things she'd ever done.'

'Well, *I* get claustrophobic after a while,' Sameera said. 'I'll change before we go out, but do you mind if I call Tara first? I want you to listen to what I'm going to tell her.'

That quick exchange of parental glances again. 'You mean there's more?' Mom asked.

'Just a bit.'

'Go ahead, Sparrow,' Dad said.

Tara answered on the first ring. 'Hi, Sammy! Excited about our road trip tomorrow? Marcus said Sammy's blog entries about the convention got more hits than any of his previous posts. He's already working on material for tomorrow's post.'

So some Americans *did* expect their candidate's teen daughter to be stuck at adorable, bouncy, and friendly. But Sparrowblog wasn't going to be anything like that. It was going to be a place where Sameera could cox the truth as she saw it, and anybody who wanted to could climb into the boat with her and yell right back.

'That's fine,' Sameera said. 'I wanted to let you know that I'm going to start writing a blog of my own about the campaign.'

'WHAT?!' Tara sputtered.

'There's so much I'm learning and thinking about and experiencing. I want to hear what other teens like me have to say, answer their questions, and maybe even find some answers.' She was explaining all of this more for her parents' sake than for Tara's, and she noticed that Dad was nodding thoughtfully.

'But—but you already have a blog, Sammy.'

'Wilder writes that one, Tara. There's nothing in it that's... well, got to do with the real me. Plus, there's no room for comments, which is one of the things I like best about blogging.'

'Marcus carefully crafts each piece to avoid any controversial subjects. And since it's a page on our official campaign website, we don't allow lunatics to comment and post their crazy opinions.'

'Well, I *want* to hear from the loonies,' Sameera said. 'They're Americans, too.'

Tara's tone was frosty. 'If you decide to write a quiet little online journal of your own, Sammy, go right ahead. I know a lot of girls your age are into that. But we can't host it on your official site. And you definitely can't use the name "Sammy Righton". I don't think you should even use "Sameera Righton". Two blogs written by the same girl will only cause massive confusion out there.'

'Don't worry. I won't use Sammy's name at all.' *Now THAT'S an easy promise to keep.* 'I won't mention or discredit the SammySez.com site either. Wilder can keep writing posts for all

I care.' It was harder to accept the command to avoid using her real name even though she knew 'Sparrowblog' sounded catchier than 'Sameerablog'. 'And I won't use Sameera, either. I promise,' she added, trying to keep the reluctance out of her voice.

'Let me take this crazy idea to Cameron,' Tara said. 'He'll have to clear it. I'll talk it over with him on the bus when we get a chance. We leave at nine from campaign headquarters, so I'm having a taxi sent to your place by eight tomorrow morning. You can get dressed and put your makeup on in the bus; there's a dressing room on board. You've got the stuff we bought for you in L.A., and Vanessa's sending along some other outfits, but we might have to do some shopping ourselves on the road.'

*I've already done some shopping,* Sameera thought, remembering the gifts from Muhammad's Attire that were safely stowed in her dresser drawer.

Her parents had been listening silently to her end of the conversation. 'You write a blog?' Mom asked once Sameera hung up.

'Oh, Miranda and I and a few other friends have been chatting back and forth around this little blog I've been writing for a year. My buddies read my posts and comment on them. Well, now I want to take some of those posts and publish them for everybody to read.'

'You don't get any of those weird Internet lurkers, do you, Sparrow?' Dad asked, frowning.

'No, Dad,' Sameera said, trying not to sound impatient. My myplace.com blog is only accessible to a list of twenty-nine friends. I might get weirdos visiting my new blog, which will be open to the public, but don't worry, I—'

'Know how to handle them,' her parents chimed in, and the three Rightons grinned at one another.

'May I read your posts, Sparrow?' Dad asked.

'Of course, Dad. And you, too, Mom. I'd love to get comments from you guys; it would certainly make the conversation more interesting.'

'Sounds to me like you're on the move, Sparrow,' Mom said. 'Now that my report's done, I'm looking forward to figuring out how *I* can make some good things happen.'

Sameera noticed that the word 'freakin" had finally left the scene.

'Sounds to *me* like you know what you're doing, Sparrow. As usual.' Dad reached for another cracker, spread some Brie on it, and handed it to Mom. She responded by popping a grape into his mouth.

*Oh good,* Sameera thought. *No more squabbling.* 'Let's go clink those glasses,' she said. 'I'm starving.'

# Thirty-five

The campaign team had renovated two forty-five-foot VIP luxury coaches that were now proudly bearing the RIGHTON FOR PRESIDENT slogan on each side. Each bus had two bathrooms, a dressing room, a galley, flip-down TV screens with satellite programming, and leather reclining seats. A regular bus full of media people followed them on the journey, ready to pour out of the funnel of their door every time the Rightons would stop and disembark.

As soon as they boarded, Tara led Sameera to the dressing room. She made a few suggestions but left Sameera alone to change and put on her own makeup. Sameera brushed out her hair and checked herself out when she was done; she liked the fall look of the pumpkin-coloured linen blouse, brown jeans, and matching boot combo. The toned-down body-shaper she was wearing looked great underneath the outfit.

'Nice job,' Tara said approvingly when Sameera emerged. 'Now, Liz, it's your turn.'

Mom did an equally decent job of getting herself ready, and she and Sameera banged fists after Tara gave Mom a thumbs-up.

The buses crisscrossed through Virginia first, stopping at restaurants, diners, schools, and malls for Q-&-A sessions and rallies. Dad was great at this, Sameera realized again, watching him expertly work the crowd and give off-the-cuff speeches. Everywhere he went, he connected with people, made them feel welcome, captured their imaginations with his talks, and gave them his full attention when they spoke. Mom, too, took the time to make people feel welcome, and Sameera did her fair share of schmoozing with people she'd probably never see again. At senior centres, she even blew a kiss here and there; she'd decided to reserve them for the over-seventy crowd, who seemed especially delighted to receive them.

'Did you ask Cameron about my blog yet?' Sameera asked Tara as the caravan of buses continued to careen down 1-95. 'I'd like to get it started ASAP.'

She'd just finished her first on-the-bus tutoring session with Westfield, who was taking a break with a glass of milk and five oatmeal scotchies from yet another tin sent from Maryfield.

'Not yet,' Tara answered. 'But I will.'

'Could you do it now?'

Tara rolled her eyes. 'Fine. But I've been waiting to tell Marcus first.'

The Marketer of Cool was sitting a few rows behind them, hunched over his laptop. 'I'll tell him myself,' Sameera said, heading toward him.

'No! Let me—Sparrow! I'll do it!' This time, Tara had used 'Sparrow' without catching her slip of the tongue.

But it was too late. Sameera had already taken the empty seat beside Wilder. Tara stood in the aisle, grasping the seat for balance as the bus made a turn.

'Didja read your last post, Sammy?' Wilder asked. 'You blogged about—'

'That's great, Wilder,' Sameera interrupted. 'But I want you to know that I'm starting my own blog—a separate one.'

'WHAT?!' He turned to Tara. 'Does this mean I'm no longer needed? Because I—'

'No, Marcus,' Tara said quickly. 'You know how much we need you. We've got visitors coming to SammySez.com, and we still want you to spin Sammy's official blog.' She explained the stipulations, reiterating that Sameera was going to avoid using the name 'Sammy' and even 'Sameera Righton', along with any mention of the official SammySez.com website.

'Oh fine, then,' he said huffily. 'Let her do what she wants. I knew she never really liked my work.'

*And you were absolutely right,* Sameera thought, getting up.

Tara immediately slid into the vacated seat. Unlike Sameera, though, Tara sat *really* close to Wilder. *Hmmmm... looks like Mom was right about Tara and Wilder. Wow. Love can definitely make a girl do strange things.*

'Don't worry, Marcus,' Tara was saying softly. 'If they stumble across "Sparrowblog", people will probably think some fan is writing it instead of Sammy. You told me yourself that even though fans set up sites all the time, a celebrity's official website has the final word.'

'Really?'

'Really.'

Sameera left the two of them in their intimate huddle. Why not? They were a couple of thirty-something singles. She wished them the best, but Tara's taste in men had certainly deteriorated since JFK Junior.

Cameron gave his green light to Sameera's new site, too, when Tara came back to ask him. 'It's fine by me,' he said. 'The more pro-Righton blogs out there the better. As long as we keep only one of them official to avoid confusion.' He agreed that she should avoid using her real name as well as 'Sammy' in the new blog, and Sameera nodded ruefully. There was no avoiding it—she was going to have to reveal herself as 'Sparrow' to the entire planet—including Bobby.

Cameron cleared his throat. 'Now, James. I hate to interrupt, but we need to discuss a sensitive subject. How are you going to answer questions about religion? People on this journey are bound to ask you questions about that. We've been deflecting them so far, but there's no way around it now.'

Dad had been talking to Mom in a low voice a couple of rows back. He stood up and moved into the aisle, as though he'd been expecting this question and was more than ready for it. 'Here's what I intend to say. All forty-plus of our American presidents have had a strong faith in God. Some of them, like Lincoln and Reagan, were transformed during their terms and emerged as praying men. That's my hope—that I'll become more of a praying man as a president, relying on my faith for strength and hope. But when it comes to using the power of the office to impose my views on other people, I draw the line. The president of the United States is not an emperor like Julius Caesar or Constantine. He's not a dictator like Hitler or Stalin. Many beloved sons and daughters have died for freedom in this country, and I intend to make sure that freedom—including the freedom to worship—will endure.'

The entire bus burst into applause.

'Okay, who wrote that one for James?' Cameron asked, looking around. 'I'm giving that person a raise.'

Dad raised his hand. 'I did,' he said.

'Without help?' Cameron asked.

'Not entirely. Sparrow got me started. But when it comes to faith, I have to figure out what I believe before anybody else starts figuring it out for me.'

'I'm impressed, James,' Cameron said. 'I thought you wanted your speeches handed to you polished and perfect, like you used to in the old days, but that may not be giving you the scope to get your creative juices flowing.'

Mom was the only one who looked concerned. 'James, you're sure you're not saying that stuff just for the campaign?' she asked when Dad sat back down. She kept her voice soft so that only Sameera and her father could hear the question.

'No, darling,' Dad whispered back, pulling Sameera closer, too. 'You can't consider a terrifying responsibility like the presidency without grappling with your faith. I've been thinking hard about it for weeks—and praying, too. Every word I said is true.'

'James, I'm so glad,' Mom whispered, and Sameera saw tears sparkling in her eyes. *Which is weird, because Mom hardly ever cries.*

Sameera was barely keeping herself from dancing the bhangra on the bus. Her talk with Dad had helped! He'd listened to her message from Poppa and had done some thinking of his own. *See? Even a person without all the answers can be spiritually useful,* she told herself. *The next time Mom and I have a late-night faith quest, I'll make sure Dad's invited.*

# Thirty-six

The convoy finally reached Williamsburg, where they planned to stay the night in a hotel. Sameera had smiled so often during the pit stops that her cheek muscles ached. She got online as soon as she was alone and sent an email to info@ SARSA.GW.

> Okay, SARSA, the blog's a go for me. I'm attaching a copy of a rant I wrote about slave trafficking for you to review. I'm starting this blog, though, whether or not you guys decide to link to it, and here are my ground rules: I'll post a paragraph once a week to get the conversation started. Then I'll respond to the first two legitimate comments that come in. After that, it becomes a free-for-all forum where everybody can speak their mind.

She took a deep breath before writing the next part:

> The code name I'm going to use on the blog is 'Sparrow,' and I can't mention 'Sameera', 'Sammy', or 'SammySez.com'—those were the campaign team's stipulations. So here's the link to my blog:

> www.sparrowblog.com. I bought the domain name myself, and I'm staying in charge of it. I don't want my real blog hosted on anybody's website but my own. Sparrow's been my nickname for years, if you're curious. Oh, and by the way, I miss you guys. Haven't had a good cappuccino in days.

Sangi had written back by the time Sameera checked her messages again.

> Go for it. We're behind you all the way. Nadia said your post about slave trafficking made her bawl. We'll be sending the link out as soon as you've posted your first entry. Can't wait. As for the nickname, most South Asians have one. Mine is 'BABY', can you believe it? I'm sending you our cell phone numbers; we promise to keep yours a secret if you ever call us. We'd decided not to ask you for yours because we didn't want to invade your privacy, but I can see that we were playing it too safe.

Sameera smiled; she was probably going to have to widen her myplace.com inner circle to include five more members, but she'd wait until after the election. Her circle of twenty-nine would already be overwhelmed, what with reading and commenting and voting on her posts—getting to know five new people might be too much to handle.

After Williamsburg, the next stop was Durham, North Carolina, where Sameera wrote and posted her first entry on the new Sparrowblog site she'd set up. When it came to design, she stuck with simple, easy-to-read fonts and only used two colours. The one graphic on the page was a big coxswain's megaphone with the words SPARROW SPEAKING! LISTEN UP! emanating from the wide end. Her circle of twenty-nine had voted on the following post to jump-start the site:

> Cyber-greetings, America. I'll be posting my thoughts on this site once a week. Ground rules: The first two legitimate questions get answers from me, and then everybody's free to jump into the discussion. I promise to tell the truth, the whole truth, and nothing but the truth when it comes to this blog, and I'm expecting the same from you.
>
> Here's my first question. How long does it take people to drop that ethnic adjective we put before the word 'American'?
>
> White kids get to do it after they lose their parents' accents, and they don't introduce themselves as Polish American or German American anymore. But Chinese, Japanese, Koreans, Blacks, Hispanics, American Indians, South Asians—we stay Asian American or African American or Native American or Pakistani American (I'm not even sure if I should use hyphens or not) for several generations, until (or if) our descendants intermarry with white people and stop looking 'ethnic'. So, an African American person can have a granddaughter who is described as just plain American—if she's light-skinned enough

> and her blood's been mixed enough times with white people? I don't get it.
>
> Readers, what do you think? Remember: keep your comments short, clean, and to the point. Peace be with you. Sparrow.

She'd known that the most difficult thing about relaunching her blog was going to be the public unveiling of her nickname. *Widen the circle,* she admonished herself, and clicked on publish.

It didn't take long to get a response; the SARSA networks had already sent out emails about the Republican candidate's daughter's REAL blog launch with the link on their Listservs. The first question that came flying back was a predictable one: *Tell us about your adoption.*

*Easy one,* Sameera thought, fingers flying in response as she sat in a North Carolina hotel room and thought of that day long ago on the other side of the planet. She'd heard the story so often she knew it by heart.

> I don't remember anything about the orphanage I lived in until I was three. It's closed down since then, anyway. I've seen video footage of younger versions of my parents visiting a scrawny toddler who had been deposited there since birth (me). Mom and Dad and I watch it every year on my 'Homecoming Day', and celebrate by going out to a fancy dinner.
>
> But it isn't just my homecoming day we're celebrating. It's my parents' love story, too. 'You arranged our

marriage, Sparrow,' they always say. It's true, in a way. They were both stationed in Islamabad, Pakistan, where Mom was serving as a consultant to some NGO for six months, and Dad was a political officer at the U.S. Embassy. Neither of them had much time to date. They did make time, though, to take a tour of an orphanage—on the same afternoon. We all met for the first time that day. Coincidence? Maybe. Mom's sure it was divine intervention.

After that, they both made time to visit me, running into each other at the orphanage and going out for a bite to eat afterward. Slowly, the desire to adopt me was growing in each of them, taking them both by surprise, I think, since they were single. The bad news was that it was almost impossible for foreigners to adopt from Pakistan, and single people over thirty-five absolutely had no chance at all. Mom and Dad started talking about getting married, jokingly at first, and then pragmatically, and then, as Dad puts it, the 'sparks started flying'.

Three months after we met, the pastor of the international church in Islamabad presided over their wedding. In the meantime, the orphanage was shutting down. Only three children remained under their care, then two, and then one—me.

Who knows why nobody wanted to adopt me? Because we were meant for each other, Mom always says, but still, a person wonders. The director of the

> orphanage submitted proof that no relative had ever claimed me, that nobody inside the country wanted to adopt me, and that they were about to shut their doors forever. Finally, the government of Pakistan made a special exception—James and Elizabeth Righton could take me back to America and adopt me there. Which they did. And we lived happily ever after. I hope.

She almost deleted the more personal part, about wondering why she hadn't been wanted, but then she decided to leave it in. It was true, wasn't it? Most kids who were adopted wondered why their birth parents had decided to give them up for adoption. Some found out, some didn't, but most of them wondered.

Question two came in:

> How do we know this is really you and not a fake? You have that other blog, too.

A harder question this time, but it had a much shorter answer:

> Stick around and keep reading. You'll have to decide for yourself.

# Thirty-seven

Westfield stopped making Sameera write essays once she'd visited Sparrowblog. 'We'll work on analytical writing in the fall,' she said. 'For now, keep writing from the heart, Sparrow; you've got a great voice.' After that, an extremely supportive, articulate visitor named 'poli_tutor' commented on Sameera's posts regularly, and it didn't take Sameera long to figure out that Westfield was leaping into the circle of conversation.

Everybody on the bus was starting to go a little stir crazy. The banter among members of the campaign staff reminded Sameera of how the members of SARSA teased one another. Or the way her crew guys harassed their teammates (minus the swearwords in five different languages). Even the reporters seemed more silly and relaxed on the road, and the Rightons were starting to recognize faces on the media bus and getting to know their names.

Dad's campaign in the South was a big success. 'We like Righton's record of integrity and the statement we've heard him make about his personal faith,' religious leaders declared. 'We believe he's the man for the job.' His skill at working a crowd paid off, and people who met him were not only charmed but also even more convinced of his integrity.

When the team discussed the best way to approach each upcoming event or debate, Sameera tuned in. It was interesting to think about finessing campaign strategies in each region; she'd known there was diversity from state to state in America, but she'd had no idea how different they really were.

Mom spoke up when the conversation turned to fund-raising, and everybody always listened. Elizabeth Campbell had a reputation for being able to convince the most miserly people on the planet to hand their money over to a good cause. For Dad's campaign, she recommended that they shift their focus away from big donors to recruit five- and ten-dollar bills from everyday folks. 'Those add up,' Mom said. 'And when people give their hard-earned money to something, they want to help it succeed. You'll get their votes.'

'Put a button on our site that links to an online money transfer system like Pay Friend,' Sameera added.

'Great idea,' said Cameron, and Sameera noticed Wilder glowering three rows behind him.

The fast-moving conversation shifted again, this time toward the problem of attracting the younger generation to Righton's side. 'They're saying that younger voters are going to show up in droves this fall,' another staffer said. 'And we'll lose them all to Banforth if we don't make some changes. That son of hers has put most of the twenty-somethings in her pocket.'

Sameera took stock of all the thirty-and-above faces in the bus. 'How about recruiting a few younger people to join the campaign team?' she suggested. 'And adding a bit more international flavour? My generation's a lot more into cultural melding than yours.'

'I like the idea of hiring a few younger interns,' Cameron said thoughtfully.

'But what do you mean by "international flavour", Sparrow?' Dad asked. 'We're fairly multicultural on our team; I've made a point of that.'

'But everybody on this bus was born in America, right?'

They all nodded.

'What about newer Americans?' she asked. 'People who speak English with accents, even? Dad, you'll be able to show off your ability to connect with people from other countries.'

'Cameron's on top of demonstrating your father's strengths to the American people, Sammy,' Tara called from her seat beside Wilder, laughing. Sameera half-expected the windows of the bus to shatter in response to the irritating sound. There were some things she appreciated about Tara, but that pseudo-laugh still drove her crazy.

'How about hiring a couple of younger interns who are also immigrants?' Cameron asked.

'Bingo!' Dad said. 'That's a great idea.'

Sameera's next blog post included the job description for the internship, and to everybody's amazement, hundreds of applications poured in. Cameron carefully chose two interns to join them on the bus—Guillermo, from Colombia, and Fatima, who was originally from Iraq. They were both twenty-one, fresh out of college, and passionately patriotic about the country of their new citizenship—the United States of America. Guillermo, unfortunately, turned out to be a climber who followed Cameron around like an eager campaign-manager-in-training, but Fatima was a great addition to the team. When she and Sameera started sitting together on the bus, the time on the road passed even more quickly, thanks to the good conversations they had.

Sameera called Bobby as they were driving through South Carolina to let him know they were in his territory. It was a good excuse to hear his voice again. And again.

'Hey, we have tons of new members in SARSA nationwide, thanks to your blog, Sameera.'

'That's wonderful. I keep checking my site stats, and I can't believe how many people are visiting.'

'It's because you make visitors feel like they're actually chatting with you. I couldn't believe all the people who shared the stories of their adoptions, and how *they* felt about it. I stayed up late last night reading through the comments.'

'Me, too,' she said. 'But we got our share of nasty comments, too. Some people hate Dad so much, it's scary.'

'Do you want us to moderate the conversation? George said he could easily set up a membership programme on the site. That way, only members could post, and every angry person and their brother can't jump into the conversation to harass you.'

'No. Let's keep it open. I can handle it. I only have to answer two questions a week, and there are enough supportive commenters to take on the trash talk.'

'You've got guts,' Bobby said. 'But I knew that the moment you dragged me out on the bhangra floor. We'll have to go dancing again when you come back to D.C. Still got your disguise?'

'It's expanded. I own two burkas now, and a real head covering.'

'You do? Where'd you get them?'

She told him about her visit to the store in D.C., and how meeting Uncle Muhammad's family had led to her decision to write the blog, and he responded just as perfectly as she knew he would: 'It's good to pay back our debts, Sparrow. Hey, is it okay if I call you Sparrow?'

'It's fine,' she said. *Seems like there's no way around it; Sparrow I remain when it comes to my nearest and dearest. And for now, that's okay.*

'NO WAY! WE JUST PASSED THE EXIT TO CREIGHTON!' she shouted. Fatima had been keeping an eye out for it, and she elbowed Sameera violently when the green sign flashed by.

'I know exactly where you are then. But my town's an hour away from the exit.'

'I'll wait for you to give me a tour.' There was something about this guy that made her heart escape from its normal location (safely hidden inside her chest cavity) and turn up on her sleeve.

'It's a small town,' he said. 'A tour takes about three and a half minutes.'

'Walking through Maryfield takes four. I love how everybody down here sounds like you. I'll call you soon, Bobby.'

# Thirty-eight

Campaigning was like coxing, Sameera decided. The more you did it, the more your confidence grew and the better you got. She was feeling more sure of herself when it came to style, too, discovering that streamlined skirts, feminine but simple blouses, and tailored jackets made her the most relaxed in front of a crowd. And when she felt comfortable, she stopped focusing so much on what she looked like and was able to think about the questions people were asking. And about the people themselves.

She was slowly easing her natural shape out of the padded undergarments. Every girl on the planet didn't need to wear tight clothes; Sameera's genes were Pakistani, even if her jeans were American. And miraculously, her breasts were making a minor appearance. *Better late than never,* Sameera informed them when they were alone together in the shower.

Thanks to SARSA's nationwide grassroots promotion and the help she got from her circle of twenty-nine to hone her posts, word had spread about Righton's daughter's real blog. Sparrowblog.com was starting to get thousands of hits—and comments galore, mostly from young people. It was easy to come up with a new topic every week, since nothing was taboo.

Passionate debates raged over the issues that Sameera raised, and she jumped in whenever she could. The questions she was getting were challenging; sometimes she'd have to answer, 'I don't know what I think,' and the possibilities would keep her up late into the night.

The team flew from Montgomery to Chicago, where Dad and Senator Banforth were scheduled to have their first debate. Just before entering the University of Chicago auditorium, Sameera's mother was stopped by a reporter.

'Could you comment on the morality of a woman—Victoria Banforth, I mean—who bore a child out of wedlock and wants to lead our country, Mrs Righton?'

Mom lost it. 'How *dare* you judge that woman? She has lived her life with grace, and she is a *huge* success. Every woman in this country is proud of her.'

The reporter looked flustered but not yet defeated. 'And what if your own daughter decided to use Senator Banforth as a role model, getting pregnant without being married first?'

'Have you *witnessed* how Thomas Banforth has stood by his mother through this campaign? I'd be *proud* if Sparrow chose a woman like Victoria as a role model of what fresh starts and second chances mean to every one of us.'

Sameera and the entire Righton entourage listened, glazed-eyed and open-mouthed. Had they just heard the Republican candidate's wife *championing* his opponent? As Mom swept into the auditorium and took her seat, several staffers looked pale and tense, including Tara Colby.

But they shouldn't have worried. The next day, the press was nothing but positive. 'Elizabeth Righton speaks out for single mothers who overcome the odds, including her husband's political opponent, Victoria Banforth.' Mom looked regal in the television coverage, exhibiting a one-two punch of strength and beauty as she faced down the obnoxious reporter.

Sameera, in turn, blogged about how proud she was of her mother *and* her father, who had debated his opponent well. Unfortunately, despite Dad's eloquence and courtesy, the win seemed to go to the earthy, witty Victoria Banforth, who had made the entire nation laugh several times during the debate.

The next day, to Sameera's amazement, she received a comment from tbanforth@yale.edu.

> Hey, Sparrow. Tell your mother thanks for standing up for mine. When this is all over, I'd love to take you out to dinner. We can share some of our best campaign horror stories. Peace backatcha. Tom.

Both Bobby and Miranda called Sameera immediately after they read that surprising comment. 'Who does that Banforth dude think he is?' Bobby asked. 'Why doesn't he stick to women his own age? He's twenty-two—he could get arrested as an online predator.'

Was that *jealousy* she heard? 'He's a good guy, Bobby. You can still like a person even when you disagree with their politics.'

'I know,' Bobby said, sighing. 'I'm just tired of all the attention he's been getting. He's definitely the hot guy on the political scene right now. Even Sangi, one of the most rabid Republicans I know, is losing it over him.'

Miranda, too, sounded a bit swoony. 'I *loved* that "backatcha". How tasty was that? I wonder if he'd like to take *me* out to dinner… '

Sameera blogged her way through Illinois, Michigan, and Indiana on trains and buses. The buses didn't venture into Ohio; Dad's support there was so strong, they didn't need to worry much about getting votes. At a college in Grand Rapids, Michigan, after Dad finished giving his speech, a voice called out: 'We love you, Sparrow!'

With a shock, Sameera realized that a visitor to Sparrowblog was in the audience. Sparrowbloggers, as the campaign team called them, started popping up everywhere—in Arkansas, Texas, Colorado (where Dad won the second debate), Kansas, New Mexico, Arizona, Nevada.

Cameron finally called a conference about Sameera's duelling blogs. 'Should we get rid of SammySez.com?' he asked Tara.

'Oh, no,' Tara answered quickly, glancing at Wilder's sullen face. 'It's still getting a fair amount of hits. Most of the public thinks that SammySez.com is Sammy's official site; there's been no mention at all of her other blog in the traditional media yet.'

Other blogs had been linking like mad to Sparrowblog, so it was only a matter of time before the mainstream press picked it up. *That's the operative word,* Sameera thought. *Yet.*

'What is a "fair amount" of hits?' Fatima muttered in her ear. 'Thirty? Three hundred? Or three? Nobody I know *ever* checks out his site.'

'Some of our discussion on Sparrowblog is way too controversial for the campaign's official seal of approval, anyway,' Sameera told Cameron. 'Too many four-letter words in the comments.'

She didn't want the campaign to co-opt her site; it was sure to be tidied up, censored, made politically correct. The free, wild, unexpected blogginess of it might be sucked out.

Every now and then, while she was typing on her laptop, she'd look up and catch Wilder's frenzied eye. He was continuing to produce SammySez blog entries once a day; she only had to post once a week and then respond to two comments. He was looking more exhausted and getting more snippy as the days passed. *It must be draining to pretend to be someone else all the time,* Sameera thought, actually feeling sorry for the guy.

What with campaigning, lessons, blogging, spending time with Fatima, and talking to Miranda, Bobby, or Sangi on the phone, the days spun by in a whirl. Sameera was so busy she didn't have a chance to sneak off in 'Muhammad's Attire', but just the thought of an armour of invisibility tucked inside her suitcase was comforting.

*If I need to disappear, I can,* she told herself more than once, waving at crowds of people until her wrists felt like they had permanent carpal tunnel syndrome. *I can be Sparrow, Sammy, or Sameera. I can be invisible or turn heads. I am one of those mutant X-Men with special powers. No. I am… Wait a sec. What's that ancient women's lib song Aunt Bev likes to sing at the top of her lungs while she's gardening? Oh yeah—I AM WOMAN, HEAR ME ROAR!*

# Thirty-nine

November finally came, and the weary Rightons crawled back to D.C. for a day of rest before election day. Mom stayed around the apartment, announcing that 'she wanted to spend the whole day alone with her daughter for the first time in weeks'. This was a bit frustrating to Sameera, who'd been hoping to don her burka to visit Mariam and her family. Now she'd have to wait for another opportunity, and she had no idea when that would come; she'd been concentrating so hard on the Big Day that it was hard to imagine a future beyond it.

'Aren't you going to start consulting again, Mom?' she asked. 'The campaign's officially over now, isn't it?'

'Depends on if your dad wins tomorrow,' Mom said. 'Right now I'm still focused on getting the IDPs what they need from the NGOs. A first lady might have a bit more clout to make that happen.'

*Good thing I speak acronym,* Sameera thought. Basically, what this meant was that Mom had taken every chance during the last few weeks to champion internally displaced people, regardless of the original topic of conversation. At a banquet sponsored by the Daughters of the American Revolution in Pennsylvania, for example, she'd started with a long, patriotic, touching speech, and segued into her IDPs with something like this: '… And as we think of our forefathers who fought so hard for freedom, we remember others who don't have that kind of freedom right now—take the internally displaced people in Burma, for example…'

'Is Dad going to be home late?' Sameera asked. 'He needs a good night's sleep before tomorrow.'

'Not too late, I hope. The team's planning how we're going to spend election day.' Mom was making herself a sandwich. 'I'm *so* glad the campaign's finally over, I'm not sure I even care about what happens tomorrow. You hungry, Sparrow?'

Sameera shrugged. 'Not really.'

'I'll make you a sandwich, too, just in case.'

Sameera watched her mother slather pieces of whole grain bread with mustard, mayo, salt, and pepper, and then stack turkey, cheese, sprouts, and tomato slices in between them; Mom had *never* spent time in the kitchen when they lived overseas.

Suddenly, she was ravenous. 'Mom? Could you and I stay up late tonight like we used to? I've got some stuff I want to ask.' *Like: Can a person who believes strongly in God still have doubts or questions? Do you? How do you handle it?* She could pose questions like these sort of generically on her blog, of course, but somehow a heart-to-heart conversation with Mom seemed to be a better setting for them.

'I'd love to, Sparrow. It's been a while, hasn't it?'

She handed Sameera a sandwich with a flourish. 'Ready to get metaphysical?'

'Yeah, but let's wait until after we eat, okay? And maybe we can watch a movie first, too? Something funny and sweet that we've seen at least a million times?' There was nothing more relaxing than eating dinner on the couch and watching a chick flick with someone you loved.

The two Righton women were doing just that, enjoying the romance between Audrey Hepburn and Gregory Peck in *Roman Holiday,* when Dad came home.

'Looks like the race to the finish line is going to be close,' he announced, hanging his coat in the hall closet.

Mom pressed the pause button on the remote. 'Sameera and I are done with campaigning, James,' she said sternly. 'And we're right in the middle of this movie.'

'Okay,' Dad answered meekly. 'Can I join you?'

'Sure. Want a sandwich?' Mom asked, obviously relenting.

'One of those? Definitely. I'm starving.' Mom left the room, and Sameera found herself feeling sorry for her father. He looked so *woebegone* standing there in the hallway.

'Are you worried about losing, Dad?' she asked.

Dad loosened his tie and joined her on the couch. 'Not really, Sparrow. I want to win; if I do, I'm hoping to get some great things accomplished during the next four years. But when it comes to our family life, a victory's the beginning of another rollercoaster ride. For all of us.'

She groaned. 'I know, Dad. We'll be heading to the… White House.' She made her voice sound evil, as though she were saying something creepy like the 'Cavern of Horrors'.

Dad grinned. 'Dum, dum, dum, DUM. It might be fun for you, Sameera, and especially if Miranda comes for a visit. There's a bowling alley there somewhere, and a movie theatre. Susan Ford was about your age when she moved in, and she had her high school prom there.'

'Things are a bit more complicated for me now than they were for Susan Ford in the last century.' She remembered the photo Tara had shown her of the blonde, beautiful girl washing her 1970s-style sedan outside the White House.

'President Ford's daughter couldn't put on a burka and disappear when she needed to, now could she? But things haven't changed that much. It's always been rough to have a political parent, or a political spouse. That's one of the reasons I didn't get married while I was serving in Congress.'

'Well, you're definitely married now. And stuck with both of us.'

He pulled her head toward him and kissed the top of it. 'And blessed with you, you mean. Oh, well, Sparrow. We might never move into the White House; I might lose by a landslide.'

'Forget about that for now, Dad. Wanna stay up late tonight with me and Mom, talking theology?'

'Maybe. Or better yet, I'll listen while the two of you unlock the mysteries of the universe and give my ageing brain a rest.'

'No way. You stay, you play. Or pray, depending how the night goes.'

Mom came back and handed Dad the sandwich. He took a big bite, chewed with gusto, and finished it off in about four bites. 'Let's start the movie again. Nothing like a good family night at the movies to take a break from heated topics like politics and religion,' he said, putting one arm around his wife and the other around his daughter. 'Just kidding, y'all. Count me in for later on.'

# Forty

The Banforth-Righton race brought out more voters than any election in history. Both candidates were respected, even if people disagreed with their politics, because neither had resorted to the ugly smearing and hate ads that had marked previous campaigns. Bloggers everywhere were noting that this year, it seemed like Americans were voting *for* a candidate instead of against one.

Dad came back to the hotel suite late on election day, where Sameera and her mother were jubilantly watching the last results come in. It was starting to look like a sure win; they'd just snagged several key states in the Heartland. Commentators were saying that Righton only needed a couple more states in the Midwest to clinch the victory.

'Dad! You should be bursting in here with a bottle of champagne!' Sameera said. 'Why do you look so worried?'

'Yes, James,' Mom added, jumping up to hug him. 'This is absolutely fantastic. Your first lady in waiting wants a presidential smooch.'

But Mom's kiss didn't erase the look of concern on Dad's face. 'A huge number of people just trolled SammySez.com at the same time,' he said. 'We have no idea why they'd try that stunt so late in the day.'

'What does "troll" mean?' Mom asked. 'It sounds ugly.'

'They blitz the site with millions of hits at once. Your official website crashed, Sparrow; it's going to take a while to get it up and running again.'

'That's weird,' Sameera said. 'Because Sparrowblog is working fine.' She'd been commentating on election day results and happenings with periodic posts all through the day.

'I know,' Dad said. 'The timing of an attack like this doesn't make sense. The election's almost over.'

The phone rang, and Dad picked it up. 'It's Marcus Wilder, Sparrow. And he wants to talk to you.'

Sameera was surprised. Wilder hadn't ever called her before; he'd always preferred using Tara as his mouthpiece. 'Hello?'

Words from the other end came hurtling at her like air gun pellets. 'You talked your hokey relatives into doing this, didn't you? To convince your father that your blog was more effective than *mine?* Admit it!'

Sameera hardly recognized the voice—Wilder was so upset that it almost sounded like he was crying. Her parents were looking at her curiously, so she went into her own room and shut the door. 'What are you talking about?'

'Once your father clinched this election, you got your… people to attack my site.'

'What? I did not.'

'Don't play games with *me,* young lady. I've lost my job, thanks to you. And more than that. Much more.'

Now it was Sameera's turn to get angry. 'Back off, Wilder,' she said. 'I did no such thing. Let me talk to Tara.'

'She's not here. She left, after—' This time, he did burst into tears, and hung up.

'Sparrow!' Mom called from the living room. 'Come out here, quick!'

Her parents were standing in front of the television with their mouths open. On the screen, a dozen members of Maryfield Ladies' Aid, including Gran, were holding up signs that said 'Let Sparrow Sing!' As they watched, all twelve of the grey-haired ladies, dressed in peasant skirts and T-shirts that had a picture of Sameera emblazoned on them, started singing an old 1970s rock song: 'If I leave here tomorrow, would you still remember me? 'Cause I'm as free as a bird now, and this bird you cannot cha-ange. Woooo-oooh. And this bird you cannot cha-ange.'

Aunt Bev was strumming a guitar in the background. Sameera recognized the venue: it was the Maryfield High School auditorium, and the ladies were singing onstage.

'FREE BIRD! FREE BIRD! FREE BIRD!' the Maryfield Ladies' Aid started chanting, punching their fists and signs in the air. The camera panned the crowd in the seats, and Sameera glimpsed more and more familiar faces: the Presbyterian minister and his wife, Miranda, Poppa, Mayor and Mrs Thompson… everybody in town seemed to be there, and now they were joining the chant: 'FREE BIRD! FREE BIRD! FREE BIRD!'

At first, the coverage of the Maryfield protest looked bad for James Righton: 'Now that it looks like their golden boy is about to win this election, the people of Maryfield, Ohio, want answers. They claim that Sammy Righton's "official" website is a fake, and that the real Sammy Righton has been blogging at Sparrowblog.com. They organized a grassroots email campaign asking people to troll the official blog once Righton got the win.'

Dad switched the channel. It was still bad. 'Breaking news. James Righton hires marketing guru to write his daughter's blog. Democrats claim this confirms that Righton would do anything to win votes, even compromise his own daughter's integrity.'

Switch. 'Sammy Righton's official website came down late today when thousands of people "trolled" or "flamed" it in response to a protest started in her mother's hometown. On another note: Righton appears to have clinched this election with a win in New Mexico and Idaho, but stay tuned for final results.'

Sameera called her cousin to get the scoop on what was happening in Maryfield.

'Mrs Graves got the entire Ladies' Aid started on a huge email campaign,' Miranda said. 'You know; forward this to ten friends, and so on. They told everybody that it wasn't you writing that SammySez.com blog. "READ Sparrowblog! IT'S THE REAL THING!" they said. "TROLL THE FAKE BLOG AFTER FIVE O'CLOCK ON ELECTION DAY!" They even started selling those T-shirts that say "free bird" under a photo of you, and they're making a bundle—enough to pay for three new computers in the library.'

Next, Sameera called Tara. 'Wilder phoned me. I didn't have anything to do with the trolling, Tara.'

'He called you? That jerk! I know; I told him not to bother you.'

'Tara? Did you break up with him because of me?'

Tara sighed. 'No, Sparrow. It's been coming for a while. I fall for these temperamental, artistic types, and then they end up being way too high-maintenance.'

'I'm sorry.'

'I'm the one who should be sorry. You keep going with your blog; we're getting rid of the whole SammySez website, now that the campaign's over. Wilder's blog never got the kind of traffic he promised to generate, and I learned a big lesson, thanks to you. I *don't* know the American people as well as I thought. Maybe I should spend some time with your Maryfield folks.'

'I'm sure you'd be more than welcome,' Sparrow said, trying and failing to picture Tara at a Ladies' Aid meeting.

'Sparrow? Could you do us a favour?'

'Sure.'

'Could you sort of... clear up this mess on your blog soon? Looks like we've won this election, but we don't want your dad starting his new job on the wrong foot.'

*You're asking ME to fix something for YOU. Wow. We've come full circle, Ms Tara Colby.* 'I'll do my best,' Sameera answered.

The post she came up with while Mom and Dad were getting ready for the celebration party was excerpted on her loyal SARSA sites, quoted on television, discussed on the radio, and even assigned as required reading for students in schools around the nation.

> Hey, America, you voted my dad in! Thank you, thank you, thank you! I can promise that you won't be sorry. He's going to be the best president this country has seen in a long time. We're about to go party, so you'll see me on television soon, but I wanted to clear something up first. By now, you may have read about my fake blog. You might be wondering why a

person like me, who tries always to write the truth, would give up my voice to someone else.

Let me explain. Some members of my father's campaign team (NOT my father himself) were worried that I—the real me—wouldn't be 'American' enough for you. That I might damage Dad's campaign because I was born in Pakistan and look 'foreign'. That's why they created 'Sammy Righton'—because they thought America wanted someone who wasn't anything like the real me. But thanks to YOU I've had the great satisfaction to show them that they were wrong.

So here I am, America. Sameera Righton—your new first daughter. I may not be your typical all-American girl, but then who is? I'm an American because I get to blog like this, to say what I want, to tell the truth as I see it, even if my father ends up becoming the most powerful person in the country.

I'm sorry I let someone else steal my voice—I'll never do it again. Think you can forgive me? (This one time, forget our usual rule: you can make comments that are long, nasty, and completely off-topic. Sparrow.)

The American people did forgive her. The site received only a few insulting or unrelated comments, and those critics were quickly torn apart by other commentators leaping to Sameera's defense. 'The ultimate teen town hall,' the site was described by the *New York Times*. 'Moderated by a young woman who seems wise beyond her years—Sameera Righton.'

ZTV NEWS: 'From every corner of the country, you responded to Sameera Righton's candid, sometimes provocative insider's take on this presidential campaign. Pundits think that her blog might have had an influence on the election outcome—even older Americans seem to trust this savvy young woman's opinion of her father.'

CNN: 'James Righton has now won enough electoral votes to clinch this race. Senator Victoria Banforth is conceding defeat and thanking her supporters. Meanwhile, Republicans are going wild in the ballroom of the Four Seasons Hotel, where Righton is giving his acceptance speech.'

LOS ANGELES TIMES ONLINE: 'After giving Righton and his wife, Elizabeth Campbell, a standing ovation, the packed ballroom supporters spontaneously began to chant one name in unison: "Sparrow! Sparrow!"'

The roar when Sameera joined her parents onstage was huge. Balancing easily on three-inch heels and wearing comfortable lingerie (with just a bit of padding) underneath a glittery blouse and a tailored brown pantsuit, she was already composing her take on the event for her blog:

> ... I was waving and smiling, yes, but my feet were killing me, and I was already mentally filling in my calendar. I'm off to Maryfield for the holidays, the inauguration's in January, and we move into the White House right after that. Four years in the most luxurious prison in America. Am I going to survive? What do YOU think? Remember: keep your comments short, clean, and to the point. Peace be with you. Sparrow.

Turn the page for a sneak preview of Mitali Perkins's fabulous sequel to

*Extreme American Makeover*

# *White House Rules*

FIRST DAUGHTER Book 2

Sameera opened her laptop with a sigh of relief. Sparrowblog readers were getting restless for the insider's take she'd promised over two weeks ago, and her fingers were eager to provide it. She powered up, logged on, and started typing.

> Wow. It's good to be back. Dad's ten-day inaugural extravaganza kept me so busy I couldn't take even the briefest of breaks into cyberspace. Lots of you have been asking what it's actually like to live in The House that's on the back of every twenty-dollar bill. Well, I've been here for over a week now, so here's a taste of the Good, the Bad, and the Ugly.
>
> **THE GOOD**
>
> 1. Mom and her lady-in-waiting (sparrowcode translation: Wonder Woman Tara Colby) passed some redecorating over to Miranda and me. We've been assigned the bedrooms at Camp David, our suite in the White House, and the living quarters on Air Force One. For two Home and Garden Channel addicts, working with fab Designer David has been awesome. We've settled on California minimalist for Air Force One because Dad likes streamlined, Ohio farm cosy in the White House bedrooms so Ran and

I can chill, and global-import-trendy at Camp David, because when on vacation, I LIKE sequins, paisley, incense, silk, mosaic, batik, and squashy ottomans with tassels. Don't ask why. I just do.

2. I get to work out in the White House gym with a trainer. Coxing never pumped the body much, so I'm hoping to display toned triceps the next time the razzi catch me sleeveless. (BTW, I can't decide between 'razzi' or 'pappaz' when it comes to the hordes behind the huge lenses. What do you think?)

3. We've been splashing in the indoor pool at midnight, which is especially great when it's snowing outside. It's tempting to skinny-dip, but Cougars are ever on the prowl (sparrowcode translation: Secret Service dudes).

4. At the First Bowling Alley the other night, Ran and I trounced a couple of Penguins (sparrowcode translation: valets in tuxes). I got two strikes, thanks to my already enlarged triceps.

5. The in-house theatre is lined with leather recliners, and we get to choose from thousands of movies, even first-run feature films. I refuse, however, to watch any flicks or television reruns that involve a president—it's freaky watching some ultra-gorgeous Hollywood starlet playing a first daughter now that I've morphed into the real thing. I do accept the gobs of buttery popcorn served by an Orca (sparrowcode translation: maids who might be voluptuous, but that

didn't earn them the name; they wear black and white uniforms that are amazingly killer-whale-ish).

6. Good news for tiny bladders: unlimited access to thirty-five bathrooms. Wahoo!

7. Note to self: when bored, try baking with state-of-the-art appliances, unlimited ingredients, no need to clean up, and five Pandas at your service (sparrowcode translation: Gourmet Chefs). Ran and I wandered into the kitchen and wangled our way into making oatmeal scotchies for Mom's first official tea in the East Wing. After the prime minister of Sweden's wife gobbled six of them (from MY batch), she begged the Penguins and Orcas to give her the recipe. She even came into the kitchen and accosted the Pandas. My cousin scribbled something down and handed it over, but it won't work. The real product can be made only by Campbell hands.

8. We walk Jingle two times a day around the South Lawn. Yes, my cousin brought the farm pooch along for the whole six months she's here. Thanks, Gran and Poppa, for loaning me the world's most wonderful Labrador retriever. Yes, he is sleeping on my bed. Or am I sleeping on his? It's hard to tell which one of us owns the place.

**THE BAD**

1. We have to memorize the names of the hundred-plus people who work at the House so that we don't

hurt anybody's feelings. This is hard, as many dress in identical uniforms. Several are also still in love with the previous residents. Mom and I have overheard muttering about missing the Adorable All-American First Children and Perfect First Mom who were forced to move out the day before WE moved in. Turns out those chicks—and that mother hen—were likeable in private AND in public. Wonderful.

2. If I ever leave on my own, I'll have to fill out forms in triplicate and will be accompanied by armed Cougars. My visitors get frisked from head to toe and are forced to give out enough personal information to make even the Dalai Lama worry about identity theft. (Not that he's visited. But he might. And then he would get stressed out.)

3. This house might be where we live, but it belongs to the American people. Tours start at six-thirty in the morning; we can get over five thousand visitors a day. I prefer to stay closeted on the third floor until the sightseers exit, playing hearts with my cousin and any available Penguins or Orcas with time on their hands. Judging by his expression, one of the younger Cougars wants to join our game, but it's against the rules. Stay on the prowl. Always.

4. No school. No gossip. No crew. No friends. Good thing Ran's here for now. I'll have to figure something out in June when she heads back to Ohio. Any ideas?

5. Dad's office is in one wing of the House, Mom's is in the other, and they've both been working nonstop. This must end. This will end. Leave it to me.

**THE UGLY**

1. Sparrowhawk, bird hunter, pakipoacher, listen up. I've read your furious flames and visited your rant-filled sites. I know you're griping about the 'self-centred brat' who's moved into the White House. You're hoping I'll use my position to change the world, but that isn't going to happen. Sameera Righton is NOT employed by the United States of America, people. James Righton is, so here's the link to his website. Vent your thoughts about his policies there. But feel free to keep commenting here, too, because I intend to post MY opinions as openly as ever. BRING IT, because a good battle keeps things hopping out here in the blogosphere.

2. To those of you who've been wondering if we're related, I'm not going to compare your DNA with mine. I might head back to Pakistan someday to find out more about my origins, but I'll wait until Dad's no longer president. I'm not going on a journey THAT intense with a thousand pappaz and razzi tagging along. So you'll have to wait a few years to find out if I'm your niece or cousin. And I'm sorry, I can't get you a visa in the meantime.

3. To Bobby. I haven't heard from you in two weeks. Maybe you've seen one too many of those

movies about presidents' daughters and their dating traumas. Maybe you don't want to be hounded by the media and labeled something horrible like 'Sparrow's Southern Boy Toy'. But you might at least answer ONE of my emails or phone calls. Did I just imagine the spark that sizzled when our eyes met? Didn't you rest your hand for a few extended, more-than-needed, wonderful seconds on the small of my back the last time we headed out to bhangra on the dance floor?

Sameera stopped typing, sighed again, and deleted the last paragraph she'd written. She was committed to being honest on her blog, but she wasn't about to let a gazillion readers mull over the details of her thwarted love life. Was the ultimate Southern gentleman backing off because he was intimidated by her newly acquired first daughterhood, or because he just wasn't interested? George Washington University's South Asian Republican Students' Association would be meeting tomorrow in their usual highly caffeinated location. She could join them there, confront Mr Bobby Ghosh, and ferret out the truth about why he'd been avoiding her. All she needed was a way to sneak out of her luxury prison without a posse of Cougars tracking her every move.

*Hmmmm,* she thought. *It's a good thing I bought that extra woolly winter burka at Uncle Muhammad's shop last August. I had a feeling it might come in handy.*

## It's Funky, it's Fun, it's YOU!

HarperCollins India presents a new and exciting range of titles for Young Adults

## *Potato Chips*

Anshuman Mohan

**'Students are like potatoes... Only the finest of us will get made into chips!'**

When Aman Malhotra is made to change schools, he knows that his goose is well and truly cooked. From the easygoing, friendly atmosphere of Akshar, he is thrust into the big, bad world of St Xavier's. The reason, according to his parents: a big school prepares you much better for your future, i.e., IIT. Things, Aman realizes, are about to change and not for the better. The progress graph of his life plunges downwards in a sudden freefall—his grades suffer, his classmates snicker at him, his teachers think he is a brat.

Struggling to make sense of his new, high-pressure surroundings, Aman casts his net far and wide for friends and finds Shubho, a boy with a crafty drop-shot and a mean backhand. As Aman gets to know Shubho and tries to help him out, he also begins to get his own life back on track. A hero, he finally understands, comes in the most unlikely of guises and isn't necessarily the most popular kid in school.

An honest, in-your-face story of school life and adolescence—the highs, the lows, the pranks, the exams, the friendships, the fights—*Potato Chips* is crisp and smart, fresh and funny.

## *How to Salsa in a Sari*

Dona Sarkar

Issa Mazumder, a nerdy half Indian, half African teenage girl who lives in the US with her single mother, has just been utterly destroyed because the gorgeous Cat Morena, Latina princess, Issa's worst enemy and the most popular girl in school, has stolen Issa's equally nerdy boyfriend Adam. And there's worse to come – Issa's mother announces that she and Cat's father are getting married. And they are moving into Cat's huge mansion.

Cat has no respect for Issa's traditions and makes Issa's life hell. But Issa gets some tough advice: if she wants Cat Morena to welcome *her* traditions, Issa had better learn to salsa in a sari!

# Body Talk

Anjali Wason

**Real Girls Ask Real Questions About Life, Love and Everything In Between**

Sex. Girls. Boys. Bodies. Relationships. Being a young woman can be confusing, but *Body Talk* is here to offer some clarity…

Are you afraid to tell your parents about your boyfriend? Do you wish you were more confident about yourself? Or do you just want to know how to flirt?

*Body Talk* features over 400 questions that girls just like you have asked across India; it brings together real voices from the real world, in which everyone is curious about life, love and sex. Packed with advice on everything from how to use a condom to cyber dating to sexual harassment, *Body Talk* is an essential guide for any young woman interested in understanding her feelings, her body and her life.